NO BODY IN BLACKBERRY COVE

BLACKBERRY COVE MYSTERIES
BOOK 1

BEN COTTERILL

1

OCTOBER 21ST, 11:04 AM

At first glance, she was no one.

Her face in the photograph was so disfigured, Gregg could imagine any woman's features in its place, even his daughter's. Found in the basement of a vacant house, she'd been tied up and fired at with a nail gun, repeatedly. Her clothes were pierced, her skin impaled, until finally one nail hit her windpipe and brought the torture to an abrupt end.

The depth of the wounds—quite shallow—meant the killer fired from at least a few feet away. They wouldn't have meant to hit her throat intentionally. Their aim would have been too remarkable.

Rachel Milgram slid another photograph across Gregg's desk. This time not of the dead woman, but of a rugged man. A bead of rainwater trickled from Rachel's loose and parted hair, dampening the picture. Boston's rain was frequent and heavy, and the faulty heating in Gregg's office ensured clients were always soaking his furniture and dripping on his floor.

"This man—Liam Watts—disappeared on the night she was

murdered," Rachel said. "We believe he was murdered as well, but his body was never found."

Gregg studied the file. "The town's in Vermont?"

"Yes, Blackberry Cove."

Rachel adjusted her silk scarf and tucked the ends into her trench coat, which she then unbuttoned. Beneath, she sported a black sweater. She wasn't law enforcement. Another private citizen was hiring Gregg's services. The only strange thing was, his PI services usually involved cheating husbands or workers' comp scams, not murder investigations.

Gregg tapped the pictures of the dead woman. "Tell me about her."

"Mayor's wife—Clementine Stannard. Originally from New Jersey. Met the mayor when they studied in Montpelier. Got married shortly after. Loved by everyone, according to the reports."

"What exactly do you want from me?"

Rachel reached into her pocket and revealed a sheet of folded paper which she uncrumpled and placed on the desk. She slid it closer, but Gregg didn't have to read it. He'd recognize that article anywhere.

Next to the column of texts were two pictures. The first was of him dressed in his suit, standing next to his old partner, Jim. The second picture showed a smiling twelve-year-old girl named Emilie Jones.

The article reported the story of how young Emilie had been missing for nearly twenty-eight hours. She disappeared after her dad dropped her off at school. The teachers said she never showed up for class, and none of the other students remembered seeing her.

The BPD questioned Emilie's uncle, establishing he had been molesting the girl for years. They'd focused all their attention on him, believing he killed her after deciding she was old enough to talk about the abuse.

Gregg, however, as the article retold, explored a different

theory. Thinking the uncle's wife knew more than she was letting on, he went back to interview her. He believed that not only did the aunt know about the abuse, but she also blamed Emilie for taking away her husband. He found the twelve-year-old girl in the trunk of the aunt's car, gagged and beaten. Barely breathing. A couple more hours, the paramedics said, and she'd have had no chance.

"So, what?" Gregg asked. "I got lucky nearly a decade ago, and now you think I'm Batman?"

"It must have been a great feeling," Rachel said, "to find that girl alive."

"After the birth of my daughter, it was the happiest moment of my life."

"You didn't find her by luck. You have a unique perspective on things, Mr. Hunter."

"Miss Milgram." Gregg glanced at his watch. "The job?"

"I want that unique perspective on the missing man in Blackberry Cove."

Gregg stood. "Sorry, Miss Milgram. I don't leave Boston. Send me copies of the case files if you want an assessment."

Rachel remained seated. "Since the woman was the mayor's wife, Blackberry Cove's police force has focused all their resources on finding her killer for three months with no luck. They're barely investigating the missing man."

"I can't."

"I'm willing to pay you—"

"It's not about money. Family priorities. I'm sorry." He shuffled around the corner of his desk and opened the door to his office.

Though his daughter probably wouldn't, Gregg liked to be nearby on the off chance she might call and ask to see him, perhaps for dinner or a movie. She was the only reason he still solved cases. Trying to prove to her—even without his badge and after the divorce—that he still could.

Rachel dragged herself to the door. "I thought you helped

people, Mr. Hunter. This man needs help, and no one is doing anything about it. You didn't even ask anything about him. Don't you care?"

"If you've read that article, you know the answer to that," he replied.

Rachel expelled a short breath, then buttoned her coat. She forced a polite smile that was tinged with frustration and left the office. Gregg grabbed his umbrella and followed suit.

Noon was fast approaching, and Gregg's thoughts were focused on meeting his daughter for lunch. She'd be home alone since his ex-wife had spinning classes on Saturday mornings and her boyfriend worked weekends. Besides, his office was windowless, the size of a janitor's closet, and so bland he couldn't stand to be in there more than a couple of hours.

He made it to his old home in Watertown, but Boston's notorious traffic got him there too late, and his ex's car pulled up as he arrived. Sarah stood at the doorway, hands on hips. The silver-colored designer shoes on her feet reminded him of how much he lost in the divorce.

Gregg stepped out of the car. "I'm here to see my daughter."

"That isn't in our custody agreement." Sarah's favorite response. She was always ready with it.

"I drove all the way from the city to have lunch with her." He raised the bag from the local deli, containing Silvia's favorite meatball sandwich. "Since I'm here, why not?"

"You shouldn't have come in the first place. You get her every second weekend, Gregg; that's all. You can't stop by whenever you want."

"I thought she'd be eating alone."

"Well, I'm here now, so she won't be. You can go now, Gregg." The door slammed shut.

"Dammit, Sarah!" He thrashed his umbrella against the pavement, regretting it immediately when the cheap metal bent under him.

He'd arrested fathers just like him when he was a cop—seedy

guys who refused to follow a simple custody agreement and couldn't leave well enough alone. He used to shake his superior head, oblivious to the fact his perfect life was on its way to turning him into one of them.

He caught a glimpse of his daughter from her bedroom window with that all-too-familiar look of disappointment on her face—the one that said he had lost her.

A few months ago, he had stepped into her room for the first time since the divorce and it felt like a stranger's. Her trophies from netball and violin no longer took center stage but hid at the back of shelves. The collection of Sherlock Holmes books they used to read together was nowhere to be seen. Even the poster he had bought her of Acadia National Park, where they used to go camping, was ripped and faded.

He knew she was growing up and moving on, as he expected her to. After all, it had been six years since the divorce, and she was now a distant teenager. But it hurt to think that the memories he cherished so dearly may have disappeared from her mind, just like they had from her bedroom.

Gregg had to show Silvia that he had improved, that he no longer let the divorce and loss of his badge ruin his life. It would be a long process, as his daughter had witnessed him during quite a few depressive episodes. But he was a private investigator now, and his forensic psychology qualifications got him back in as a consultant with the BPD. He was going to prove he could still be Silvia's hero.

Gregg got back in the car and pushed the strands of blond hair out his eyes. A man in a brown suit and sunglasses sat in a parked car behind. Without giving it a second thought, Gregg drove off.

7:46 PM

That night, like most nights, The Orchid awaited Gregg. His usual stool all but had his imprint on it. Tucked away from the bustle of the waterfront yet close to his house, it offered a refuge where he could unwind and savor the silence with a cold beer in hand.

His head spinning from his encounter with Sarah, he fished out a pen from his pocket and grabbed a napkin from the counter. Writing often helped him release his anxieties and shift his attention elsewhere. Thinking back to his conversation with Rachel Milgram, he jotted down some words that came to mind regarding the case she had described and took a swig of his beer. Before he could drink or write any more, he got a phone call from his daughter.

"Silvia, I'm really sorry about the scene I caused earlier," he said immediately. "I just lost it."

"I thought you were doing better, Dad; taking cases again and drinking less."

"I am." He looked guiltily at his surroundings.

"Then why were you shouting at Mom?"

"I just… I know what she says to you about me."

"That doesn't matter. I can think for myself."

"I feel like I'm losing you, and it's tearing me apart."

"You're not losing me, Dad."

"I'm trying to be a dad that you can be proud of, Silvia."

"You don't need to fix the world for me to love you. I just want you to be there for me."

"I'm here anytime you need me."

"Can I see you now?" she asked.

Gregg smiled in surprise. "Yes. Of course. I would love that."

"Great. Can you park on the corner?"

"Sure thing."

"See you soon, Dad."

Without a second though, Gregg left his drink on the counter and made his way towards the door. When he heard someone call, "Mr. Hunter," he stopped.

It took him a second to recognize the dark-haired woman at the bar.

"Rachel..." he muttered.

Dressed in a form-fitting black dress and towering platform shoes, Rachel looked particularly striking. Her hair was styled in an artistic bun, and her vivid green eyes sparkled with warmth and kindness, while the curve of her lips hinted at a gentle smile.

"Funny seeing you here. We could discuss my offer further over drinks," she said.

"I'm sorry, but I'm on my way out. And please, don't pretend you're here by coincidence."

"So, you won't be joining me?" She pulled back the chair beside her.

"I appreciate how greatly you want me to accept this offer, Miss Milgram, but I'm not interested in the job if it takes me from Boston."

Rachel's smile dropped, replaced by a steely expression. "No, Mr. Hunter, what you're interested in is your daughter. And that's precisely why you should accept my offer. Because her life depends on it."

2

THE MAN IN THE BROWN SUIT HAD SILVIA AND HER MOM TIED TO their dining chairs.

After the phone call with Dad, Mom was upstairs, and Silvia was about to lie and tell her she was going out with friends. There had been a knock at the door, so Silvia went to answer it first.

A man with short, fuzzy hair, a little older than her father, yet in slightly better shape, stood at the doorway. He wore sunglasses that concealed his eyes, and his face bore an expression devoid of any emotion.

"Hello?"

"Are you Silvia?" he asked in a stern monotone.

"Who are you?" she asked, feeling a sense of unease.

Coldness radiated off him. "You look like the photograph."

Silvia shrank back in fear, turning to call for her mother, but the man quickly covered her mouth and barged into the house, locking the door behind him.

Before long, the man in the suit stood over her and Sarah, clearly indifferent to the tears streaming down their cheeks. He held a gun, complete with a silencer, or she assumed as much based upon the hours of cop movies with her dad.

He dialed a number and put the call on speakerphone. "Milgram," he said. "Have you secured the subject yet?"

"Gregg Hunter is with me right now," a woman's voice replied. "And you, Fury?"

"I'm here with the collateral," Fury replied.

Surely, that's not his actual name, Silvia thought, but soon was distracted by the very real fact there was a man who had a gun pointed at them.

"Collateral?" she heard her father ask on the other side. "You-you mean Silvia?" He sounded horrified.

"Dad, is that you?" Silvia asked meekly.

"No talking," Fury yelled.

"No, let her talk," Milgram said. "Hunter here needs to understand the gravity of the situation."

"What are they doing to you?" Gregg's voice crackled over the phone.

"T-there's a man here," she replied, "and h-he's holding a gun to my head. He keeps saying he'll have to eliminate-eliminate anyone who m-might notice. I think he means Mom and Noah."

"That's right," said Milgram. "Do you have the adults?"

"Just the mother," Fury replied. "The boyfriend has yet to return home."

"Stay strong," her father urged over the phone, but Silvia could only whimper.

"She'll be fine, Hunter," Milgram reassured him. "So long as you don't try to be a hero."

Behind her, Silvia saw her mother attempting to wriggle her hands free from the restraints.

"Gregg, what the hell is going on?" Sarah demanded.

"I'm not sure right now, but I'll figure it out. What I do know is that you have to get away if you—"

Silvia heard a thud and a muffled grunt, then the call disconnected.

Silvia screamed, "Dad? Dad?"

"Shut up," Fury barked. "Call's over."

Sarah managed to free her hands. She made a grab for Fury's gun, her legs still tied to the chair. Silvia's heart pounded in her chest as Fury and Sarah wrestled over the gun. Fury yanked it from Sarah's grip, causing her chair to topple over. Sarah grabbed Fury's ankles to trip him, but he kicked her in the face, and she fell silent.

Silvia screamed. Fury told her again to shut up and smacked her with the butt of his gun, with enough force to topple Silvia's chair, breaking its legs. Silvia's feet slipped out of the rope, and she sprinted up the stairs, searching for a phone.

Fury went after her, not running but going at a brisk pace. Silvia frantically searched for a place to hide while struggling to free her hands from the rope. She heard Fury's footsteps closing in on the top of the stairs.

"Hold it right there," he said.

Silvia froze and slowly turned to face him, fear gripping her entire body. Then, they heard the front door open. They both peered down the staircase and saw Noah, Sarah's boyfriend, entering the house. Startled by the sight in the living room, he dashed to Sarah.

Fury pulled his gun away from Silvia and aimed at Noah. He was poised, ready to squeeze the trigger, but Silvia ran at him, pushing him into the banister, and causing his shot to miss.

Silvia rushed down the stairs and caught the attention of Noah. "Silvia, what's going on? Was that a gunshot?" he asked.

Fury leapt down, landing at the bottom of the stairs, like some sort of flying demon. Noah picked up a nearby table lamp, and shouted, "Run, Silvia!"

He ran at Fury, swinging the lamp. Fury effortlessly caught it mid-air and then delivered a powerful headbutt, sending Noah tumbling to the ground. Fury then struck him once more with his gun, knocking him out cold.

Sarah was still unconscious on the floor. Silvia looked to the front door. Someone else approached the house. She ran for the back exit in the kitchen.

As she dashed out the door and into her backyard, she collided with someone. She screamed, only stopping when she saw he was in uniform with an officer's badge. Finally, she was safe. "Thank God you're here! Help me, there is someone trying to kill me!"

"It's going to be alright. I'm here to help."

Fury appeared, kicking open the backdoor. Silvia went to make a run for it, but the officer grabbed her by the arm.

"What are you doing? Let go of me!"

To her horror, Fury seized her other arm, and they both covered her mouth. Together, they dragged her to a waiting car parked on the street corner and forced her inside.

The car's door slammed shut, and Fury sat in the driver's seat. She pulled the door's handle, but it was locked. The man in the brown suit drove her away.

3

RACHEL MILGRAM'S VAN PULLED UP OUTSIDE A WAREHOUSE ON THE outskirts of Boston. Two men in suits pulled Gregg from the van. They followed Rachel to the warehouse and dragged Gregg along with them. He clasped his throbbing cheek from where he had been punched.

Not to his surprise, Rachel hadn't answered any of his questions. Upon entering, they were greeted by two uniformed officers standing over two people covered in plastic. It seemed Rachel had people everywhere. Even if Gregg managed to call for help, he wasn't sure whom he could trust.

It wasn't until he got closer Gregg realized that the two bodies were his ex-wife and her boyfriend. They were alive and struggling to break free from the tightly tied layers of plastic sheets.

Gregg dashed to help but the two men grabbed him by each arm. From beneath the plastic sheets, he could hear muffled screams of terror coming from Sarah and Noah.

Gregg felt himself grow hot and his body shake with rage and worry. "Where's my daughter? What have you done with her?" he shouted, his voice croaking with dryness.

"Be quiet," someone said. The man in the brown suit from

outside Sarah's house appeared from another door. He stepped closer to Sarah and Noah and pulled out a handgun. It was Gregg's handgun, which he kept in a safe at the office. "Recognize this?"

Gregg nodded, too stunned to speak.

The man held the gun to Sarah's skull and pulled the trigger. Just like that. Then he did the same to Noah. Their wriggling stopped.

Gregg felt his body go limp, and he fell to his knees. The room around him was spinning, and he thought he might be sick.

Rachel crouched in front of him. "If you go to the police, we'll make it look like you did this and kidnapped your daughter. We'll see to it her body disappears and no one ever finds her."

"I don't understand." Gregg clasped his head. "Why are you doing this?"

"Listen to what I'm saying," Rachel said. "You don't need to understand. Just listen."

Gregg took a deep breath. He had to pull himself together for Silvia's sake. "If I do what you say, you'll give her back to me?"

"Yes. We'll take care of the bodies and make it look like your ex-wife and her boyfriend took Silvia on vacation. That'll buy you some weeks to solve the case."

Gregg rocked back and forth with his head held in his hands, then nodded in submission.

4

OCTOBER 22ND, 11:11 AM

THE SUITCASES FIT IN THE CAR LIKE *TETRIS* PIECES. WITH THE LAST one strategically placed inside, Gregg slammed the trunk shut.

His daughter's kidnappers were planning to frame him for Sarah and Noah's murders. The worst thing was that he had been such a wreck after the divorce, even those closest to him might have believed it.

No, surely no one could ever think him capable of murder. He loved Silvia and would do almost anything to be with her, but he'd never force her from the home she'd always known. People would believe the truth, he told himself, if he came forward.

Could he trust the police to get Silvia back, though? They could waste all their time interrogating him, thinking he knew where Silvia was, while the real kidnappers disposed of her. He'd be no use to them if he was in prison, and so they'd have no reason to keep her alive.

Puddles splashed against footsteps behind him, and he turned to see Rachel walking across the apartment block's car park.

"What are you doing here?" Gregg asked.

"Just wanted to see you off. Got a problem with that?"

"Depends what you want."

"Just to remind you of something," she said casually. "This job you're about to go on, it won't be easy, and it won't be what you're used to. Trust me."

"Trust you?" Gregg smirked. "I did that before and look where it got me."

"Stop complaining. I swear all you do is whine." She never lost her nonchalant manner.

Gregg felt his blood pressure rise, but he bit his lip. "Apologies, ma'am. Anything else?"

"Remember, when you find Liam Watts, you contact me immediately. The authorities are not to poke their noses in this. Once everything is resolved to my satisfaction, you can have what you want."

At this, Gregg's voice broke. "Can I see her? Please? Even if just for a—"

"No," Rachel interrupted sternly. "Not until the job is done. The agreement was quite clear."

Gregg fought back a tear and forced a smile. "Crystal clear. I want a picture sent to me when I get there to know she's still alive."

"You'll get it." She presented a file. "This is Blackberry Cove."

Gregg took it and flipped through the pages. It looked like something out of Mayberry, probably complete with a soda fountain and a store that sold penny candy. "So, this is where it happened?"

"Indeed, it is. A sleepy little mining town where the grass is green, the picket fences are white, and the doors are left unlocked at night. The ideal place to carry out a murder."

"I can hardly believe that he came from a place like this," Gregg said, taking in the serene surroundings of the mining town. The papers contained pictures of residents followed by descriptive paragraphs, which he'd examine more carefully later.

"Now, now, appearances can be deceptive. Take me, for example."

"I don't know, you look like a cold bitch to me."

Rachel's expression remained unamused, her lips frowning ever so slightly.

"Where will I stay when I get there?" he asked.

Rachel flicked through the pages in his hands, landing on the profiles of an Irish couple—Richard and Hannah O'Doyle. They ran the local B&B. "I hope you like the sound of the place. Options in town are quite limited for holidaymakers."

He put away the papers. "I'll be hearing from you soon, I suppose."

"Indeed, you will. Now off you go—Blackberry Cove awaits."

3:10 PM

The drive to Vermont was a few hours, but Gregg only stopped once, for gas and a quick toilet break. The majority of the journey was through open country, made up of meadows and pastures. Once he entered Green Mountains National Forest, he knew he was in a different world. The majestic mountains and dense forests extended for miles and miles, like a scene from *The Sound of Music*.

The only road to town was a dirt track that spiraled through gaps in the mountains. Outside the car window, crisp golden leaves fell from the surrounding trees that swayed gently in the autumn wind. The sky was crowded with clouds, allowing the sun's light to break out only in bursts. Despite the stunning scenery outside his window, Gregg failed to appreciate it. His gaze remained fixed ahead, his eyes tired and puffy.

He briefly glanced up at the only thing that kept him going—a photograph attached to the dashboard, showing a cleaner-cut version of himself with his ex-wife and their teenage daughter. A life Gregg no longer knew.

Upon rounding the corner, a sign came into view, reading

Welcome to Blackberry Cove. Gregg felt relieved to arrive at his destination, although the circumstances left little room for celebration. As he began to contemplate his new job, however, his thoughts were abruptly interrupted. The car was slowing down, making struggling noises. Eventually it came to a stop, steam blowing from the hood.

"Damn it." He took his hands away from the steering wheel and stepped out of the car.

He made his way to the front and lifted the hood with difficulty. Coughing, he cleared the white smoke away with his hand but still couldn't see the problem. He sighed, turned around, and looked for help. Unfortunately, there was nothing but forestry hugging the road. Ahead of him, a car was parked on the roadside. Squinting, he continued to search until he eventually spotted a figure near the vehicle—a man perched in a nearby bush.

The man had a camera hanging from his neck and binoculars in his hands. He was using the binoculars to spy at the top of a tree, appearing to be waiting patiently. A small, blue bird landed on the branch, causing the man to smile. He carefully and quietly lifted his camera, about to take a picture...

"Excuse me?" Gregg called over.

The man jumped, turning his gaze away from the target, and the bird took flight. The man sighed and flung his arms into the air. "What are you doing, sneaking up on someone like that? Do you have any idea how rare it is to see a Steller's jay this far east?"

Gregg took a step back. "Um, I'm sorry."

"Those birds come from the west. Did you know that? They come from the California deserts and the Grand Canyon. Maybe they make it as far as Colorado, but not here. Do you know what it means to see them here?"

Gregg shrugged.

"It means global warming's happening even quicker than we realize."

"Fascinating," Gregg lied.

The man stared, annoyed, then asked, "What do you want?"

"My car broke down, and I need to get it fixed."

"Well, isn't there someone you can call?"

"Even if I did know anyone here, I haven't had a signal for miles."

The man groaned. "I can give you a lift into town. There's a garage there that can fix your car."

"Thank you," Gregg said, feeling relieved.

"Yeah, yeah, yeah," the man muttered to himself, walking towards the road.

Gregg followed. He sat in the passenger seat, and the stranger drove them towards town. A golden locket hung open from the interior mirror, showcasing a green-eyed brunette. A sleeping bag and muddy hiking shoes were scattered on the backseat.

The man's eyes flickered towards Gregg's suitcase. "I'm surprised to see someone planning on staying in our little town. We get few visitors or new residents these days. Was it the scenery that drew you in? It's an attractive place to live to me anyway. Plenty of nature to acquaint myself with."

Gregg felt the fondness with which the man was speaking but shook his head. "I'm actually here on an investigation." Gregg retrieved the ID from his pocket.

"Private Investigator," the man read.

Gregg offered out his hand. "Gregg Hunter."

"Bernard Neumann. I take pictures for nature magazines." He briefly glanced away from the road to shake Gregg's hand. "So, what are you investigating?"

"Missing person, declared a cold case here some months ago. I've been asked to look into it."

"Missing person, eh? You're thinking murder! Ha, which one?"

"Excuse me?"

"Oh, it was quite the scandal here a couple months ago. Two

18

people disappeared mere hours apart. They found the woman the next day—murdered. The man they never found."

"Well, I'm here to look for the one they never found."

"Liam Watts, eh?"

Gregg nodded.

"I take it you haven't got a place to stay yet," Bernard said, changing the subject.

"I read about a place called the Swan Inn."

"No place finer for visitors. Not that it's got so much business since the… well, what you're here to investigate."

"I'll take your word for it."

"What can you tell me about the town?" Gregg asked.

"I would call it peaceful, but some might say silent and remote. It was a mining town in the nineteenth century. Once the mines ran dry, the townspeople had to find another way to make their bread. Since the town is located in the center of the Green Mountains, they thought they could attract tourists. So, they built a hotel and a railway line to Bennington, luring tourists here with promises of hunting trips and hiking trails. Blackberry Cove never became the hotspot that the townspeople hoped it would be, and it nearly became unincorporated when the hotel and railway line closed, but it managed to limp on as the people in town refused to leave their homes. They were completely self-sufficient for a while. Once the roads were built, the town managed to begin attracting a small number of tourists again, this time from cities further afield, like Boston."

Gregg scanned the scenery of trees outside. "How large is the forest?"

"More than four hundred thousand acres," Bernard replied. "When you're on the edges of town, trees are as far as the eye can see. It certainly makes you feel separated from the rest of the world."

They left the woods and entered the main town, crossing a covered bridge to get there. Beneath them was a fast-flowing river, perfect for kayaking. The town was small and homely and not very modern. There was a towering white church, a small bank, bookstore, and clothes store. No sign of a decent restaurant, movie theater, or of the many other luxuries one would consider a necessity in Boston. Bernard pulled over outside an old-fashioned, Tudor-looking building. It displayed a rundown sign out front, which still appeared much newer than the rest of the B&B, reading *The Swan Inn*.

"They will have the number of the local mechanic," Bernard said.

Gregg thanked him and stepped out of the car.

"Good luck with the investigation."

Gregg thanked him yet again, then shut the door and allowed the man to drive off. He made his way down the cobblestone pathway, wearing shoes that were meant for a bit more action, and entered the Swan Inn.

5

RICHARD O'DOYLE WAS LIVING THE LIFE HE ALWAYS WANTED. ONLY problem was, he hated it.

He and his wife owned a bed & breakfast—the only bed & breakfast—in a small Vermont town surrounded by acres of woodland and meadows. Hannah had decorated the upstairs bedrooms homely. Across from reception there was the entrance to their traditional-looking inn, with an open fireplace, ceiling beams, and a bar where the locals gathered nightly. They served country meals and had built a good reputation in town for both their cottage pie and lamb stew.

He stood in front of the reception counter, his hands resting on the wood that was a wormy chestnut, or so his wife said when they had furnished. He pretended he was instead stroking the surface of that old, shabby breakfast table from their cramped New York apartment, pretending he was somewhere far away from his current reality.

All he could think about lately was leaving behind the business they had worked so hard to establish, and the countryside they had forever dreamed about escaping to.

Richard considered it was maybe a midlife crisis, but he knew that was just an easy rationalization. The fact was, he felt trapped. Trapped in a tumultuous marriage with a woman he fought with constantly. Trapped in an isolated town, serving the same locals every night, listening to the same mundane conversations and petty gossip. Trapped in a failing business. Tourists were much harder to come by than they expected, and the locals coming for evening drinks weren't enough to keep them afloat. All the money they had saved up and spent on buying the place and doing it up, thinking they'd earn it all back in no time, had never come back, and it looked like it never would.

"You haven't done the dishes? There are no clean plates in this whole damn place," his wife shrilled in her thick Irish brogue as she entered the room. It seemed all they did was bicker lately.

Hannah had a pretty face, but it was tired with deep rings under her eyes. Her blonde hair was pulled back into a ponytail, a few strands escaping.

He argued back, "So what? Let the employees do it. It's what we pay them for."

"It may have escaped your notice, but we haven't been paying them. There's barely an employee left in this freak'n ghost town!"

"And why do we have no money to pay employees? Because we have no customers so why do the dishes need to be washed?"

"Because we're professionals! I left you a note, telling you specifically—"

"Oh, you left no note," he said, grunting.

"Maybe you would've noticed if you weren't sitting on your ass all day!"

"Hey! I work damn hard to make this place what it is!"

"And look what it is! A laughable failure! This place is—"

"Honey," Richard yelled, suddenly spotting someone at the door.

"Um, hi," a tall, blond man said, dressed in jeans and a buttoned blue shirt.

Richard and his wife looked at him, slightly shocked, and both feigned huge smiles.

"Hi!" they exclaimed in unison.

"Welcome to the Swan Inn, may I take your coat?" Hannah asked, not waiting for an answer before immediately hanging the man's jacket up on a nearby hat rack.

"Thank you," the man said, appearing a little startled.

Richard, now standing behind the desk, dinged a little bell. "Hello, sir. We are the O'Doyles. Welcome to the Swan Inn, where family is everything. Would you like a room?"

"Um, yes please."

"Name?"

"Gregg Hunter," the man replied.

Richard wrote it into the book. "And how long will you be staying, Mr. Hunter?"

"I'm not sure yet. Put me down for three weeks."

Richard and his wife's eyes widened with shock.

"I'll give you a forest view room." Richard handed the man a key.

Hannah added, "We can discuss your bill later. Will you want dinner tonight? Our restaurant offers a wide selection."

"Sounds good." Gregg pocketed his key. "Do you know the number of a mechanic? My car has broken down."

"I'd be happy to get that for you, sir." Richard clicked through an address book. Meanwhile, at the other side of the counter, his wife picked up something from the ground—a note.

"Aha!" she exclaimed. "I told you I left a note!"

"Well, if it's on the floor, how do you expect me to see it?"

"I want a divorce," she grunted.

"Yeah, keep saying that, maybe a lawyer will hear you." He snatched the note from her and wrote down the number of a mechanic. He turned to Gregg with a newfound smile and handed it to him. "Here you go, sir."

"Thank you, Richard."

Gregg turned to leave.

"Richard?" he questioned. "I don't think I told you my name."

"Right, the guy who gave me a lift here told me: Richard and Hannah, the local innkeepers," Gregg said.

Satisfied with the answer, Richard and Hannah resumed their normal state of quarreling.

6

It was an unusual sight to see a stranger at the Swann Inn, but there he sat, ordering from the menu with Hannah.

As Blackberry Cove's therapist, Timothy prided himself on knowing people in town, as well as all their secrets. It gave him a sense of distance and control. Even while shopping for meat at the grocery store, he knew those he passed in the aisle better than they knew him. So, to encounter someone at the inn he knew nothing about left him feeling off-balance. Power was like a knife—if not in your own hands, you could always be stabbed in the back.

As the blonde stranger got up from his table and made his way to the restroom, he passed where Timothy was nursing a beer.

Timothy quickly stood, blocking the man's way. "Oh, b-beg my pardon."

"It's alright," the outsider assured him.

"Excuse me, but I don't think we've met before. I'm Dr. Timothy Holst, the local therapist." He extended his arm, and the man shook it warmly.

"Gregg Hunter."

"Are you new to town?"

"Yes. I'm actually here to investigate the disappearance of Liam Watts," Gregg replied. "Maybe I could ask you a couple of questions?"

"Oh. A-are you a private investigator?"

Gregg nodded, and Timothy tried to hide his discomfort. Not only was this man a stranger, but he was also a snoop, here to learn the town's secrets, and maybe even Timothy's. That would not do.

"I was a friend of Liam. He didn't have family or many friends. Who hired you?"

"I'm afraid I can't say."

"Well, it's a-all a mystery to me. Liam was a nice guy, kept to himself mostly. I don't see why a-anyone would have wanted to hurt him. If you a-ask me, there is nothing here to investigate."

"What do you mean?" Gregg asked.

"Well, it's possible that he simply moved on. He had no real ties to this town."

"But the reports suggest that he didn't take anything from his house."

"Perhaps he had nothing worth taking," Timothy said.

"And it was coincidence that he disappeared on the night of the murder?"

"Coincidences do happen."

Gregg nodded thoughtfully as he considered Timothy's words. "Excuse me, Doctor," he then said, pointing to the restroom.

Dr. Holst stepped out of the way. "Oh, I'm sorry. I suppose I'll be seeing you soon."

"Probably." Gregg went around him and entered the restroom.

Timothy stepped out of the Swan Inn to the main street of Blackberry Cove. He immediately took out his cell phone, looking around to ensure no one was watching.

"Hello," he said into the phone. "I'd like to speak to the mayor please. There is something I think he'd like to know."

The mayor was busy, so he left a message with his secretary.

He walked down the street, sick to his stomach and struggling to breathe, as if an anchor was weighing down on his chest. A private investigator was in town. *Fuck.*

Timothy had stuttered like an idiot, probably already making the detective suspicious. Hopefully, the mayor would do something about this. After all, Timothy wasn't the only one with something to hide.

His thoughts were interrupted when a young woman with dirty blonde hair approached.

"Afternoon, Dr. Holst," the local girl said.

The therapist looked up at her, nodded and tried to smile, but it didn't last long.

"How are things?" she asked.

"Oh, they're…they're fine."

"Things better with Mrs. Holst?"

Dr. Holst repressed a curse. Instead, he nodded with another brief and false smile. "Oh, yes, thank you."

"Well I should be off. Have a good day, Doctor," the woman said, continuing on her way.

Dr. Holst stopped and thought, *Yes, I'm not the only one with something to hide.*

He turned to her. "Chloe."

The woman twisted her head back to face him. "Yes?"

"There's a detective."

Chloe's smile dropped, and she went pale.

7

GREGG RETURNED TO HIS DINNER IN THE SMALL LOUNGE OF THE INN. He had to be careful not to allow any slip-ups again as he had with saying the innkeeper's name. He took out the photograph that had been on the dashboard of his car and held it tight to his chest.

I have to keep focused, he thought. *The sooner I solve this case, the sooner I can see Silvia again.*

Richard came over to light the fireplace, and Gregg put the photograph back in his pocket. Despite Richard's imposing stature and bushy beard, he exuded a gentle demeanor, perhaps due to his smooth voice and musical accent.

Richard looked up to him. "So, you're investigating the disappearance of Liam Watts?" He must have overheard his conversation with the therapist.

"That's right."

Hannah arrived with another drink and chimed in, "That was such a terrible tragedy. Are you also here to look into the murder of Clementine?"

"My employer is only interested in Liam Watts," Gregg replied. "But it is possible the two cases will overlap."

Hannah looked somber. "I truly hope you're able to bring

justice for Clementine. Her death was a devastating loss for everyone. She was such a young mother, you know?"

As Gregg opened his mouth to respond, the door swung open and a man in uniform strode in. He wore a gold badge on his chest and a hat that mostly concealed his silver hair.

Hannah turned to face him. "Hello, Sheriff. Can I get you a beer?"

"I'm here on business," he replied curtly.

"That doesn't usually stop you." Hannah smiled teasingly.

But the sheriff didn't return the smile, clearly focused on his task at hand. "Actually, Hannah, I'm here for him," he said, pointing to Gregg.

Gregg tilted his head. "Me?"

"The mayor wants to see you."

"Can I finish my dinner?"

"People don't usually leave the mayor waiting."

Gregg was curious to meet this mayor, and so he followed the sheriff outside.

5:18 PM

At the town's city hall, a secretary showed Gregg to the mayor's office. The first thing he noticed about her was her skin, as white as a porcelain doll. She was dressed in long pants and a sweater, with a collared shirt underneath. Introducing herself as Isabella Blake, she stepped aside and opened the door to the mayor's office.

"He's here, sir," she announced meekly.

"Good, send him in," the mayor replied.

The mayor sat behind his desk, dressed in a white shirt and skinny black tie, his tall blond hair carefully styled. The deep wrinkles on his forehead suggested he was slightly older than one might at first think. A gold plaque upon the desk read *Nathan Stannard*. Gregg recalled from Rachel's background files that Nathan was also the owner of a local sugar house, held by the family for generations.

The mayor wasted no time. "Hello, Mr. Hunter, I'm Mayor Stannard. I heard you have been asking questions about one of our town's former residents."

Gregg nodded. "I've been hired to investigate the disappearance of Liam Watts."

"That sounds like a good idea," Isabella said, while carrying around files at the back of the room, "bringing in the extra help. Our investigators reached dead ends in both cases."

The mayor waved at her dismissively. "You know what I think sounds like a good idea? Coffee. Two sugars. Make it snappy."

Isabella nodded and walked over to the coffee machine in the corner of the room.

"May I ask the identity of your employer, Mr. Hunter?"

"My employer would prefer to remain anonymous during my investigation."

The mayor's expression turned sour. "Mr. Hunter, my father was the mayor of this town before me, and his father before him, and so on. Nobody cares more about the welfare of this town and its citizens than I do. What makes you think you're more qualified than our own investigators? We happen to have a very competent sheriff."

"We've met," Gregg reminded him. "And I mean no disrespect to your investigators, but I'm sure they haven't dealt with anything like this before. Missing persons cases are rare in such small towns, especially ones connected to a murder. I deal with such instances all the time in Boston."

Isabella looked over from making the coffee. "Wow, you must see some interesting stuff."

She played with her long, brunette hair and smiled at him with twinkling eyes, revealing a row of uneven teeth that looked almost vampirish. *Laying it on a bit thick,* Gregg thought.

He gave her a gentle smile and turned back to the mayor. "I

only want to help. It would be much easier with your coop-eration."

"What makes you think the cases are connected?"

"They occurred on the same night. Most likely, that's not a coincidence."

Nathan nodded, contemplating the words. He appeared lost in a moment of distress and sadness at the sound of the disappearance being connected to a murder, his wife's murder. He lifted his hand as if it were holding a cup, however looked down to find his hand empty. Looking around confused, he asked with disdain, "Why aren't I drinking coffee?"

Isabella dashed over with a mug. The mayor took it from her, had a sip, and then said, "Very well, Mr. Hunter. I see no issue with accepting your assistance. I will instruct my sheriff to provide you with access to the case files."

"Thank you, sir," Gregg replied before departing from the office.

6: 12 PM

Gregg returned to the Swan Inn. He approached the entrance, walking beneath the starry night sky and moonlight. As he came to the door, a young woman with dirty blonde hair exited. She looked like a typical country girl, dressed in a red plaid shirt, denim shorts, and taupe boots. She possessed an innocent and unblemished beauty that reminded Gregg of his former wife during their college days. Despite her obvious charm, she walked awkwardly with her eyes down, seemingly unaware of her own allure.

He smiled. "Evening."

"Good evening," she replied, returning the smile.

And then she was gone, disappearing into the night. Upon entering the inn, Gregg made his way into the bar area where he found some of the town's locals enjoying drinks. As he scanned the room, he spotted Bernard Neumann, the man who had given him a ride into town, sitting alone and waving at him. Gregg reciprocated the gesture and walked over to join him.

On his way, he passed a short man with glasses and thinning hair. It was Dr. Holst, the therapist he met, dressed in the same white shirt and gray slacks. The therapist stood. "Oh, Mr. Hunter, good to see you again. I'd like for you to meet my wife."

No stutter this time, Gregg noted. He looked to see a woman with curly blonde hair sitting with the doctor.

"Nice to meet you." He shook her hand.

"Elaine," the woman introduced herself.

Gregg glanced back at Bernard and said, "If you'll excuse me, Doctor."

"Oh, of course."

Gregg took a seat beside Bernard, who was drinking a beer, but Gregg noticed a second glass on the table with lipstick on the rim.

"Is someone sitting here?" Gregg asked.

"There was," Bernard replied, "but they left."

Gregg thought back to the young woman he passed outside; she had been wearing the same shade of lipstick.

"You settle in okay?" Bernard asked.

"Sure, this place seems nice. And the mechanic is fixing my car."

"Great."

Hannah walked over. "Can I get you a drink, Mr. Hunter?"

"It's Gregg," he told her. "And a beer, please."

She went to get his order.

Bernard took a sip of his drink, and then asked, "Any progress with your investigation?"

"I met the town's mayor. It was a little intense."

"The investigation is personal to him. Besides, after what happened to his first wife, he's probably worried about voters suspecting foul play."

Gregg's spine tingled, and he spun to face Bernard. "What do you mean? Are you saying Clementine was the mayor's *second* wife?"

Bernard nodded.

"What happened to his first wife?"

"This all happened a long time before I moved here, but, as I understand it, she just disappeared one night with a full suitcase. The mayor hired private investigators to track her down, but they all came back empty-handed."

"His first wife went missing and his second wife was murdered," Gregg summed up. "What's the odds?"

Bernard shrugged and took a swig of his beer.

"I also don't understand how he knew I was in town. I just got here."

Bernard shrugged. "I didn't say anything."

"The only people who knew I was here were you; the innkeepers, who I spent all afternoon with; and..." He glanced over to Dr. Timothy Holst and his wife enjoying their drinks.

"What? What are you thinking?" Bernard asked.

"I'm wondering why Dr. Holst would feel so threatened by me being here," Gregg replied, staring at the therapist.

He excused himself from Bernard, needing to make a phone call, and exited the inn. He slid his cell phone out of his pocket out on the cobblestone pathway and dialed.

Soon, Rachel Milgram answered. "Ah, I was just about to call you."

"I'm here, just as instructed."

"I know. Find anything yet?"

"No. Everyone appears so nice."

"I thought I told you: appearances can be deceiving. Don't trust what your eyes tell you. At least one of those people is a killer. And one of them killed Liam Watts."

"Noted. Now, where's my picture?"

His phone vibrated, and he looked at the screen to find a text had come in. He opened it to find a photo of his daughter tied to a chair, still wearing the clothes she had on when she was taken.

Gregg's breathing became heavy as he felt tears stream down his face.

"This could have been so much easier," Rachel said, "if you just accepted the job to start with."

"Why me?" Gregg asked.

After a brief pause, Rachel replied, "Call me when you have something."

The call ended, though Gregg continued to stand there, staring at the photo of his daughter on his phone.

In despair, a woman was found dead,
Her face disfigured beyond any med,
With a nail gun, she was shot,
And her killer vanished, not caught.

A man missing, tied to the crime?
Was he the culprit or a victim of time?
Perhaps a serial killer roams free,
Claiming souls in a murderous spree?

8

OCTOBER 22ND, 4:58 PM, (YESTERDAY)

BERNARD NEUMANN STOOD IN THE FOREST, SNAPPING PICTURES WITH his camera.

Bernard felt tired. He always felt tired. Sometimes he wasn't sure the world around him was real unless he took a picture. An overwhelming feeling of sadness seemed to have taken up permanent residence in his chest. A disorganized cloud assumed all capacity of his mind, as if a thick fog had descended upon it, disconnecting him from the world.

He snapped some more pictures. The camera lens gave him a view of the world, but at a distance. It gave him a perspective that was somehow safer. It protected him. At the more comforting angle of a camera, he could create a different reality, one that he could control and manipulate to his liking. In a better reality he would not have seen what he had seen or done what he had done.

As he took more pictures, Bernard couldn't help but think about the life he used to have before everything went wrong, stripping him from his life and prospects, leaving him as the walking corpse he now was, isolated from the world.

He stopped in his tracks and looked down, spotting something. Bending down, he took some closer pictures.

Hearing another rustle of leaves from behind, he looked up and said calmly, "You can stop hiding now."

Behind him, Chloe Mason stepped out from behind a tree, but Bernard didn't turn to face her.

"Why are you following me?"

"There's a detective in town," Chloe replied; he could hear the nervousness in her voice.

"I know. I drove him here."

"You what?"

"His car broke down on his way here. So, I gave him a lift." He paused before asking, "How do *you* know?"

"It's a small town. News travels fast."

Not that fast, Bernard thought.

"What are you doing out here?"

Now, Bernard turned to face her. He held up his camera.

"No," Chloe simply replied, looking irritated. "You're searching, aren't you?"

Bernard looked away again.

"You promised you wouldn't. It isn't safe, especially now with a detective here."

Bernard merely nodded.

"We said we'd look out for each other."

Bernard's gaze slowly returned to her. He yielded a gentle smile. "Okay."

"Come on then."

Chloe turned and walked off, as Bernard called after her that he was coming.

Before he followed her, Bernard briefly turned back to what he had been looking at. Holding his camera up, he snapped some final pictures, and then turned away to follow Chloe.

What he had been taking pictures of remained behind. It was a trail of dried blood.

9

OCTOBER 23RD, 8:20 AM

BLOOD.

It was all Richard O'Doyle saw when he closed his eyes. It was the real reason he felt trapped lately. He saw everything differently, now that he had seen something his mind couldn't erase. It was something he thought about, whether he was walking the dog, pouring the locals their evening drinks, or changing the guests' bed sheets—*blood*.

It had been so red. He tried washing it from his hands, but it was glued permanently between the fine valleys of his fingerprints. When he tried wiping it away, it spread all over his clothes, all over the walls. Everywhere he looked, he saw it.

He had to escape.

Richard's eyes shot open. He looked around, remembering that he was in a therapy session with his wife sitting beside him on the couch. Dr. Timothy Holst sat across from them, listening attentively to her ramblings. Richard let out a loud yawn, and both his wife and Dr. Holst turned to look at him.

"Do you have something to add, Richard?" Dr. Holst asked.

Richard, who still saw everything as a slight blur, replied, "No, not really."

"See, Doctor? This is exactly what I'm talking about. He never listens or takes anything seriously anymore. He just doesn't care." She spoke sadly, with some anger biting behind her words.

"Richard, did you hear anything that your wife said?" Timothy asked.

Richard released another yawn.

The therapist, taking this as a *no*, said, "I think the root of your problem is a lack of communication—"

"Lack of communication?" Richard interrupted. "We communicate too much if you ask me."

"Not healthily. Not anymore, anyway. But all problems start somewhere. Surely there was a time when you made each other happy. There was a reason why you fell in love and got married in the first place."

The couple looked at each other.

"If there was a time like that, I don't remember it," Richard admitted.

"Well, start remembering it. Reminisce. Tell each other these things without shouting," the therapist instructed.

"Without shouting?" Hannah asked, as if the concept was foreign.

"You need to open up to one another," Timothy replied.

"Are you talking sex?"

"No!" the therapist exclaimed with a sigh. "I mean emotionally. Let the other know how you're feeling. If you're angry, tell your spouse why you're angry in a safe and calm environment. Deep breaths, count to ten, and then talk. Discuss your problems. Discuss these things before they annoy you more."

The couple glanced at each other begrudgingly and looked away, arms crossed with identical expressions of anger on their faces. Neither of them was happy with the supposedly therapeutic advice.

Richard thought back to when he first met his wife, trying to recall his initial feelings. He met her at a college party in Dublin. She was studying business with dreams of opening her own hotel. He had just become a college dropout, choosing instead to spend his days playing video games and smoking pot. At first, he hid this from Hannah, telling her that he was still in college.

After two weeks of dating, however, Richard realized he couldn't possibly go on lying to her. She was unlike any girl he had ever met. Hannah was someone he could picture himself settling down with and who made him want to be a better person. She had forgiven him on the condition that he never hide anything from her again. He promised to always tell her the truth for as long as he'd love her, which he said would be forever.

The days when Richard could tell Hannah anything felt like a lifetime ago. She had been the most beautiful girl he'd met, and during that first meeting he had butterflies in his stomach. Now, eighteen years later, Richard wondered what happened to that flutter.

He didn't get much sleep lately. Whenever he lay down and closed his eyes, trying to picture him and Hannah happy, it never lasted for long. He would see them holding hands, and then the picture would go red. Their smiles would fade. They'd release their hands, as the redness seeped between them, forcing them apart.

10

GREGG BARELY SLEPT DURING HIS FIRST NIGHT AT THE SWAN INN. That was typical whenever he started a new case. He would stay up, debating theories in his head, and then when he finally dozed off, he'd wake up with possible solutions that had come to him in his sleep.

But he wasn't thinking about the case this time. He was thinking about the people who had his daughter. *Who was Rachel Milgram? Who were the men she worked with? Why is finding Liam Watts' killer so important to her? How is she even sure there is a killer, and Liam Watts hasn't just run off? And most importantly, why me?*

Gregg knew he was a good detective but kidnapping someone's daughter seemed like an excessive measure to get them to cooperate. Gregg shook these questions from his head, knowing he was letting himself get distracted. He had to focus on solving the case; that was how he would get Silvia back.

His mobile phone rang from atop the bedside desk. He got out of bed and picked it up. The caller was Rachel Milgram.

"Good morning, Hunter."

Gregg didn't respond.

"Do you have any news for me?"

"Not yet," Gregg replied. "How is she?"

"Don't waste time, Hunter. You know what I have and what will happen if you don't get the job done. So, let's not dwell on it. Stay focused. When I call for an update, I expect a response longer than two words. So, where are we? Who are the suspects so far?"

Gregg tried to listen for any noises in the background. Maybe something could give away Rachel's location. Unfortunately, he heard nothing. "I've only just met people."

"First impressions are everything," Rachel reminded him. "Their reactions to seeing you for the first time are key, because it's the only time you meet them, and they aren't expecting it. So, don't tell me you don't already have suspects. I know you do."

"The mayor."

"Why?"

"He seemed too distant from his wife's murder. But also, guilty. He only agreed to me seeing Liam's case files after I brought up the murder."

"See if he was having an affair."

"You didn't tell me he was previously married."

"I didn't think it was relevant."

"Not relevant?" Gregg asked, astounded. "Don't you know spouses are the most common culprits? The fact his first wife went missing only makes it all the more likely he had something to do with the murder of his second."

"Yes, but you are being asked to solve the murder of Liam Watts, not the mayor's second wife. Keep focused on the case at hand, Hunter. Now, tell me who else is a suspect."

Gregg gave a deep sigh, making a note to ask the mayor about the circumstances of his first wife's disappearance in case it turned out to be significant. "The mayor's secretary, Isabella Blake."

"Why her?" she asked.

"She was being coy. Plus, we know from her background file that she has a record."

"Theft and prostitution, right?"

"Yes."

"Okay. Go on."

"Bernard Neumann," Gregg said, remembering the man he met in the woods. Not only had he asked about the investigation on the drive into town, but he also requested an update when they had drinks last night.

"Who is that?"

"Photographer for a nature magazine."

"I don't remember his file."

"There wasn't one. He must be new to town."

"I'll see what I can find. Anyone else?" Rachel asked.

"There's also Dr. Holst."

"The therapist? Why?"

"He's threatened by me being here."

"Anything else?"

"That's it for now. I'll work on their connections to Liam. And look for more potential suspects. Then I can find out who saw him last and work out a last known location."

"Good. We'll speak soon, Hunter."

"Milgram, if anything happens to her, just know—I'll be coming for you."

Silence.

"Get to work." She hung up.

Gregg exited the inn, dressed in another blue collared shirt, tucked into jeans. He walked the town road. Mayor Nathan Stannard headed his way, holding hands with a small boy.

"Good morning, Mr. Hunter," Nathan greeted.

"Morning." Gregg nodded.

"I'd like for you to meet my son, Raymond."

Gregg looked down at the small boy, dressed in a shirt and sweater with perfectly combed hair, who waved back shyly.

"Say hello, Raymond," his father ordered.

"Hello," the boy said barely in a whisper.

"Do you believe it? I have a secretary and a nanny, yet I'm the one taking the kid to school," Nathan said. "Can I help you with something, Mr. Hunter?"

"Actually, you can. I was hoping you could tell me a little about your first wife."

Nathan waved a hand in the air. "I don't like to talk about that. What else can I help you with?"

"What about your second wife?" Gregg asked. "Will you tell me about her?"

"Why should I? You're here to investigate Liam Watts, correct?"

"They could be connected. We've been over this."

The mayor returned a glare. "What do you want to know?"

"Do you miss your wife?"

"Excuse me? Of course, I do! What the hell kind of question is that?"

"Well, your wife died three months ago but you aren't lonely at night, are you?"

"What?" Nathan went red. He looked at his son, and then back at Gregg.

Before the mayor could say anything further, Gregg pointed down to Nathan's shopping bag. "You bought NasoSpray. Who are you keeping up at night? What's her name?"

Nathan glanced at the snoring medicine at the top of his shopping bag and cast an enraged look. "Is this really appropriate, Mr. Hunter? In front of my son! The boy just lost his mother for fuck's sake!"

Gregg averted his gaze, feeling a wave of shame wash over him. He reflected on his own painful experience of his wife cheating on him before their divorce, and imagined how hurt his daughter would be if she found out in the same way as Nathan's son just did. Although he was anxious to get his daughter back and knew that catching people off-guard could be effective, he realized that he could have approached the conversation with the mayor in a more appropriate way. What had he accomplished by pointing out the medication? Nothing. Not even a name.

"Come on, Raymond," Nathan said, shaking his head and mumbling in frustration while he led the small boy down the street.

Gregg turned away. He found Bernard standing a few paces away, apparently having been waiting for him.

Bernard presented a bakery bag. "Hey. I have donuts, and they have jelly. Figured all this investigating might be making you hungry."

"It's only been a morning. And I've only had a meeting with the mayor, which was just as pointless as the last one. But hey, I'll bite, how've you been doing?" He took a donut.

"Nothing much. The Steller's jay never returned, thank you very much."

Gregg looked at him blankly.

"The bird you scared away," Bernard reminded him.

"Oh, right. Sorry about that."

"It's okay," Bernard assured him. "And you? Find out anything more?"

"Why are you so interested?" Gregg asked, though he had no problem humoring him. It wasn't unheard of for suspects to inject themselves into investigations to find out what cops knew about the case. This usually worked in the favor of the investigators, allowing the suspects to make a mistake close-up. Gregg wasn't convinced yet that Bernard was a serious suspect, but at least someone in town was actually happy to talk to him.

"Oh, you have no idea how exciting this is. This kind of thing never happens here. The last mystery we had was when a bottle of wine was stolen from the church. It ended when we found Old Ted passed out on one of the pews."

Gregg chuckled. "I think it's going to be a hard case to be honest. Liam appears to have had no friends or family, no one I can question properly or help provide some answers."

"Well, I don't know about family, but you could always try his girlfriend," Bernard suggested, taking a donut for himself.

"Liam had a girlfriend?" Gregg asked, surprised. Taking out his pad and pen, he was ready to write down the name of another potential suspect. "Who?"

"Chloe Mason. She works part-time at the grocery store and takes care of her father full-time. I can give you her address if you'd like; she doesn't live far. No one does here."

Chloe Mason's house looked like all the others in Blackberry Cove, cozy and modest, with white picket fencing. It was painted a sunny shade of yellow, matching the warm shades of the other dwellings on the street, though noticeably more weathered than the others, and the yard appeared neglected, with overgrown shrubs and grass.

In fact, it was the only house on the street that didn't look like it belonged on the front cover of a real estate magazine. It was still beautiful, however. The minor imperfections merely made Gregg think the people who lived there actually had lives to live. How other people had time to live a life and have their home constantly looking immaculate, he would never know.

He approached the home and knocked on the door. The young woman with dirty blonde hair he had seen the day before answered the door, wearing a blue plaid shirt and jeans, and the same taupe boots.

"Hello," she said.

He showed his badge. "My name's Gregg Hunter, and I'm investigating the disappearance of Liam Watts."

"Oh." Her face showed a mix between surprise and fear.

"Do you mind if I come in?"

"Sure." She opened the door and led him down the hallway as he thanked her.

"We passed each other last night, right?" the young woman

said. "I was wondering who you were; we don't get many new faces around here."

Gregg simply nodded.

"Can I get you something to drink?"

"No, thank you."

When they entered the living room, Gregg was a little startled. There was a pale, elderly man sat in an armchair. His hair and clothes looked freshly cleaned, but his skin looked like death.

"This is my father, Harry."

"Pleased to meet you, sir." Gregg extended an arm.

The old man didn't even move his eyes.

"Oh, he can't respond. He had a stroke a couple years back," the young woman said.

"And you care for him by yourself?"

"Sure." The girl took a seat. "He can't speak or move, but he can hear me, or so the doctors say."

"I'm sure he understands and appreciates what you do for him."

Chloe smiled.

Gregg cleared his throat. "So, I was told Liam was your boyfriend. Is that right?"

"It was a fling. Nothing serious. I don't have any idea where he might be."

"I stopped by the grocery store where you work on my way here, Miss Mason. Your colleagues mentioned that you were frequently upset with Liam."

"Flings can be frustrating, especially when one of you wants something more."

"Who wanted something more?"

"I did," she replied.

"Did you see Liam the night he went missing?"

She nodded. "Yeah, we were on a date earlier that evening."

"Take me to where you had the date, please."

. . .

Chloe took him to the town park, where a small café was located in the middle, surrounded by a children's playground and impeccably maintained flowerbeds.

"So, this is where you last saw Liam?" Gregg glanced around the quiet area of oak trees and green grass.

Chloe nodded and led him to a park bench, shaded under the tall branches of an autumn tree. "This is where we, um, made out, when I last saw him." Chloe blushed slightly. "Which is all we ever really did."

"Did anything else happen between you two?"

"This is where I broke it off."

"Oh, I'm sorry," Gregg replied, making a mental note of their breakup happening on the same day Liam disappeared.

"Don't be. All I did was finally have the courage to end an awful relationship, and I was happy to do it."

"I thought you wanted the relationship to get more serious?" he asked.

"That was earlier in the relationship, before—"

"Before you grew too frustrated?"

"Before I realized what kind of guy Liam really is."

"And what kind of guy is that?" Gregg asked, realizing that she was referring to Liam in present tense; either she had nothing to do with his murder or she was being clever.

"Not a nice guy," Chloe replied with a mixture of sadness and anger. "I had got him a keychain engraved with his initials as an anniversary present. He didn't get me anything in return, of course." Gregg noted that someone who was only a fling gave anniversary gifts. "He threw it away after I said it was over." Suddenly, she collapsed to her knees and burst into tears.

At first, Gregg stood frozen, not sure what to do. "Um, I'm sorry." He then tried placing his hand on her shoulder.

Chloe shrugged him off and struck the ground with her fist. "I hate him!" she screeched. "I hate him!" She gave the ground another punch and collapsed, lying in the grass, sobbing, too pained to say anything more.

She cried silently as Gregg watched over her, stunned by the outburst. Awkwardly, he picked her up, sliding his hands beneath her arms and carried her over to the bench without protest, where he sat beside her.

"Are you okay?" he asked.

Chloe didn't say anything; she merely continued to cry into Gregg's shoulder. Confused, he simply sat there and let it happen.

He remembered one time Silvia came over to his apartment from a party, crying. She had said that there would be no boys at the party, but Gregg had known she was lying. Silvia had been spending time with a boy named Kyle from her class. He hadn't spoken to his daughter about it, mainly because he wouldn't even know where to start. Shouldn't her mother be the one to discuss boys and relationships with her?

He always thought if a boy ever upset her, he'd be filled with rage. But when she came over, crying from that party because Kyle kissed another girl, he wasn't. Kyle was just a dumb kid and wasn't worth his fury or his daughter's tears, not because he was a bad kid, but because he was a kid who hadn't meant to hurt anyone.

He sat beside his daughter and let her cry into his shoulder for nearly an hour, and then they just sat and talked. Gregg told her how when the right guy came along, she would know it, reciting stories of silly, but meaningful things he had done for her mother, like the time in college he wrote and played her a song with his guitar to first get her attention. When they were finished, his daughter hugged him and gave him a smile that made his stomach flutter, and his insides beam warm—there was no greater feeling in the world. In that moment, he had felt like he would always be able to protect her.

Now, sitting on the park bench, with the young blonde crying into his shoulder, Gregg realized how much he wanted to feel that way again.

7:40 PM

The day eventually ended. Gregg sat in the bar of the Swan Inn, having a drink with Bernard, and recounted his meeting with Chloe.

"That's crazy," Bernard commented. "Do you think she had something to do with his disappearance?"

"I don't know who to trust. But no, I don't think she had anything to do with it. From what I saw today, she isn't calculating or controlled enough."

"Anyone else? How *did* your talk with the mayor go?"

"Well, he isn't as innocent as he claims. Nor was he loyal to his wife," Gregg replied.

"You didn't say that to his face, did you?"

"Of course I did."

"It would be a bad idea to alienate him," Bernard said.

"I don't have time to consider people's feelings."

"That's just it," Bernard explained. "The folks here aren't used to people who don't have time for that. This isn't the city. The people here stop in the street to ask each other about their days. Everyone has time for everyone here. If you want these people to tell you anything, you're going to have to work on your people skills."

Gregg knew Bernard was right. Getting along with people was never his strong suit. He hadn't gotten along with anyone on the force other than Jim.

Bernard finished his beer and stood. "Well, interesting as always. I'm going to call it a night."

"Night," Gregg told him as Bernard walked off.

Gregg continued to sip at his beer alone when he heard a woman from behind say, "Excuse me, Gregg."

He turned to see Chloe Mason standing.

"I wanted to apologize for earlier," she said. "I acted like such a nutcase."

"Well…"

"It must have made me look guilty, but I didn't have anything to do with Liam disappearing if that's what you're thinking, I swear. Although I am still angry at him."

He gave her a smile, and she smiled back.

"Maybe I could apologize by buying you dinner. Up here all alone, it must get boring."

"You don't have to do that," he replied.

"I want to."

Gregg believed she was being friendly, but perhaps that was because he didn't want to see any strain to her smile. Either way, he accepted the dinner invitation as, just like the picturesque town, if there was ugliness hidden beneath the surface of Chloe Mason's smile, it wouldn't take him long to unmask.

With her dark hair and piercing green eyes,
Rachel Milgram, a kidnapper in no disguise,
Cold and frightening, her demeanor so stark,
Her motives and plans hidden in the dark.

Cold and calculating, Rachel's game,
But he won't let her win the fame,
Of taking his daughter and leaving no trace,
He'll find her and put her back in her rightful place.

11

OCTOBER 24TH, 8:15 AM

Nathan Stannard poured a bowl of cereal and cup of coffee in the shiny and modern kitchen of his large home. The Stannard mansion had been passed on through the generations, as well as it seemed the mayorship title.

Nathan was happy to keep up traditions but insisted on bringing his own flair to the home. The dull exterior bricks had been painted blindingly white, as had the columns. Tiled floorings were implemented, and the large wine cellar had been turned into an indoor swimming pool, equipped with a hot tub, sauna, and steam room.

He passed the cereal down the breakfast bar—made of faux, black marble—to Raymond, keeping the coffee for himself.

"So, I'm meeting with your teacher today. What can I expect to hear?" Nathan asked.

Raymond shrugged, crunching his corn flakes.

"Are you struggling with anything? Reading? Math?"

The boy shook his head.

Nathan smiled. "Good. That's what I like to hear. You need to get ahead of the competition early if you want to succeed in life."

"Is that how you became mayor, Dad?" his son asked.

"You better believe it."

"Well, I wanna be like you when I'm older."

"Then you need to be tough. Never let anyone see you as a victim. You understand?"

Raymond looked as though he was thinking this over and then nodded.

Nathan smiled. "Good boy."

After leaving Raymond with the nanny, Nathan made his way to the school. Although parent-teacher night had been held the previous evening, Nathan's busy schedule prevented him from attending. As the mayor, Nathan believed that the teacher would understand his predicament, and she had graciously agreed to meet with him the next morning.

He sat across from Raymond's teacher, Miss Daisy. She was a slender, young woman with curly hair tied up in a bun and thick, blue glasses perched on her nose. Miss Daisy clearly hadn't gone to a lot of effort on his account, wearing a crumpled skirt and a pink shirt with a coffee stain on the sleeve. Nathan ran his hand down the black, slim tie attached to his pristine white shirt, indicating his attention to detail in his attire.

"Raymond is reading at a fifth-grade level. You must have read to your son from an early age," Miss Daisy said.

"Well, I'm certain either the nanny or his mother did. At least one of them, I'm sure."

"Like I said, his grades are very good. But Raymond does still seem to be having some problems outside the classroom."

Nathan sat forward. "What do you mean?"

"With another student, Max."

Nathan sat back in his chair and waved the air. "Boys tease each other. It's part of growing up."

"It's more than that, Mr. Stannard. Yesterday I found Raymond out on the playground in tears. He wouldn't say why he was crying, but some of the other children said Max had been picking on him."

Nathan shook his head. "You're wrong. My son is not a sissy. He can defend himself."

"Mr. Stannard, I have moved the boys apart, but—"

"You did what?" Nathan asked, frowning. "What good will that do? Raymond can fight his own battles! He doesn't need you helping out, and he certainly doesn't need to be taught to run away!" Nathan stood up and unbuttoned his shirt collar, feeling a wave of heat wash over him.

"Mr. Stannard, please, that is not what this is—"

"Toughness in young boys should be fostered and encouraged, yet people today insist on ruining them with safe spaces and participation trophies. My wife was just the same. She coddled him, and he's no better for it."

"Mr. Stannard, we can talk about this."

Nathan slammed his fist into her desk and made her jump. "Just keep your nonsense out of the classroom and leave me to worry about my son."

―――――

Gregg made his way through the narrow hallway of the sheriff's station, eventually coming to the main office. It included a large desk and a couple of small jail cells, both empty.

Sheriff Johnston sat on his chair, feet resting on the desk. He had a mug of coffee in one hand and a donut in the other. Once the sheriff spotted him, the sheriff immediately threw the donut at a nearby bin, but missed, and put the coffee down on the desk, repositioning himself to appear more professional.

"I hope I'm not interrupting something, Sheriff," Gregg said, looking at the sprinkled donut on the floor and smirking.

"Not at all. Is there anything I can do for you?"

"Actually, yes, I need everything you have on the Clementine Stannard case."

The sheriff frowned. "I already gave you all the case files we have on Liam Watts. As you've made perfectly clear, that is *all* you are here to investigate."

"That's still true," Gregg admitted. "But there's a chance the two cases intersect, and I've always suspected it would come to this."

The elderly sheriff squinted. "You know, I don't like that you think you can come in here and start running this town like you know what's best for it. We don't need no city folk poking their noses in. Blackberry Cove was doing just fine under my watch."

"I do hope you're not forgetting what I'm here to investigate, Sheriff: one murder and one missing person case, both unsolved, and both happened under your expert watch."

"I don't like you, Hunter," the sheriff said simply.

"Well, it doesn't take a genius to figure that out. Rest assured, Sheriff, once I have everything I need, I'll be out of your town for good. I do hope *that* is incentive enough for you to make the right decision."

Still squinting his eyes, Johnston said, "You'll have everything you need on Mrs. Stannard by this afternoon."

While Gregg waited for the files to be ready, he decided to delve further into Mrs. Stannard's case by paying a visit to her husband. The mayor wasn't there to greet him, however. Instead, an older, large woman welcomed him. She introduced herself as Felicity, the nanny, and offered to get him some coffee but he turned her down. "I was just hoping to ask a few questions about the late Mrs. Stannard," he said.

"Anything I can do to help the Stannards will be my pleasure," the woman answered. "Like most people here, I've lived in this town all my life. In all that time, never has anything like this ever happened. Would you like to go into the sitting room?"

"No, that's alright. This won't take long," Gregg replied,

preferring to stay in the entryway. "Have you worked for the Stannards long?"

"I've been that boy's nanny since he was born, and before that, I used to babysit the mayor for his father."

"You must have worked here when the mayor was married to his first wife."

Felicity glanced at the floor. "That was a long time ago."

"Can you tell me a little about her, please?"

"Anna moved to Blackberry Cove almost twenty years ago, already with a little girl. The mayor's father didn't like that. He was a very traditional man. The mayor was young, not quite ready to go to college, and fell in love with Anna instantly. They got married, but she ran off less than a year later. Personally, I got the impression she just wasn't suited for family life."

"What do you mean?"

"She was always cold with her little girl. Not at all like a mother should be. And I never got the feeling that she loved the mayor."

"Then why did she marry him?"

Felicity shrugged. "She seemed to be in quite a desperate situation when she arrived."

"What happened to the girl?"

"She went to live with her father. After all, the mayor and the girl's mother had only been married less than a year. I don't think the girl really took to Mr. Stannard. He was too young to know how to be a father."

"You must have some loyalty to the family after working here so long," Gregg remarked.

"Everyone in town does."

"What do you mean?"

"Mr. Stannard's grandfather was the mayor during the Second World War," she explained. "Everyone knows that great man kept this town going."

She stopped as if to check that he wanted her to continue, and Gregg nodded, signaling she should.

"Well, a lot of the men were off fighting, so Mr. Stannard's grandfather encouraged the women to take over their jobs, especially on the farmlands. He doubled the labor on those farms, also to help the neighboring towns. Ever since then, it seemed fitting that a Stannard should run this town."

"I see. And have the Stannards always been good to work for?" Gregg asked.

"I never saw much of Mr. Stannard before his wife's death," she replied. "He was working a lot. But Mrs. Stannard was a delightful woman. She was the kind of person who genuinely wanted to talk to you and know how you were getting on. That's so rare these days. At first, I think she felt quite intimidated by the town. Mr. Stannard was late going to college, so he was quite a few years older than Mrs. Stannard when they met. Still, they married almost immediately. It took her a while to find her voice. Once she did, everyone fell in love with her, and she fit in with the town perfectly."

"Were you working here the night she went missing?"

"Yes, in fact, I was the one who reported Mrs. Stannard missing to the sheriff."

"You did?"

"She was off on her nightly run and asked me to watch Raymond as usual. Mrs. Stannard usually returned after an hour or so from her run, but she never did. Eventually, I got worried and called the mayor. He said to phone the sheriff."

"What time was this?" Gregg enquired, jotting down notes into his pad.

"It was nearly eleven by the time I called," she said, almost ashamed, like she thought maybe calling earlier would have saved Mrs. Stannard's life. Gregg was never good at comforting witnesses, so he didn't attempt to do so. "The sheriff didn't find her until the next morning. By then, it was too late."

"Where was Mr. Stannard at the time you called him?" he asked.

Felicity's eyes started to water. She took a handkerchief from her pocket and dried her eyes. Once finished, she folded it immaculately and placed it back. "He was at the office."

"At eleven o'clock? Is it usual for the mayor to be working so late?"

"Yes, it is," she replied. "Like I said, the mayor is a busy man."

"Was he alone when you called?"

She looked down at her feet.

"Felicity?"

"I don't know if I should answer that."

"Please do," he urged her. "Anything you tell me will be held in the strictest confidence, and you never know what may end up being useful to an investigation."

"The mayor spends a lot of time with his secretary," she responded meekly.

He smiled. "Thank you, Felicity."

12

Breakfast at the Swan Inn was Bernard's Tuesday treat before he'd go on a hike through the Green Mountains, overlooking Little Rock Pond. Sometimes he'd take a few days, bringing a tent along with him. It depended on what wildlife he hoped to see. While the animals were largely reclusive, over the years Bernard had managed to find many of their hideouts, including moose, coyotes, and black bears.

He dug into his Full Irish Breakfast, thinking about how good they must eat in Ireland. Although he had heard that a true Irish breakfast consisted of oysters and Guinness, he was content with the savory sausages, crispy bacon, and other indulgent fried foods that he was currently enjoying, even though sure his arteries probably weren't.

Richard and Hannah's dog, Sparky, bounded into the room and beelined straight for Bernard, eagerly anticipating his usual doggy treat. Bernard took one from his pocket and fed it to the white husky. He rubbed the happy dog's head before it ran off, having gotten what it wanted.

Bernard took the locket out from his other pocket and clicked it open, staring fondly at the image of Flora inside. A tear trickled down his stubbled face. After a long gaze, he closed it and placed it back. He ran a hand through his short, unkempt hair and looked to see Sparky still running around the inn.

The dog stopped at Richard and Hannah in the back of the room, expecting another treat, but Richard shooed him away instead.

"So, what was it you wanted to talk about?" Hannah asked her husband.

"Pack your bags," Richard said happily.

"Why?" Hannah asked.

"I can't tell you, it's a surprise."

"This is awfully sudden."

"If it wasn't sudden, it wouldn't be a surprise," Richard said.

"I don't know."

"Hannah, please. I'm really trying here. I just want a romantic couple of days away with you. Can you grant me that?"

After a moment's thought, Hannah relented, "I suppose so."

"Great! Pack your bags!"

"But what about the inn?"

"What *about* the inn?"

"We need someone to run it, and the only staff members we have are a bunch of inexperienced teenagers."

"Well…" Richard surveyed the room and spotted Bernard sitting nearby. "Bernard can run the bar. Can't you, Bernard?"

Bernard looked up from his plate, egg still in his mouth. "Huh?"

"You can run the bar while we're gone, right? It'll only be for a couple of days."

"Sure, I guess," Bernard agreed, sensing Richard's excitement. Knowing they had problems, he decided to stay and do his hiking another day. "I can even keep an eye on Sparky, if you'd like."

The husky's eyes widened at the sound of his name, perhaps half expecting another snack.

"Fantastic! Settled. Tara can keep the rooms; she's been here the longest. There's no reason we shouldn't go."

"Well, okay! I'll go and pack my bags," Hannah said, her face suddenly lighting up with excitement.

Richard leaned forward and gave his wife an awkward kiss before she turned away.

Bernard continued eating his breakfast. He wondered silently if the couple's sudden trip had anything to do with Gregg's arrival in town.

After he returned to the sheriff's station, Gregg and Johnston looked over a vast number of files, all of which were laid out for him on the office's main desk.

"So, what do you think the connection is between these cases?" the sheriff asked.

"I don't know, I just know it's no coincidence that one was murdered, and one disappeared on the same night."

"Maybe Liam Watts killed her and ran off," Johnston suggested. "Maybe they were having an affair."

"No."

Johnston scorned. "Why not?"

"Did you not read their character descriptions? Their personalities are too different, too incompatible. I doubt they were having an affair."

"They say opposites attract."

"We're talking about people, not magnets." Gregg looked at pictures of the crime scene. The body of Clementine Stannard was tied to a chair with a puddle of blood on the floor beneath her. "The killer left all of that, but no fingerprints or DNA?"

Johnston shook his head.

"No clues whatsoever?" Gregg asked.

"Well, there could have been at the time, but it would have all been cleaned up by now."

"Where were these images taken? Where was she killed?"

"The basement of a vacant home in town. But the real estate

agents have already had the place completely hosed down. They wanna hide the fact a murder took place from any potential buyers. Not that it stopped word getting out. No one's had any interest in that house since. People put flowers on the front lawn, treating it like a monument to our late First Lady."

Gregg scanned the pictures and noticed blows to the victim's head. He pointed. "That's not from a nail gun."

"No," the sheriff replied. "She was also beaten over the head by a blunt instrument."

"It doesn't make any sense."

"What doesn't?" the sheriff asked.

"The killer, that's what. He planned everything in advance. He had the basement all prepared, knew the victim's running schedule, and figured out a way to take her to the basement without being noticed. He was even careful enough to restrain her and wore gloves to avoid leaving any fingerprints. If it's the same person who killed Liam Watts, then he covered his tracks by disposing of Liam's body. This all suggests that he is an organized criminal, in control of himself. But these blows to the victim's head appear out of control. And he left a chaotic crime scene behind."

"So, what are you thinking? Two killers?" Johnston enquired.

"Not necessarily. It may not be that simple. Perhaps Liam stumbled on what was going on, the killer pursued him, killed him, got rid of the body, and then had no time to go back and dispose of Clementine's body."

"But the time of death was about eight thirty that night. We weren't even looking for Mrs. Stannard until about three hours after that. If he didn't have time to dispose of her, then Liam must have been keeping him busy for a *long* time."

"That's a possibility. Pursuing, killing, and disposing of a body can take longer than one might think. And this killer is organized, but he's not experienced. The messy means of a nail gun show that. Do you have any kind of profile constructed?"

"Just that he's probably a sick fuck," Johnston said.

Gregg rolled his eyes.

"Oh, also that he's probably a white male, between the ages of twenty-five and forty-five, and all the usual crap."

"The murder demonstrates a lot of pent-up anger. Also, he felt more comfortable knocking Clementine out on her walk rather than luring her in using his social skills, meaning he's probably a loner and antisocial. But there was no sexual assault or any other evidence to suggest this was about sexual pleasure or repressed fantasies. Maybe, he has successful sexual relationships. But he feels powerless in other aspects, such as a menial job which he feels is below his skills and intelligence.

"The crime scene doesn't portray the image of a highly intelligent offender. He likely has an unrealistic image of himself and believes himself to be due more than what he has. This crime was all about power; it was about him releasing his resentment towards a world that has never recognized what he has to offer. And the victim was carefully selected, so he personally knew her and *hated* her, or she's a surrogate for the real target of his rage, such as an abandoning or emasculating mother."

For the first time since they met, Johnston looked at Gregg with almost an air of respect. "I always thought profiling was a bunch of nonsensical guesswork."

"Never guesswork," Gregg replied. "And it can be a useful investigatory tool if used right and along with other means. Did anyone have reason to hate Clementine Stannard?"

Johnston frowned. "You may think I'm just a dumb hick, Hunter, but I've been sheriff here for many years. I checked thoroughly for any enemies Mrs. Stannard may have had and came back empty."

"What about Liam Watts? Could he have hated Clementine Stannard?" Gregg asked. "Tell me about him."

"Actually, you just did," Johnston replied.

"What do you mean?"

"I mean your profile described Liam Watts perfectly. That's why I was impressed. He's a good-looking guy, in a relationship with a good-looking girl. Not very friendly. In a job he hated, at the local shop. He's not the smartest guy in the world, but not stupid; he could have pulled this off. From what I remember, he had a rough time as a kid too. Mother left him and his old man when he was five, he was bullied at school, and his dad died when he was still young. So, there you have it, the profile matches. Liam probably killed Mrs. Stannard and then ran off, probably out of the state by now."

Gregg nodded and continued to flick through the crime scene photos. "A dusty basement floor and lots of blood, but no footprints?"

"The killer wore plastic bags over his feet," Johnston replied.

Gregg turned to him.

"I know." Johnston nodded. "Like you said, he was organized."

"He had been fantasizing about it for a long time," Gregg replied. "He had time to perfect almost everything until he could hold the rage no longer." He stopped at a photo of the scene and stared at it.

"What is it?" Johnston asked.

Gregg handed him the photo. It showed the floor in front of Clementine's body, where the killer would have been standing. But in the back corner, there were three distinct imprints in the dust, at an angle.

"What is that?" Johnston brought the photo closer, but then his eyes widened as he realized. He turned to Gregg. "Is that from a camera?"

Gregg nodded. "A camera tripod, yes."

"Do you mean that this sick fuck filmed the killing?" Johnston asked.

"That's exactly what this means. He needed a way to relive the killing over and over to release his rage again and again." Gregg's eyes turned to the window. "That video is out there somewhere."

13

NATHAN KNEW THAT PEOPLE WOULDN'T UNDERSTAND. THEIR LOVE was pure, but if word got out, people would misjudge the relationship he had with his secretary. The local paper would report it as a sex scandal, even though it was his marriage which had been ungodly.

Clementine was only interested in his money and good looks. She never appreciated who he was as a person. The only reason he married her was to make his father proud. He'd have been ashamed of him for knocking a girl up and not marrying her. Besides, it would have destroyed the family image, meaning he'd never have become mayor.

Now that he finally had a beautiful woman who truly loved and understood him, he wasn't prepared to let her go for anything. That was all he wanted, ever since his mother left him as a child—for a woman to truly love him and to never leave him.

It was a terrible thing to have a mother disappear in the night. As a child, Nathan blamed himself for her leaving. His father was no help. Nathan often wondered if she would have stayed had he been a better son. But he no longer had to worry about any of that with Isabella at his side.

Four months ago, Isabella suggested they run away after another of his wife's phone calls interrupted one of their nights together. She was sick of being Nathan's hideaway, she said, and of being the person he had to make excuses to his wife and son about. She loved him and wanted the world to know it. Nathan was worried Clementine would take his son from him; he was the one good thing to come from that whole damned relationship. He couldn't lose Isabella, that much he knew. She gave his life the meaning he longed for his whole life. He had to find a way to keep both her and Raymond, and so the two of them formed a plan.

Now, four months later, Nathan had both Raymond and Isabella as he wanted, but things weren't exactly as he imagined them to be.

As he returned home from the school, Felicity greeted him. She, like many in town who lived there all their lives, had an unbreakable respect towards his family. She had a way about her that made Nathan feel good about himself, as if her respect reinforced his belief that he was meant to be this town's mayor.

"The PI stopped by," she said.

Nathan frowned. "What did he want?"

"Had some questions about Mrs. Stannard."

"Hope you told him to beat it. Now, where's Raymond?"

"In the lounge doing his homework, sir."

Nathan marched into the room, and Raymond glanced over from the small desk he used for school studies. "Hi, Dad."

Nathan sat beside him. "So, your teacher told me about Max. Is Max being mean to you, Raymond?"

The small boy shook his head.

Nathan sighed. "The only way to deal with bullies is by showing them you're tough. That they can't mess with you. That if they hit you, you hit back harder. Do you understand?"

Raymond nodded.

"Good."

Nathan stood and headed out of the room. He asked Felicity, "Has Raymond seemed okay to you lately?"

"Well, he's been a bit sad, but… excuse me, sir, I don't think it's my place to say."

"No, say it."

"Forgive me, sir, but I think that with all that's happened lately, what the boy needs is for his father to be more present."

Nathan felt a lump in his throat, surprised and angry she would say such a thing. He frowned. "You were right; it's not your place. I am there for my son. I've always been there for him."

He made his way to the office, where he knew Isabella and a bottle of scotch would be waiting.

Isabella sat reading in the corner of the room. Her lips stretched into a pleasant smile once she saw him. She stood and handed him a glass as he sat and explained his morning.

"Can you believe it," he shouted. "I didn't raise my son to be a wimp, to be pushed around by other kids!"

"Well, no offense dear, but you didn't exactly raise him at all," she replied.

"This is all Clementine's fault, bringing him up with all that wishy-washy nonsense. He needs discipline and strength. I want my son to be a man one day and one like myself. I didn't get where I am by being pushed around!"

"Have you considered maybe there is more to this than you think?"

"What on earth are you talking about?" Nathan asked. "Women, you always speak in riddles."

"Maybe Raymond isn't sad lately just because he's being bullied."

Nathan furrowed his brows.

Isabella pulled some ruffled–up pieces of paper out from under some files on his desk.

"What are they?" Nathan asked.

"They're pictures that Raymond drew for you to look at, but you never did," Isabella informed him.

She handed him the pictures. Nathan looked through them to see a scene of a little stick man walking hand in hand with a stick woman, who appeared to have wings.

"What the hell is this meant to be?" Nathan said.

"It's Raymond and his mother as an angel."

Nathan scoffed. "She's no fucking angel."

"No, but she *is* dead. You see, this isn't about you, Nathan. This is about your son. He misses his mother, and he is hurting."

Nathan stared at the picture, listening to her words. She was right. Now that Isabella was in his life, Nathan was desperate to keep her there. Maybe too desperate. Perhaps, he had clung to that desire too tightly, and it was his son whom it had hurt.

14

Having taken Chloe up on her offer, Gregg sat with her for dinner at the Swan Inn. While it was nice of the girl to keep him company, he wasn't in much of a sociable mood.

"So why would anyone come here?" Chloe asked. "It's so boring."

"You don't care for the town?"

Chloe shook her head. "I hate it here. If my dad didn't need me to care for him, I'd have left long ago."

"You're a good daughter," he said.

"I figure I owe it to him."

"That's good. Family's important. What about your mother?"

"She and my sister died in a fire when I was little. Only my dad and I made it out. He came into my room, picked me up in my blanket, and carried me out. The flames were too bad for him to go back for my mother and sister."

"I'm sorry. Were you and your sister close?"

Chloe paused. "I like to think we would have been had we both had the chance to grow up. She was a few years older than me, and I always saw her as this perfect person I would never be as good as. We fought all the time. Mostly over nothing. What about you? Do you have a family?"

"It's complicated," Gregg uttered.

"What do you mean?"

Gregg didn't answer. He took a swig of his drink. "How is working at the grocery store?"

"Well, I'm sure it's not as fulfilling as what you do, but I suppose it's nice getting to talk to everyone in town. Some of the older people don't get out much, so I try to chat with them. I like to think that we all have the power to make a difference in people's lives, even by the smallest gestures."

Gregg nodded, taking another sip.

"So how is the investigation going?" Chloe asked.

"It's proving to be difficult. But I'll find who is responsible."

Chloe smiled at this.

"Actually," Gregg said, "I know this is meant to be a casual dinner, but it'd help if you told me a little about Liam."

"Well, if it'd help."

"It would."

"What do you want to know?" she asked.

"How did you meet?"

"Well, I always knew him around town," she replied. "But I suppose I first noticed him at a bar five years ago."

"Did you hook up?"

She averted his gaze, blushing, and then nodded.

"Five years is a long time for a fling," he pointed out.

Her eyes turned back to him. "It was quite off and on, never serious, but you're right, I wasn't entirely honest with you. I'm sorry."

"Serious enough for anniversary presents though."

She looked at him again, this time as though she was a little girl caught eating a piece of candy before dinner.

"Was Liam your first boyfriend?"

"I suppose," she said. "I had a thing in school with a boy from town, but we drifted apart. He's the town's deputy now."

"I haven't met a deputy."

"He's on a fishing trip but will be back in a few days. You'll likely meet him then, unless, of course, you've already cracked the case."

"Let's hope so," he said. "Did Liam do any filming?"

She arched her eyebrows. "Yes, he went to film school but dropped out. Said it was a waste of time. Why?"

He ignored her question and asked, "Do you know what school he went to?"

"Burlington College."

"Did he work on any film projects after film school?"

"He was especially interested in horror and used to occasionally make videos at the park," she replied. "He said he wanted me to star in them and was going to make me famous, but I wasn't interested in that."

Lucky for you, or you might have ended with a nail in your neck.

"Why is this important?" she asked.

Gregg stood. "I'll get us more drinks."

Behind the bar, Bernard appeared a little frazzled. He was grabbing glasses, pouring drinks, and taking the orders all by himself. Gregg wasn't too sympathetic, considering he used to work bars in Boston to help pay his school fees. Now, a shift by the waterfront on a Saturday night—*that* was frazzling.

Dr. Holst and Elaine stood in front of Gregg. While the therapist ordered a glass of red wine and his wife ordered a gin and tonic—probably the most complicated cocktail Bernard would have to worry about—Gregg took out his phone and started to research what he could about Burlington College.

Liam Watts, a film school dropout so strange,
Loved horror movies and gore beyond range.
He filmed gruesome scenes, disturbing and vile,
Making people uneasy, and sometimes rile.

But now he's missing, and the town's in dismay,
A prime suspect in the mayor's wife's foul play.
Did he commit the murder, or is he a victim too?
Only time will tell what's really true.

15

OCTOBER 25TH, 9:58 AM

GREGG FOUND A CONTACT NUMBER FOR BURLINGTON COLLEGE'S Film Studies class. He called them that morning and asked to speak to the course instructor, to see if they remembered Liam Watts. But the professor—Dr. Marek Galt—had retired and moved to some northern state; the woman at the university's office didn't remember where exactly. She said she'd try to pass on the message, but Gregg wasn't very hopeful about getting a response.

He made coffee for him and Bernard, who appeared lost in a world of his own, staring down at the picture of the woman in his locket. Gregg mixed the hot drinks silently, eyeing Bernard in the corner of his vision. It was apparent whomever Bernard was mourning, he wished to do so in private. In fact, everything about Bernard was a mystery, and that's exactly why Gregg wanted to get to know him better.

As he approached with the drinks, Bernard dried his eyes and closed the locket.

"Where were you this morning?" Gregg sat down and placed the coffees on the table. "I tried calling earlier to meet."

"Oh, I went for a morning walk. I never bring my phone, sorry." Bernard took a sip and thanked him.

"See anything interesting when you were out there?"

"Nothing unusual... What did you want to speak to me about?"

"Well, you spend a lot of time in the forests and mountains around these parts. If someone *had* killed Liam and buried him, I'm thinking out there would be a good place to do it. Secluded. You've never seen anything worth mentioning?"

Bernard paused for a moment. "Just the beautiful wildlife."

Bernard was hiding something, but Gregg wanted to keep him as a friend. No point in pressing and alienating him, like he had the mayor. He gave a disappointed expression, hoping Bernard would latch on and provide him with something.

"I could show you Liam's place," Bernard said. "He lived in a cabin on the outskirts of the forest. It belonged to his father."

"My employer told me. I have no one I can contact for permission to go inside though."

"No law against looking through the windows, right?" Bernard asked.

Indeed, there wasn't, and so after finishing their coffee, Bernard drove them up a country road towards Liam's cabin, declaring they would have to be back before the inn's bar opened.

The house was at the edge of the forest, Bernard said, and they had to walk a little from the road to get there. Green Mountain National Forest surrounded most of Blackberry Cove, and it was vast. Gregg saw that on his drive to town, but walking through the woodland gave a whole new perspective, making it appear truly endless.

"How come you know where you're going?" Gregg asked, wondering if Bernard had been to the victim's house before.

Bernard looked back over his shoulder. "The cabin is north of town. Liam told me that when I first moved here and asked for hiking tips."

Bernard walked at a rapid pace, and Gregg struggled to keep up, though he didn't dare show it. He breathed through his nose to avoid the sound of heavy panting. Since losing his place on the force, he had let himself get out of shape a little.

He was going to ask how Bernard knew they were even heading north but figured that was a silly question. Bernard probably studied the forest's maps enough to know where everything was located. Also, Gregg vaguely remembered from his brief time in the Boy Scouts that certain outdoorsy people could find north by studying the moss and tree branches. If anyone knew about the stuff, he was certain Bernard did.

"You ever done any tracking?" Gregg asked.

Bernard stopped and looked over his shoulder. "Like animal tracking?"

"I have no doubt you can identify different animal tracks. You need to find the animals before you can take their pictures," Gregg replied. "I was thinking more about tracking people."

"Why are you asking?" Bernard said. "I hope you're not thinking Liam is out in these woods and you want me to find him."

Gregg shrugged. "I'm just curious."

Bernard kept walking. "A few years ago, I was in Brazil and hired a guide to take me into the Amazon. On our first day, he pointed to his boot's footprint in the mud and said not to lose him. After that, he liked to test me by disappearing between trees and having me follow his tracks. I learned animals, too, can help when tracking someone, by the sounds they make. Sometimes hunters wonder why deer stay away, even after they've been creeping slowly. It's because birds, squirrels, and other animals make warning calls to each other, and the deer can understand it. Animal calls are like ripples in the water, carried on by other animals."

"I never thought of that," he said.

"What about you?" Bernard asked. "Any tracking experience?"

"Back when I was a detective for the BPD, a little girl went missing—Emilie Jones. There was this FBI tracker. Native American trained. I was amazed by the things he knew. He explained, footprints are a lot like fingerprints—no one walks exactly the same. Some people drag their heels or walk more on one side. He could even take a good guess at the person's height and weight just from their footprint. He knew if the person was walking or running, or if they were lost. I kept in touch with him after the case was over and picked his brain as best I could."

"Did you find the girl?" Bernard asked.

"Alive."

"That's good," Bernard said. "Let's hope the same happens with Liam."

"How did the town get its name?" Gregg asked, scanning the surrounding trees and mountains. "Seems like an odd name for a mining town in the forest."

"The first settlers here were lost in the stony mountains. Once they came across a river, they followed it. Eventually, they found an inlet in the shoreline of the river that led to a field of blackberries. Apparently, they were near starvation and the berries kept them alive, so they decided to build their homes next to the field. Personally, I doubt how true that story is, but it's the one people tell."

"Well, that's important. Sometimes, when working a case, what people say and believe is more significant than what actually happened."

When they finally arrived, it was a worn-looking cabin, sitting lonely, the wood scratched away, and the windows obstructed by inside shutters.

"So much for looking through the windows," Gregg remarked.

He stepped onto the tattered welcome mat, feeling stones underneath, and pulled the door handle. It opened. Surprised, he took a stride closer.

There was an open planned main room with a kitchen, dining

area, and living section with a television and sofa. The dated furniture was shabby and covered in dust, and Gregg realized that, even before his death, Liam probably never replaced or even cleaned his parents' décor, though décor was too generous a word for what this was.

The living area's dustbin was filled with small pieces of paper. They were train tickets from Manchester, Vermont to Albany, New York. Dozens of them, going back months before Liam's disappearance. Gregg pocketed a handful.

He walked past the master bedroom and bathroom, coming to the smaller bedroom, where—judging by the unmade but well-used bed—Liam Watts had still been sleeping. Inside, there was a desk with a computer and a camera. Adjacent to the camera, a tripod rested. Gregg switched on the camera, but there were no pictures or videos to view. Opening it up, he realized the SD card was missing.

Disappointed, Gregg scanned the rest of the room. Other than being exceptionally messy, the bedroom seemed average. A television was linked to a gaming console, with game discs and movies strewn about everywhere. There were a few horror movies, but there were also plenty of science fiction, superhero movies, and old classics, as well. In fact, they were mostly movies Gregg enjoyed himself.

Atop the bed was a poster of some cheap horror movie that caught Gregg's attention. The picture depicted a screaming brunette, blood dripping onto her face from a knife that hung above her. The woman in the picture looked just like Clementine Stannard, or at least what he remembered from the post-mortem pictures he had seen of her. The woman in the poster looked about ten years younger, which made him wonder if it was really her or just a coincidence.

"Bernard," he called.

Bernard appeared around the corner of the doorway. "What's wrong?"

"Look at this picture," he said. "Does it look like Clementine Stannard?"

Bernard gazed at the poster up and down. "Creepily like her."

"Everything about the place is creepy." Gregg unpinned the poster from the wall and rolled it up to take with him.

"What do you mean?" Bernard asked.

"Everything appears untouched since the death of Liam's parents," Gregg explained. "The place doesn't even look like it's been cleaned in years. The sheriff said Liam's mom left when he was young, and his dad passed away some time ago. How long ago?"

Bernard shrugged. "I really haven't lived here that long, and I was never close to Liam."

"He gave you hiking tips," Gregg reminded him, "so you must have spoken sometimes. He never mentioned anything about his father?"

Bernard appeared to ponder and then said, "Well, he did mention his father helped build the town's church. That's only about ten or fifteen years old, going by the wood, so I guess he died sometime after that. Sorry, that's all I can think of."

Gregg went into the kitchen to rake through drawers, and then went in search of a closet or outdoor shed but couldn't see any.

"What are you looking for?" Bernard asked, following him.

"Tools. I didn't exactly expect to find a nail gun lying around, but it's strange that I can't find any tools whatsoever. Especially if Liam's father was as handy as you say."

"A nail gun?" Bernard asked. "You think Liam killed Clementine, don't you?"

"It's a possibility."

"You think someone took it and the other tools?"

"Again, it's possible," Gregg replied. "But it's also possible I just can't find them, or Liam threw them out after his dad died. Though that seems unlikely, seeing as how he appears to have thrown away nothing else. This place is cluttered with junk."

"I can understand that," Bernard said. "It's difficult for some people to let go."

Gregg eyed the locket around Bernard's neck. "Is that why you're always staring at that picture?"

Bernard appeared startled. He put his hand over the ornament, as if to protect it. "My wife was gunned down in a parking garage on our anniversary. I was waiting for her at the restaurant when it happened."

"I'm so sorry," Gregg said.

"When she died, my world froze, and no one around me seemed to understand. You know when you're sick and everyone makes a fuss over you? Well at first it was like that, but eventually no one seemed to understand why I couldn't get better. They wanted me to move on and forget. But I couldn't."

"Is that why you moved here?" Gregg asked.

"The outdoors have always been my way of escaping," Bernard replied. "It's like a different world, one in which you're free from everything. One day, I just packed up and moved without telling anyone where I was going."

"You didn't tell your friends or family?"

"I came here to be alone."

"Don't you feel lonely?"

"When I first moved here, I did," Bernard said. "I'd only go out during the days for hiking, and I'd spend my nights reading nature magazines, curtains drawn, doors locked. Then one day, my neighbors—the O'Doyles—came to my door with a potted plant. They saw the moving truck outside my place a week earlier but hadn't seen anyone around, so they wanted to know if anyone actually moved in. They welcomed me to town and brought me over to the Swan Inn that night for drinks."

"Sounds like it's a very welcoming community," Gregg remarked.

"It is," Bernard replied. "It's a real shame you're only here to look for the ugliness in our town, because it truly is beautiful."

Gregg smiled, then realized he should get back to work. "You said Liam's dad helped build the church, so was Liam religious?"

"Not that I know of," Bernard said. "I think he went to church sometimes though. You think it's worth asking there about him?"

"Probably not," Gregg replied, "but I'm getting desperate."

They headed for the door and Bernard asked, "What about you? Do you have a family?"

"I have a daughter, but we're currently separated." Bernard tilted his head and Gregg thought up more to add. "She lives overseas with her mother and I'm trying to get a visa to go over there."

"Sorry to hear that. I'm sure you'll get back to each other soon."

Gregg gave him a squinted look. "What makes you so sure?"

"You'd be surprised at what people can withstand. The height of any task is only determined by our own state of mind."

"Thanks for that," Gregg said, "but it sounds like you've been reading too many survival stories."

"Nothing wrong with survival stories," Bernard replied with a smile. "My favorite is that of Steven Callahan. He spent seventy-six days adrift at sea. The only reason he survived was because his mind split into two characters: a captain to give orders, and a crewman to obey them. He would argue aloud with himself non-stop about the water and food rations, and the captain side of himself would always win."

Bernard picked up his locket and looked at it. "At first, I wasn't sure how I would survive without my wife. She was my life, and I am who I am because of her. But when she died, I *did* find a way to survive, because I discovered another side of myself. It took me a long time to find it, but I eventually did. It was holding onto it that kept me alive."

Gregg would never have thought he could survive his daughter being taken from him, so he understood what Bernard meant. Since his daughter's kidnapping, he found strength he never knew he had, for her.

"We should get back to town before it gets too cold out here," Gregg said. "I didn't bring a jacket."

"Don't worry, the temperature isn't going to get too low today," Bernard replied.

"How can you tell?"

"By the chirping of the crickets."

"Are you serious?" Gregg asked.

Bernard nodded and Gregg could only laugh. That was one they hadn't taught him in Boy Scouts.

Gregg followed Bernard out the doorway. He winced as he felt something sharp pierce his foot from underneath the doormat once more. Gregg moved his foot, but as it rubbed against the mat, he realized it wasn't rocks he felt. He crouched down and peered under the mat. There was a watch underneath, broken and stuck on the time of when he first stepped on it.

Someone wanted to know if anyone stepped inside Liam's cabin, as well as *when* they did so.

Why?

All he could think of was the camera.

Someone wanted to know when he found it.

Bernard, the nature photographer, so serene,
Hiked through the wilderness, with a locket, so keen,
A picture of his wife, with green eyes and brown hair,
Her beauty captured, with love and care.

He trekked through the mountains, with a heavy heart,
Lost in thoughts, never quite apart,
From the memory of his wife, so dear and kind,
Her picture in the locket, always on his mind.

16

Timothy received a great deal of satisfaction from helping those in town. They came to him with all sorts of problems, from marriage woes to grief counseling. So, when Nathan Stannard came to him that afternoon with his son, he was of course happy to help. Until, that was, Nathan explained what it was his son needed help with.

The mayor told him Raymond had a lack of confidence and wanted the doctor to help Raymond become more comfortable with who he was. This particular request made Timothy feel uneasy, as it clearly did Raymond, evident from his nervous eye twitches.

It reminded him of his father. A man who had never had a lasting relationship, Timothy's father had adopted both him and his brother, raising them by himself. It wasn't until they were older that Timothy and his brother realized their father was a self-hating gay man.

Bullied as a child for his lack of masculinity, his father spent most of his adult life attempting to overcompensate for this. Working out at the gym was his favorite pastime, and he was strictly opposed to any activity that might be perceived as feminine. When Timothy came home from school one day, explaining he wanted to dance, his father made him join the football team.

Timothy failed to live up to his father's expectations. In high school, he let kids pick on him. On one occasion, he was even physically shoved into a locker. In college, he refrained from confronting his girlfriend over her cheating or the man she cheated on him with. When his wife bought a house in Blackberry Cove without consulting him, he moved there without protest, even though it had taken him years to establish a respectable practice in New Hampshire.

In fact, it had been Liam who reminded Timothy of his father's words. It wasn't just because of the videos Liam introduced him to, though watching them made Timothy feel powerful. Liam had also taught him to stand up to his wife and for himself. Without Liam around, Timothy was panicking that his life would return to the same as it was—living under his wife's thumb.

Now, Nathan was looking for Timothy to shape his son into a man, just as Timothy's father had tried to do for him.

He took a seat across from the father and son, seated upon his couch, and thought of what his father would say. "Do you know why it's important for a man to be strong, Raymond?"

The small boy shrugged.

"Do you think you're a strong man, Raymond?"

"I'm ten."

Crossing his legs and sitting back in his armchair, Timothy said, "I'm going to tell you a story, Raymond, that my father told me when I was a little younger than you. It's an Aesop fable. Do you know what that is?"

The young boy shook his head.

"Use your words," Nathan ordered.

"No, Dr. Holst."

"Well, my father was a big fan of them. This particular story is about a weak wagoner who was unable to deliver his merchandise to market because one of his wagons was stuck in the mud. Unable to deliver his merchandise, he would have no money to support his family. Like my father always said, a man who does not support his family is a weak man. So, the wagoner got down on his knees and he prayed for Hercules to appear and lift his wagon for him. Then, do you know what happened?"

"What happened, Dr. Holst?"

"Hercules appeared."

"Did he lift the man's wagon?" the boy asked.

"He certainly did no!" Timothy exclaimed, causing the boy to flinch back slightly. "Hercules yelled to the weak man, 'Gods don't help those who don't help themselves!' Because being weak gets you nowhere in life. If you spend your life being weak, people will walk all over you. When a crow feels lazy and doesn't want to fly anymore, he lands on the back of a sheep and enjoys a free ride. But he doesn't land on the back of a dog. Do you know why?"

"Because the back of a sheep is soft like a pillow?"

"No, because dogs bite back! So, are you a sheep or a dog, Raymond? Because your father told me about this boy at school picking on you, and it sounds like you're a sheep."

"I'm trying to be strong like my dad."

"You have to do better than try. You have to bite back!"

Timothy stood up and walked over to the boy. "So, show me. Show me you can defend yourself." He pushed the small boy, causing him to fall on his side.

"Dr. Holst, what are you doing?" Nathan asked.

But Timothy ignored the mayor, his attention on the boy. After all, this is what Nathan wanted, for his son to be strong, as Timothy's father had wished for him to be. "If a boy did that to you, what would you do?"

"I don't know," Raymond said, getting back up.

"That's not the right answer," Timothy said loudly. "There is a part of you that wants to fight back. If you deny this part of you, things will only get worse."

Timothy pushed him down again.

"Dr. Holst…" Nathan said.

Timothy felt the nails of his fingers dig into his palms. He was getting so hot he thought he might pass out, sweat pouring from his forehead and his heart slamming against his ribcage, desperate to break free. He got up in the small boy's face and shouted, "If I did that to you, what would you do? Wouldn't you fight back? Aren't you strong enough to fight back?"

Raymond flinched, afraid.

Nathan stood up. "Timothy, stop this."

But Timothy's mind was elsewhere. "Wouldn't you fight back?"

Suddenly, Nathan launched a fist right between his eyes, causing Timothy to collapse on the floor.

"What the hell is the matter with you?" Nathan said to Timothy, and then grabbed his son.

Timothy looked at the tearful boy. Realizing what he had done, he shook his head, his mind only just returning. He apologized, not knowing what had come over him.

The father and son left the office. The therapist looked down, confused and concerned for himself. What was happening to him lately? Without Liam, his mind was falling apart. It was as if his body was being taken over. By someone violent.

There was clearly an inner fury inside him, begging to get out. Now, it was more and more frequently taking control. He feared what he might do when the rage took over.

Gregg Hunter's arrival only made things worse. Timothy was panicking he'd be caught. Quickly, he decided it was time to destroy Liam's SD card.

17

Gregg sat in his room at the Swan Inn, reading over his notes as he awaited Rachel Milgram's arrival. She had called him the previous night to express her dissatisfaction with the lack of progress he had made and had promised to visit him in person to "motivate" him.

Whenever he was about to talk to Rachel, Gregg got a fleeting feeling of anxiety. Funny, a woman had never made him feel that way before. He never got flustered around girls when he was at school or college. When he was a cop, female perps were always the easiest to break, and he generally found the female officers easier to get along with than the men.

Of course, Rachel was holding his daughter hostage. But it was more than that. There was something distressing about her very nature. He tried not to let it show, but her cold and controlled manner made him feel powerless in her presence, as if nothing could faze her.

It also made Gregg uneasy to have made such little progress on the case, but if it wasn't for being told there was a case, he wouldn't have even been sure himself; there was no evidence to suggest Liam had been murdered. This raised the question of how Rachel knew Liam was dead. He seemed to have fallen off the face of the Earth.

Liam's disappearance, nevertheless, *was* connected to Clementine Stannard's death. It was too big a coincidence for it to not be. Either Liam killed her, or someone else had taken care of them both. But Gregg put his money on the former. Unless, that was, someone wanted him to think Liam was the culprit. Finding that camera at Liam's place was just too convenient. Also, someone wanted to know when he found it, placing that watch under the mat.

There was a knock at the door and Rachel's voice soon called. He got up and opened the door.

"Shall we begin?" she immediately asked.

Gregg moved out the way and allowed his employer to enter the room.

"I see you didn't tidy up on my account."

"I've been skipping the turndown service."

"Clearly." Rachel ran her finger along a surface and showed him the dust on it. "Have you at least prepared anything?"

Gregg presented his notes. "I made a list of all the town's residents and what I know of their relationship with Liam Watts. Plus, I'm fairly certain Liam murdered the mayor's wife that night."

She took the papers. "What makes you say that?"

"Clementine's killer filmed the murder. Liam was a film student."

"Is that all?"

"No. My profile of the crime scene matches Liam."

"Your profile?"

"Observing the scene, reading people, and making connections is what I do. That's why you wanted me to do this job, remember? I've tried to contact Dr. Marek Galt, the lecturer from the college, to see if he remembers Liam."

"Why would that be useful?"

"Liam spent his entire life in this town, except for the one year he tried to make a go of film school. If I want a full picture of Liam's life, I need to know about that year too."

"And?" Rachel asked.

"No luck. Dr. Galt's retired, but the college took my message and said they'd pass it on to him."

Rachel read through his notes briefly, before smirking. "This is nothing. What have you been doing since you got here, Hunter?"

"Mostly integrating myself. I figured it'd be helpful if I'm going to—"

"I'm beginning to think your heart's not really in it. You're supposed to be the best, but this truly is a half-assed job. Tell me, do you value your daughter's life at all?"

"O-of course—"

"Because her life is what's at stake here if you fail. Do you even have a murder weapon yet? A last location?"

"Liam was at the park that afternoon with his girlfriend, Chloe Mason. And no, I haven't found a murder scene. In fact, I haven't found *any* evidence to suggest Liam is even dead. Maybe he ran off after killing the mayor's wife."

"No."

"No?"

"No, he's dead. I'm sure of it."

"How?" he asked.

"You don't need to know. All you need to know is that if I'm sure of it, you're sure of it. Got it?"

Gregg nodded.

"And have you questioned those at the park yet?" Rachel asked.

"Just Chloe."

She rolled her eyes. "Honestly, never send a man to do anything important. Well, I suggest you start there. I hope you're feeling like a trip to the park."

"I'd be delighted," he replied gruffly.

"When you're finished there, I have a surprise for you."

Gregg grabbed a jacket with a frown, and vacated the room, closing the door behind him.

At the park, Gregg found the therapist's wife, Elaine Holst, and a middle-aged man tending to the garden. They appeared to be repotting plants after someone or something uprooted them from the earth.

When he asked about the case, Elaine told him she wasn't working in the garden the night of Liam's disappearance. He made his way over to the male gardener, hoping he could be of more help.

"I've already spoken to Elaine," he said. "And she tells me you were working in the park the afternoon the mayor's wife was killed and Liam Watts disappeared."

"That's right." The gardener looked up from his knees, busy fixing some small tree back into the soil. "And my work is never over with all those young hooligans who come in and wreck everything."

"Right," Gregg said, trying to move on.

The gardener continued. "Nearly every morning I find the garden destroyed. You should be looking into those kids, not questioning me."

"That's really not why I'm here. Can you please tell me if you saw anything useful to me on the night of Liam Watts' disappearance?"

"Nah, I didn't see nuffin'. I ain't still around here in the evening. If I was, I'd catch those kids wrecking the garden, and give them what for!"

"So, you left the garden in the afternoon?" Gregg looked to clarify.

"That's right."

"Then what?"

"Then I went to the inn, like every night."

"To do what?"

"Drink!"

"I can ask the O'Doyles to confirm your whereabouts."

"You do that."

"Anything else?" Gregg asked, sighing.

"You should try talking to Shannon Alvie."

"Who's that?"

"Owner of the café." The gardener pointed to a neglected-looking building located in the middle of the park, with worn paint and unclean windows. "Shannon was probably here in the evening, cleaning up after a day of work."

Sure, looks like she does a lot of cleaning. Gregg thanked the gardener, walked across the grass, and approached the café, passing some tables with parasols still there from summer.

Entering the building, he found the place empty, except for a blonde woman sat on a stool at the counter. She was smoking a cigarette and sipping a beer. The deep circles beneath her eyes told of her weariness. She turned to face him, blowing a cloud of smoke from between her full lips.

"Are you Shannon Alvie?" Gregg asked. "The owner?"

"That's right. What can I help you with?" She put out her cigarette in an ashtray on the counter.

"I'd like to ask you some questions about Liam Watts, if you don't mind."

"You must be the PI everyone's talking about." She looked him over with a smile. "What kind of questions can I help you with, darling?"

"Did Liam frequent this place?"

She let out a brief chuckle and raised her palms to showcase the room. "Oh, my dear, no one is here *frequently*, can't you see? However, I do recall seeing Liam here during the summer. Business was better then. Everyone wanted ice cream."

"How long ago was that?" he asked, taking out his pad.

"About a month before the murder, I believe. June is always the peak of business. That's when everyone wants to sit in the gardens, licking ice cream and drinking milkshakes. By July, they're sick of it."

Gregg scribbled everything down. "Any other details? Do you remember who he was with or anything like that?"

"He was with the therapist," she replied. "I remember because it was nearly a hundred degrees and the two of them sat outside drinking hot coffee. I think they were here more to people-watch than to enjoy the café."

"What makes you say that?" he asked.

"Liam had binoculars."

"Binoculars?"

"Yeah, it was pretty creepy. At first, I thought he was looking for birds. Then, I noticed him staring in the direction of the children's playground. When I asked what he was doing, he told me it was none of my business. Then, I threatened to call over the sheriff, so he left."

"Did you notice him staring at anyone in particular?"

She shrugged. "I couldn't say."

"Do you remember if Mrs. Stannard was in the playground with her son that day?"

"Look, I'm not some female Rain Man. I don't remember stuff like that. I just remember Liam was here with Timothy and he was staring through his binoculars like a pervert. There's a good chance Mrs. Stannard was here with her son though. They were two of my best customers; ice cream almost every day—she always got pecan, and little Raymond always got vanilla."

"Do you have any other staff here that might have seen anything?" He looked around but knew the answer.

She let out another chuckle. "I moved here with my ex-husband. The café was his idea. To listen to him, you'd have thought we were gonna become millionaires. Then he got bored and left town with some little tramp. Now, I run this dump all on my own. No one else."

"Sorry to hear that," he said. "I got one more question: did you see Liam Watts the day he disappeared? He was outside in the park that day, with his girlfriend."

"You gonna give me something to answer this last question?" she asked.

He squinted his eyes. "What do you want in return?"

"Hey, I answered your other questions for free. You PI's get paid a fortune for these kind of cases. So, if I help solve the case, why shouldn't I get some of the reward?"

He shook his head. "Lady, you have no idea what the reward is for this case."

"I don't care." She crossed her arms. "Give me something, or I'm not telling you anything else. That's the deal."

Gregg had never given a bribe for information before, but never had he needed to solve a case so badly. He called up Rachel and asked her for some money, figuring it was probably insignificant to her, considering the extent she took to gain his cooperation.

Proving him right, Rachel said she'd go get the money and then meet him at the café.

She soon arrived with an envelope in her hand. He met her outside, and they went to give it to Shannon together.

Gregg took the envelope from Rachel and placed it on the counter. "A thousand dollars," he said.

Shannon's eyes lit up. She reached across the counter to snatch it. They stood and watched her count it.

Once she was finished, her smile grew larger still. "Yes. This is good."

"What did you see?" Gregg asked with a sigh.

"I saw someone that night," she said. "Someone watching the missing guy and his girlfriend."

Gregg stepped forward. "Who was it?"

"Not so fast." Shannon pocketed the envelope. "You said that you had one more question, and I answered it. Any other questions are gonna cost you more."

"Don't push it."

"Don't threaten me," she said, raising her voice a little. "Good information costs you."

Gregg exhaled in frustration and flung a plate from the counter to the floor, causing it to shatter. "We made a deal!"

"I hope you're planning on picking that up because my cleaning days are over."

Gregg squeezed his fist and felt himself grow red.

Rachel remained completely composed behind him. "Hunter, calm down."

Gregg backed off, sighing. He allowed Rachel to walk closer to the woman.

"You want more money?" Rachel asked.

Shannon nodded and smiled.

Rachel grinned back and went to pull something out of her bag. The café owner's eyes broadened in anticipation, expecting money, but Rachel's hand came back with a gun, complete with a silencer.

The woman's face dropped, and she put up her arms, screaming for Rachel to stop. Rachel fired a bullet into the woman's stomach, and she dropped to the ground. Shannon cried out in agony.

Gregg looked in horror. "What the hell are you doing?"

"She thinks she can play games with us. She's just gonna keep asking for more and more." Rachel aimed her gun between Shannon's eyes. "What did you see?"

The woman cried, "Nothing! I saw nothing!"

Rachel faced Gregg. "You said Liam was here with the girl in the afternoon, not at night. This woman knows nothing."

Gregg could sense what she was about to do. "No!"

Rachel fired her pistol once more, and the woman's crying ceased.

Gregg stared at the body in horror. "What did you do? What are we going to do with her?"

Rachel, still completely calm, put her pistol back in her bag. She casually walked to the door and switched the open sign over to closed, locked the door, and closed the blinds. "I always carry the appropriate materials in my car in case of such an emergency, Hunter."

"What kind of materials?"

"Those needed to make a person disappear from the face of the planet. And let that be a warning for you not to mess with me. Now, help me move the body. Then we'll get the drum and bleach."

Rachel began slogging the body of the woman behind the counter, and Gregg, still in shock, stood for a moment before stepping forward to help.

Gregg's world spun. Only an hour ago, Rachel had suggested he visit the park. Now, he was being wrapped up in a murder.

He had seen people killed before on the force, but never quite so unexpectedly. Rachel just pulled out her gun and fired it at the woman as if it was nothing. It was as though it was an everyday occurrence for Rachel, and Gregg realized he was only now beginning to understand how dangerous she truly was. Any chance he thought he had of him and his daughter being allowed to live once this was all over was becoming slimmer and slimmer.

Rachel told him to wait with the body while she went to get her van.

He sat down on a stool. The blood pounded in his ears. His vision was blurry, and he was going lightheaded. His beating heart slammed against his ribcage and his shaking hands grew cold and sweaty.

It felt like an eternity before Rachel returned, and the whole time he was certain someone was going to burst through the door and spot him with a dead body.

Rachel parked the van out back, and they dragged Shannon from the café.

Gregg sat in the back with the body and the drum and bleach, while Rachel turned the ignition and followed the road out of town. They drove in silence.

Once they were in the woods, Rachel pulled up and Gregg immediately burst out the doors. He dashed to the side of the road and vomited between the trees.

"Will you relax, Hunter?" Rachel told him. "I'm going to take care of everything, and no one is even going to miss that woman. My men have looked into it. She has no family in town. Everyone will think she's off on a bender, as she's done so several times before."

"You killed an innocent person," Gregg yelled. "You didn't have to do that!"

"I told you, no one messes with me. Now, calm down, because I brought something for you, something you're going to like."

Gregg wiped the sick from his mouth. "Are you sure no one is going to find out?"

Rachel nodded. "This is not unknown territory to me, Hunter. Now, do you want to know what I have for you or not?"

Gregg looked ahead to see a black van parked further up on the country road. Two men in black stepped out of the front seats. "What's happening?"

"I came to Blackberry Cove with something that I hope will lift your spirits. I brought *her*."

The two men opened the back door of the van. Silvia was inside, tied up and gagged. Gregg sprinted to the van and took the gag off his daughter's mouth. "Silvia," he uttered, tearing up.

"Dad!"

Gregg held her tight. "Thank God you're alright. You're going to be okay. I'm going to sort this out."

"Just do what they say, Dad," his daughter cried. "These people aren't messing around. That woman knows everything about us. Everything. She's been watching you for a long time, even before she wanted you to take this case. You can't mess with her."

"Enough," Rachel roared.

His daughter burst into a flood of tears at Rachel's voice,

shaking. He kissed her on the head. "Don't worry, everything is going to be alright."

"Your time's up," Rachel said.

The two men grabbed Gregg by the arms and pulled him out of the van. Silvia screamed after him.

"I will sort this out! I will see you soon," Gregg called. The men slammed the doors shut. Gregg let out all his tears and dropped to his knees.

"I hope you have been remotivated," Rachel said.

"I will find Liam Watts and his killer. Just don't hurt my daughter, please."

Rachel gave a gentle nod. "I will give you your daughter back unharmed, as long as you find me the killer. Now get back to work. Or I'll kill her."

18

Sometimes, Bernard pretended Flora was beside him while he ate. He didn't speak aloud to her—he wasn't crazy. But it was comforting to live in a world where she hadn't been taken from him, perhaps because they moved abroad like Flora had suggested when they graduated. Not that he blamed himself. He knew only her killer was responsible for her death.

At times, Bernard would imagine a child sitting at the table with them—their child—the one who could have been if their time together hadn't been so tragically cut short. During the few times they talked about kids, Bernard had mentioned he always liked the name Alex, and Flora seemed to like it too. It would have done for either a boy or girl. Back when he was a Scout Leader, Bernard had been told he'd make a great dad. He pictured himself teaching their child to use a compass, read maps, and navigate by the stars. Whenever reality struck, it pained him in the chest like nothing else.

Of course, he wasn't the same person he was when Flora had married him. He wondered, would she be proud of who he became? Of what he was doing? Or would she want him to move on?

A waitress came over with his bill. Bernard put away Flora's picture and took out his wallet to pay for the lamb stew he just had.

Richard called, "Mr. Neumann's money is no good here anymore. Whatever he wants is his."

"That's very generous," Bernard said.

Richard came over and sat beside him as the waitress took his dish.

"Nonsense. It's the least I can do for you watching this place while Hannah and I were away. If there is ever anything, please just say."

"You already helped me when I first moved here," Bernard reminded him.

"We look out for each other in Blackberry Cove."

"How was your trip with Hannah?" Bernard asked.

"It was great," Richard replied with a smile. "We talked like we used to in the old days, not about the inn, but just about whatever was on our minds."

"I almost thought you weren't coming back," Bernard said.

Richard eyed him for a moment before chuckling, as if wondering whether Bernard was being serious or not.

"What about you, Bernard?"

"What *about* me?"

Richard eyed his locket. "Hasn't it been seven years since Flora passed? Isn't it time?"

"Not yet."

Bernard felt a pang of guilt as Richard tried to decipher his thoughts with a squint of his eyes. He knew that Richard genuinely wanted to bond with him, but Bernard had never been good at making friends. He always struggled to open up and to make connections. In fact, the more he got to know people, the more distant he felt. Flora was an exception, the one person of whose company he never grew tired.

"How did you and Flora meet?" Richard asked.

"In college. We sat next to each other a few times in the library. I was taken with her the first second I saw her. Eventu-

100

ally, she caught me staring and came over to speak to me. At the time, when I asked her out, it felt like the bravest thing I had ever done. I couldn't believe it when she said yes, yet she said yes to every other date."

"What did you love so much about her?"

"That's impossible to say. I could claim I loved her because she was beautiful, but that would imply I would no longer have loved her if she lost her looks. I could say I loved her because of all the good things she did, but that would suggest I would have stopped loving her if she did something terrible. Neither of those things are true. The truth is I just loved her because I loved her. I would have forgiven her for anything."

Richard nodded in understanding.

Bernard smiled and rose from his seat. "Thanks for dinner, Richard. And listen, if you want my advice, just be happy. Work on your marriage, appreciate your wife, and live a good life together."

Richard thanked him again, then Bernard went home, ready to face another evening alone with only his thoughts and fantasies.

In a quaint corner of Vermont,
Hannah and Richard ran a B&B, their haunt,
Though they bickered non-stop,
Their love for each other never did flop.

And who could forget their white husky,
Sparky, always so happy and plucky,
A constant companion to their guests,
A friendly face to those in distress.

19

Gregg's head buzzed as he sat up in bed.

Yesterday had been too overwhelming. In the span of one day, he witnessed a murder, helped conceal a body, and been granted a visit with his kidnapped daughter. So how had he reacted? He sat in the inn all night, downing scotches while trying to make sense of Liam Watts' disappearance. Next to several empty glasses, he had scribbled down notes on what little he knew, but eventually decided that none of it was worth a damn and threw the notes into the air. He'd have to apologize to Hannah and Richard for causing such a mess.

Chloe would also be expecting an apology. Without being invited, she had sat opposite him last night. "You seem stressed, Gregg. Maybe we can grab a bite to eat or do something to cheer you up," she said.

Gregg rolled his eyes and groaned in hopes she'd leave him alone.

"Gregg?" she said.

He then stared up at her, a near deranged look in his eyes. "I'm working here!"

Chloe reached across the table and placed her hand atop Gregg's. "But everyone needs to make time for fun, right?" She smiled at him.

Gregg frowned. "Don't you understand? Don't you realize how important this is?" He slammed the table.

Chloe flinched, removing her hand as if he was likely to bite it off. "You've had too much to drink." She stood. "Maybe the reason I don't understand is because nobody is telling me anything." This said, she stormed out of the inn.

With last night's memories fading away, like lost puzzle pieces as out of reach as those surrounding Liam's disappearance, Gregg crawled out of bed to get himself a glass of water. His reluctant limbs felt heavy and unresponsive, but eventually he made it to the bathroom.

Falling to the drink when he realized his marriage was over had been the lowest point of his life. Since becoming a private investigator, he had managed to limit himself to just a few beers in the evening. It kept him going through the day knowing he'd have a chilled form of relief waiting for him at the end. Now he had fallen to it again, at the time his daughter needed him most, and he wondered how weak he really was.

The phone on his bedside cabinet vibrated against the wood, worsening his headache. He dashed to reach it.

"Is this Gregg Hunter?" a man's voice immediately said.

"It is." Gregg heard the grogginess in his own voice. "Who's calling?"

"It's Dr. Marek Galt. I'm a former professor at Burlington College. I got a message saying you were trying to reach me."

Gregg stood up straight. "Yes, I am, thank you so much for calling me back, Professor."

"The receptionist told me you were calling from Blackberry Cove, and so I had a pretty good idea what the call was about."

"You know about the case?" Gregg asked.

"Indeed," the man replied sullenly. "Terrible thing. But how can I possibly help?"

"I was hoping you could tell me a little about what Liam Watts was like as a student."

"Liam?" Dr. Galt asked. "Well, Liam was a quiet student. He never asked questions during class and always sat by himself. I don't remember much about him, really, except that he quit the class after the results of his first assignment. He insisted that he should have got a much higher grade and claimed that I just couldn't appreciate the brilliance of his work."

Fits the profile. Arrogant. Delusional.

"I must say, I'm surprised you're asking me about Liam and not about the victim," Dr. Galt went on.

"The victim?" Gregg asked.

"Clementine Stannard," Dr. Galt replied. "I read about her murder in the papers, and then when the receptionist called to say a PI in Blackberry Cove was looking to speak with me, I assumed it'd be about her."

Gregg felt the hairs on the back of his neck stand up. "Sorry, Professor, but I'm a little confused. Are you saying that you also knew Clementine Stannard?"

"Yes, of course," Dr. Galt replied. "She was in the same class as Liam."

20

GREGG KNOCKED FURIOUSLY ON NATHAN'S DOOR. AS THE MAYOR opened the door, he frowned at the sight of Gregg on his front porch.

Nathan had his sleeves rolled up and a dishcloth over his shoulder. "Can I help you?" he asked, exhaling deeply.

"I tried visiting earlier, and I also left a message with your secretary," Gregg replied. "I need to talk with you about the case."

"Yes, well, I've been busy. What can I do for you?"

"I have some questions about Liam Watts," Gregg said. "Do you mind if I come inside?"

"If you must," he replied. "Please be quick about it, though. I'm making dinner."

A smoke alarm went off from the kitchen, and Gregg followed Nathan inside, carrying a notebook in one hand and the rolled-up poster from Liam's cabin in the other. Nathan hurried into the kitchen to turn the alarm off and opened some windows, funneling out the smoke with whacks of his dishcloth.

"So, Mr. Stannard, could you please describe the relationship between you and Mr. Watts?"

"Do you really think this is useful?" Nathan asked. He brought some blackened garlic bread out from the oven. Luckily for him, his lasagna looked to be in more decent shape.

"Yes, I do."

"Well, I disagree," Nathan replied. "If you really want to make yourself useful, you could set my table for me."

Nathan pointed to a drawer of cutlery as if he actually expected Gregg to be his server for the night. He then went to grab some wine from the cabinet. Gregg followed him. "Again, sir, could you please describe the relationship between you and Mr. Watts?"

"I barely knew the man."

"And why was that?"

"I don't think he was registered to vote."

"What about the relationship between your wife and Mr. Watts?" Gregg asked.

"There wasn't one. Look, Detective, I'm afraid you're wasting your time here. Neither I nor my wife ever spoke to Liam Watts, besides possible pleasantries on the street. Now, I really am busy. If you didn't already detect, I don't cook much." He gestured to the garlic bread and proceeded to begin scraping off the burnt bits, though Gregg doubted any of it was still salvageable.

Gregg peered into the next room, looking over the passionately set table. "Is this for you and Raymond?" he asked.

"Yes. Why?"

"A little romantic." Gregg pointed to the lit candles and vase of roses on the table.

"I, um, am trying to make up for a fight we had," he replied.

Gregg eyed him for a moment, wondering if he should reveal that he knew about the affair. Both the sleeping medication and the nanny's statement had left no room for doubt. "I know you're lying, Mr. Stannard."

Nathan looked up. "About?"

"Well, by telling me Liam and your wife were never close for a start," Gregg replied. "I know they went to college together. I was confused because my employers told me your wife went to school in Montpelier, but Liam had attended a school in Burlington."

"She never graduated from Burlington," Nathan explained. "She transferred to Montpelier after a year at Burlington, and that's where we met."

"Did she transfer because of Liam Watts?"

Nathan sighed. "Okay, they dated for a little while. He didn't take the breakup too well and started following her around, so yes, that's why she got a transfer. He was a freak, obsessed with making horror movies. He used to download snuff films when he was dating Clementine, and then try to get her to watch them with him. It turned him on."

"Why did you hide this from me?" Gregg asked.

"I've hid it from everyone," Nathan replied. "My father was the mayor of this town, and Liam's father was a drunk ex-carpenter. If people knew she had dated him first, they would never respect her as a possible wife of the mayor. Do you see?"

"Not really," Gregg said.

"This is a small town, and every detail matters here, even those that seem trivial. When I came back to Blackberry Cove after college, announcing Clementine as my fiancée, I had to make sure the people would admire her. If they knew she once dated that loser, well, frankly, her image would be tarnished, and thus so would mine."

"That sounds ridiculous," Gregg replied. "You're suggesting Clementine was tainted because of her previous choice in men."

"Not exactly, but that's how people would see it."

Gregg shook his head, but perhaps he was too simple to understand the politics of the town. "If that's true, weren't you afraid Liam would talk to people about his relationship with your wife?"

"Liam barely left that grotty cabin of his. Besides, he was a pariah around here, and no one would have taken anything he said seriously."

"Why would you hide this from the police?" Gregg asked. "You've concealed a possible motive over the murder of your wife."

"What motive?"

"You said that Liam didn't take the breakup very well," Gregg said.

"They dated over ten years ago. Why would he have chosen to hurt her now? Also, if Liam even did kill my wife, then considering he isn't here to be arrested, what good would this news do the police?"

Gregg squinted his eyes and looked Nathan over. "Or perhaps you killed Liam, Mr. Stannard, in revenge for killing your wife?"

Nathan scoffed. "You're a fool if you think I cared about Clementine enough to do that." Immediately, he looked as though he regretted those words.

"Mr. Stannard, did your wife ever want to be an actress when she was younger?" Gregg asked.

Nathan screwed up his face as though he was sucking a lemon. "What kind of question is that? You really should consider a career change."

Gregg unrolled the poster, revealing the image of the young, bikini-clad brunette soaked in blood. "This is your late wife, isn't it? I found the poster in Liam's cabin. It appears he and your wife worked on some low-budget horror movie together during the time they were studying."

"Don't be ridiculous." Nathan's face went red. "That woman is barely wearing any clothes. What kind of man do you think I am, Mr. Hunter? I don't marry tarts. Clementine was an admirable woman, with self-respect. She was a role-model for all the young women in this town. She volunteered at the church and led their Sunday school lessons. She was not some failed, wannabe actress who would have shown off her legs for a chance of some petty fame and fortune."

Gregg was a little taken back. He decided to keep his final card close to his chest for now.

"Your wife must have had dreams and ambitions of her own before meeting you, Mr. Stannard. I'm not trying to suggest she wasn't happy being the mayor's wife and a Sunday School teacher, but she must have studied Film at college for a reason."

Nathan shook his fist. "As a respectable woman, her sole dreams and ambitions were to be a caring wife and mother."

Gregg bit his tongue, not sure how to respond in a way that wouldn't have him physically flung from the house. "What about your first wife?" he said at last. "Anna?"

Nathan's face crimsoned even further. "What about her?"

"I managed to learn a little more about her."

"Good for you."

"She already had a child when you met, and the marriage lasted less than a year. That doesn't seem to fit with the traditional family picture you're trying to paint."

"I'm lucky the marriage lasted less than a year. I was young and naïve. My father never spoke to me during that entire marriage. Luckily, I earned his approval back after marrying Clementine, as well as that of the voters. She was the perfect mayor's wife, and I won't have you attempt to tarnish her name by flaunting that stupid poster."

"That's not what I was trying to do."

"I think you should leave now." Nathan ushered Gregg to the door. "If there's someone you should really be investigating, it's Timothy Holst. He exploded at my son the other day, and it wasn't the first time."

"What do you mean?" Gregg asked.

"On the day of Clementine's death and Liam's disappearance, the cashier at the gas station reported to the sheriff that Timothy exploded at her for no reason whatsoever. Then, well, the other day I took Raymond to see Dr. Holst. I thought the therapist could help him with some confidence issues he's having. Anyway, Timothy started screaming at him over nothing. That certainly helped Raymond's confidence. He's about as great a therapist as you are a detective."

Before Gregg could ask anything further, the door was promptly slammed shut.

21

FIVE YEARS AGO

Dr. Timothy Holst sat for breakfast with his wife, Elaine, and their eleven-year-old daughter, Juliet. A solemn emptiness filled the air, much like every meal.

His wife and daughter's cutlery scraped against their plates as they took mouthfuls of scrambled egg and salmon. Not a word had been said since he placed their meals in front of them, not even a *thank you*.

Timothy used to beg inside his head for someone to speak, to end the uncomfortable silence that raised his heart rate and had him sitting on edge. But not anymore. Now he was used to it. In fact, now he enjoyed the quietude.

"So," his wife said finally, breaking the peace. "I have news."

"Really?" Timothy enquired. "What is—?"

"Darling, please." His wife quickly silenced him. "As I was saying, I have volunteered to be keeper of the local park's garden."

"Oh?" Timothy tried to feign interest. "And what does that entail?"

Elaine's smile dropped. "It's rather obvious, dear."

"What will you be doing, Mom?" their daughter wondered.

Emile's smile sprang back up. "Well, Juliet, Mommy's going to be redecorating the park, adding my own flair to it. I'm thinking of first giving the grass a good trim before I plant anything. After all, I wouldn't want the flowers to get over-shadowed."

Timothy sighed silently.

"I can't wait to get started!" Elaine exclaimed.

"I'm happy for you." Timothy strained a grin.

"Yes, quite. I'm going to be late home today because I plan on working in the garden into the evening. You'll have to pick up Juliet from school."

"Will do."

"And I'll need a new lawn mower, so I'm going to need you to give me money for that."

"I'm not sure we have—"

"Just write a check," Elaine ordered.

Timothy conceded with another weary smile.

"I'll pick up some seeds and flower-care tools," Elaine added.

"Sounds lovely."

"Dad?" Juliet said.

"Yes dear?" Timothy looked over to his daughter.

"I want to go to that private school that Mommy was looking at in the pamphlets."

"Oh, dear, that school's awfully far away from the house—"

"But I wanna go!"

"And I really could just barely afford the tuition for—"

Juliet pounded the table. "But I wanna go!"

Timothy fixed another smile. His daughter's screeching echoed in his head, causing his stomach to churn. He knew she wouldn't stop, and it would only cause Elaine to become further frustrated with him. God, he was pathetic. "Then that is what shall happen, my sweet."

Juliet beamed victoriously.

Elaine and Juliet stood. His wife turned to him, and they locked eyes. For a moment, Timothy thought she was trying to smile at him, but she must have been simply unable to because any trace of it soon dissipated. "Clean the table, please," she said. "I'll have to take Juliet to school on my way to the park. Oh, and I'll just take a check from your wallet and cash it." Elaine grabbed his wallet and then left with their daughter.

No one said goodbye.

Once they were gone, Timothy let out a loud sigh. The anger had once been like a hot desert storm inside his head, turning his breathing to ragged pants. But not anymore. Now, the rage left only an aching throb inside his head, as if it were now a cold winter night, freezing his body limp and making him too power-less to fight back.

He had to find a way to fight back.

His head began to clear, and he lifted his hand. His hand was bleeding. For the entirety of breakfast Timothy had been clutching the butter knife.

After taking a few deep and calming breaths, Timothy washed the blood away from his hand in the sink. He then proceeded to clean up breakfast.

OCTOBER 30TH, 8:41 AM

Timothy's life was a mundane cycle, so dull it wore him down.

That morning, he had prepared breakfast like he did every day, careful not to overcook his wife's eggs as she liked them still soft. Then, he and his family sat and ate.

While Elaine poured some coffee, she said, "Those young hooligans came by the park last night again and ruined my garden! They destroyed all my good work!"

"How do you know it was teenagers? Did you see them?" Juliet questioned.

"Oh, please, you children are always causing trouble."

Timothy continued eating his breakfast in silence.

"So, I'm going to have to stay late again this evening to fix it all up," Elaine continued. "Will you make dinner for Juliet?"

"Will do." Timothy smiled falsely.

"And pick her up from school."

Timothy nodded. Underneath the table, he practiced his anger relief by clutching his leg tightly. It was better than clutching whatever was in his hand.

"So, how is school, my darling?" Elaine asked, turning her attention to their daughter.

"Terrible," she replied. "I hate that school! Why did you send me there, Dad?"

His wife and daughter glared at him.

"I'm sorry." He clutched his leg so tightly he thought he might stop circulation. Removing his hand, he moved around his leg to restore blood flow and then gently rubbed the sore spot under his eye from where Nathan Stannard punched him the previous day.

"What happened to your eye?" his daughter enquired.

"Oh, I was w-a-alking and, I, w-a-alked into a-a streetlight," he stuttered in reply. Again. It was always so obvious whenever he was nervous or lying. It clouded his head, made him sweat, and his heart beat like a jackhammer. God, he hated himself.

"A streetlight?" his wife asked.

Timothy nodded.

"You should be more careful."

He nodded again.

"Klutz," his daughter remarked.

Elaine and Juliet stood and headed for the door, saying nothing before leaving. He got up and cleared the breakfast table. He listened to his tape play on the old cassette player while he did the dishes.

"Remember," the soft and soothing voice said, "be comfortable with who you are. Don't allow yourself to be put down.

This deficiency doesn't define you. You are a strong, confident man, and—"

There was a sudden knock at the door, and Timothy halted the tape before going to answer it. His heart sank even further to find Gregg Hunter standing at the door.

22

"I'M SORRY TO BOTHER YOU, DR. HOLST, BUT SINCE YOU WERE A friend of Liam, I was hoping you could help me out a little," Gregg said.

"I was, um, actually just getting ready for work," the therapist stuttered, still clutching the handle of his front door.

Gregg decided to put him at ease. "Please, it won't take long, and I'm struggling with this investigation. I think you could help shed some light on Liam's life for me."

It worked, and after a brief pause, Timothy smiled and led him inside. The therapist made some tea, and they sat down in the lounge.

Gregg held the cup in his hand and took a sip. "So, when was the last time you saw Liam?"

"Um, the night he disappeared," Timothy replied. "We had drinks at the Swan Inn like normal."

"He never said anything about wanting to leave town?"

"Liam spoke all the time about wanting to leave town, but he didn't mention any plans to leave on the night he disappeared."

"How late were you out?"

"Not late." Timothy shrugged. "I had work the next day, so I was probably in bed by ten."

Gregg nodded. "Do you recall how Liam got home?"

"What do you mean?"

"I went to Liam's cabin the other day and didn't see any vehicles outside. Considering it's quite a distance from town, I was wondering if Liam had a ride or some other way of getting back home."

"Liam drove a truck," Timothy replied. "Even after some drinks, he'd sometimes drive it home."

"But not always?" Gregg asked.

Timothy shrugged. "Sometimes I think he'd walk back when he felt he had one too many. In fact, he must have walked back that night, because I remember the sheriff finding Liam's truck parked in town the next day."

"Did you visit Liam's house often, Dr. Holst?"

Timothy shook his head. "No. Never. His father had always been incredibly private, and Liam was the same."

"So, you only ever met with Liam in the inn for drinks or at the café for coffee?" Gregg asked.

Timothy stared at him for a moment. "I never said anything about a café."

"You were seen there over the summer with Liam. Apparently, Liam had some binoculars with him and was caught spying on Clementine Stannard and her son." It was a lie, but Gregg wanted to see how Timothy would react.

Timothy sighed. "Look, Detective, you should know, Liam was obsessed."

"With Mrs. Stannard?" he asked. "Was Liam still in love with her?"

"No, he wasn't in love with her at all, but he was still angry about being dumped by her. He was bitter about everything he felt he missed out on because of it. He was obsessed with her life —her marriage and her child. He felt like these were things that should have been his."

The therapist's responses seemed almost rehearsed. Gregg

decided to throw him off guard with another question. "Do you ever go to Albany, Dr. Holst?"

Timothy raised an eyebrow. "I often go there to attend seminars. Why?"

"Did Liam ever accompany you to any of these seminars?"

Timothy shuffled in his chair. "Liam wasn't really interested in psychology and psychiatry lessons."

Gregg pulled out the train tickets that Liam's dustbin had been filled with. He laid them out on the coffee table for Timothy to see. "You and Liam didn't go to Albany for psychology seminars, did you, Dr. Holst? What were you doing there?"

Timothy lowered his head and didn't speak.

"It's not exactly a bustling nightlife scene around here," Gregg said. "Albany is the closest place with bars and nightclubs. Did you go there to cheat on your wife, Dr. Holst?"

Timothy's head snapped up. "No. Liam and I went to the clubs to meet women, but I never cheated on my wife."

"So, you went to Albany almost every other weekend just so you could be Liam's wingman?" Gregg asked. "That doesn't make sense."

"All I did was talk to women. I never cheated on my wife. Ever."

"You can tell me the truth. I'm not here to expose adultery. That doesn't interest me. All I want is the truth."

"I didn't cheat on my wife because I can't."

"What do you mean?"

Timothy took a deep breath. "All my wife ever wanted was a child. We came here to start a family. But shortly after we moved, I was diagnosed with an irregularly sized prostate. Getting it fixed is usually a simple procedure, but during the surgery there were complications. They had to remove my prostate gland, leaving me impotent."

"I'm sorry," Gregg said.

"We adopted Juliet not long after the surgery," Timothy went on. "And I've tried ever since to be the best husband I can be to my wife. It's the least she deserves after I failed her."

Timothy lowered his head into his hands, and Gregg wasn't sure what to say. Deciding to move on, Gregg asked, "Did Liam ever meet a woman on one of these weekends?"

Timothy nodded. "Chloe Mason. They began dating after they hooked up one night in Albany. She was there with a friend for a party."

"Were you there, too?"

"Yes, Chloe and I spoke."

"About?"

Timothy shuffled in his chair. "She told me about how she wanted to leave town and go traveling."

"That's it?" Gregg asked. "What did you say?"

"I told her traveling never interested me and I was probably too old for it now anyway," he replied. "Too old for her too, I added, and so I went to let her talk to some boys her own age, but she stopped me from leaving. She said she liked older men and wanted to keep talking. And talk is all we did. She was very nice to me, and we understood each other."

"Understood each other?" Gregg asked. "I'm not quite following."

"She knew about the issues between me and my wife," Timothy replied.

"What else?"

"I knew she had issues with her father," he went on. "In fact, I helped her find outlets for her anger when she was a teenager. I advised her that unresolved issues tend to manifest in unusual ways. I think she admired and respected me because of my advice. I believe she even felt attracted to me."

Timothy grinned, staring off at the wall, and Gregg felt his skin crawl. This man had to be more than double her age.

"Did you tell Chloe about your condition?"

Timothy nodded, his smile fading. "She told me I had to go

easier on myself and not feel like a failure to my wife. I'm not weak and powerless because of it, she told me."

"It seems like you and Chloe struck quite a bond."

Timothy's smile returned. "We did."

"So, it must have really hurt when she ended up dating your best friend?" he asked.

Timothy stared at him, frowning. "Are you suggesting that I would hurt Liam because of that?"

"I'm not suggesting anything," Gregg replied. "I'm only asking a question. Did you?"

"I never did anything to hurt Liam." Timothy began tapping his fingers anxiously on the arm of his chair, and Gregg noticed the dirt beneath his nails.

"What was that you mentioned earlier?" Gregg asked. "Something about how issues can manifest in strange ways if we don't address them?"

"Yes, that's exactly what I tell my patients," Timothy replied. "It's not healthy to bottle things up. If we don't express our anger, it can fester and lead to unpredictable behavior."

"Exactly," Gregg agreed. "It's like a ticking time bomb that can explode at any moment."

"Just to be clear, I wasn't harboring any animosity towards Liam," Timothy immediately asserted. "Both Chloe and Liam were adults, and I didn't object to their relationship."

"Perhaps not," Gregg said. "But you are harboring anger towards someone, aren't you, Dr. Holst?"

Timothy averted his gaze. "I'm not sure what you mean."

Gregg rose from his seat and motioned around the room. The walls were adorned with photographs, many of which featured Timothy and Elaine's daughter participating in Girl Scouts, rowing in a scenic lake, or starting her first day of school. However, the majority of the photographs showcased Elaine Holst and her garden. There were endless snapshots of Elaine winning various competitions that Gregg wasn't even aware of, including a butterfly photography competition, the tallest sunflower in town, and the town's largest tomato, just to name a few.

What stood out the most, however, was that Timothy was absent from every single picture. Instead, the entire house was focused on his wife's accomplishments.

"Your wife seems to have quite a bit of say in the decoration of these walls," Gregg said.

"Or perhaps I hung all those pictures because I'm so proud of my wife," Timothy rebutted.

"I heard that you had an altercation with a gas station attendant on the day Liam went missing," Gregg then said.

"She gave me the wrong change, and I may have overreacted," Timothy replied, raising an eyebrow. "But what does that have to do with anything?"

"Well, as you said earlier, our problems can manifest in unpredictable ways. I'm curious if something led to this nasty exchange. She had to call the sheriff because you wouldn't stop yelling obscenities at her, correct?"

Timothy looked down. "It had been a stressful day."

"Oh?"

"Yes, we had a family outing to the newly opened fishing museum that day. I had been wanting to learn more about fishing in hopes it could be a new hobby. I've heard it can be quite peaceful. Our day at the museum, however, was cut short by my daughter's complaints that it was too boring to bear. When it comes to picking family trips, my wife says I'm about as much use as an assassin with squeaky shoes." Timothy resumed fidgeting in his chair. "On the way back from the museum, we stopped at the gas station, and I unfairly took my frustration out on the cashier."

"Did you take out your frustration on anyone else that day?"

"Like whom?" Timothy asked.

"Maybe Clementine Stannard?" Gregg suggested.

Timothy rubbed the back of his neck and stood up. "I don't

remember seeing Mrs. Stannard that day. If that's all, Mr. Hunter, I really must get ready for work."

"One last thing," Gregg said. "I spoke to your wife yesterday. She and the other gardener said that some kids have been wrecking the gardens during the nights."

"Like you said, there's not much to do in this town." Timothy opened the front door. "So, the kids here get bored easily. Nasty hooligans. It's upsetting for my wife to see all her hard work destroyed. Luckily, I'm here every night to comfort her."

"I see." Gregg smiled falsely. "And was your wife's garden wrecked last night?"

"As a matter of fact, I believe it was," Timothy replied.

Gregg leaned in. "You really should clean under your fingernails, Doctor. Have a good day."

23

THE ONE THING GREGG MISSED MOST SINCE BECOMING A PI WAS having a partner to bounce ideas off. When working a case, he and Jim would often get dinner together to talk out possible scenarios. The only person Gregg realized he could call was Rachel. Her voice made his skin crawl, but he needed to make things clearer in his head and to hear another perspective. Besides, he was still waiting for her to get back to him about Bernard. Gregg had been given a background file on everyone in town except him, and Rachel had promised to look into it.

"Hello?" she answered. "Is everything okay?"

"Yes, I think I'm making progress with a theory," he replied.

"Go on."

"The mayor has been having an affair with his secretary. It's possible he decided to get rid of his wife."

"Why not just get a divorce?" Rachel asked, playing devil's advocate exactly as Gregg wanted.

"Being mayor means too much to him. If he left his wife for his mistress and word got out about the scandal, he might not get re-elected and that isn't a chance he'd have been willing to make."

"So, he killed his wife?"

"No. If anyone ever found about the affair, he'd be suspect number one in his wife's murder." Gregg ran a hand over his stubble. "Instead, he would have paid someone else to do it. Liam was short on cash and already held resentment against the mayor's wife for breaking up with him in college."

"So, the mayor hired Liam to kill his wife and then he killed Liam himself to cover his tracks?" Even over the phone, Gregg could feel Rachel's skepticism.

"It's a possibility."

Rachel gave a deep sigh. "It's also possible Liam got abducted by aliens. Anything is possible, Hunter. I want evidence."

"I'm working on it," he said with a grunt. "Now, you said you'd get me some information on Bernard. What do you have?"

"Right," she replied. She cleared her throat, and Gregg could hear her shuffling through papers. "Bernard Neumann. A software engineer from Boston. Did his master's at MIT, and his big break came nine years ago when the United States government hired him to work on a project. Top secret. He married Flora Evans eight years ago, a psychology student he met at college. She was murdered a year later. They never caught the killer."

"Then what?" Gregg asked.

"He moved to Blackberry Cove. Doesn't seem like he took his wife's death very well. He sold his car, possessions, apartment in Boston, and his house in Lexington, all within the year after his wife's death. The only significant purchases he made were plane tickets to South America. He made a lot of money from his project for the government, so he probably spent that time traveling to recover from the breakdown he had. Clearly, he's a mere sad sack, looking for solitude because he can't move on. I wouldn't worry about him. Now, anything else?"

"No. I'll call you when I have more." Gregg hung up the phone.

I wouldn't worry about him, Gregg repeated to himself. He didn't like to be steered in an investigation. *Why is she defending Bernard?*

Gregg returned to the Swan Inn to see if he could find Bernard there, but the place was empty, except for the gentle giant behind the counter.

"Hey Richard," he called. "You seen Bernard today?"

Richard looked up from the Halloween decorations he was placing around the inn and scratched his beard. "He and Hannah left town this morning."

"Where'd they go?" Gregg asked, curious.

Richard shrugged. "They didn't say."

"Are Bernard and your wife close friends?"

Richard nodded with a smile. "When we first moved to Blackberry Cove, I wasn't as enthusiastic about the place as Hannah. To me, a small town in Vermont sounded rather dreary, but Hannah had it all sorted out. The place was on the rise for tourism, she said, meaning we could buy a cheap place and do it up into the inn we'd always talked about in time for the boom of tourists. But once we moved, this place and I didn't click."

"And Bernard changed that?" Gregg asked, trying to see how what Richard was saying had anything to do with the question he asked.

Richard continued as though he hadn't even been interrupted. "Hannah spent a long time trying to get me to hike with her, but I wasn't interested. I was happy that Hannah was happy, but I think she felt guilty, as though she had done a terrible thing in dragging me here. Then, Bernard moved next door and Hannah had a hiking partner. More than that though, he got me to go out with them."

"How did he manage that?"

Richard pointed over to Sparky, the little, white husky, running around in a circle after his own tail.

"He got you a dog?" Gregg asked.

"Bernard told Hannah it would be the perfect way to get me outside and to make me fall in love with this place."

"And was he right?"

Richard nodded. "There's nothing I look forward to more

than my long walks with Hannah and Sparky. You'd never imagine that the addition of a small puppy could make such a difference, but Sparky has made us feel like a family and that Blackberry Cove is our home. Since then, Bernard's been a close friend to all three of us."

Gregg thanked Richard for sharing, silently wondering if he'd ever see his own family again. With every moment, his daughter inched closer to death. He could hear Rachel's patience wearing thinner with every phone call.

If he was going to solve the case soon, he needed help, and he needed it now. If Jim wasn't around, he'd get someone else.

24

I⸀ᴛ ᴡᴀꜱ ᴀ ʟᴏɴɢ ᴅʀɪᴠᴇ ᴛᴏ ᴛʜᴇ ᴇᴀꜱᴛᴇʀɴ ꜱɪᴅᴇ ᴏꜰ Mᴀꜱꜱᴀᴄʜᴜꜱᴇᴛᴛꜱ, ꜱᴏ Bernard was thankful for Hannah's company. Her friendship had been a great source of comfort during his stay in Blackberry Cove, along with the breathtaking nature there. It was nice to spend time with someone who enjoyed hiking and appreciated the world's beauty as he did. It made him feel much less alone.

"Thanks for coming with me." He glanced away from the road only briefly.

"Of course." Hannah smiled and looked over at the flowers. "They smell lovely."

"That's carnations you're smelling," he told her.

"Oh, the flower of love."

"Yes. The story goes that the first carnation blossomed two thousand years ago on the day of Jesus' crucifixion, in the exact spot where Mary wept for her son."

"That doesn't sound like a very happy story for such a beautiful flower."

"Well, only what gives us joy can give us sorrow." Bernard grasped his locket.

Once they reached their destination, Bernard parked the car by the side of the graveyard. Hannah said she'd stay in the car to give him privacy. Bernard took his flowers and placed them gently on Flora's grave.

It had been too long since his last visit, but living in Blackberry Cove, he couldn't get down as often.

"I still think of you every day," he said aloud. "I know you'd want me to move on, but I need to finish what I started first."

It wouldn't be much longer. The finish line was within sight.

The last piece of the puzzle had come to town—Gregg Hunter.

25

GREGG TRIED CALLING CHLOE ALL DAY TO APOLOGIZE FOR HIS behavior the other night, but there had been no answer and she hadn't responded to any of his messages. He approached her house in the darkness, all the while trying to organize his words. But he still had no idea what he would say.

He knocked on the door, and as soon as Chloe opened it ajar, he let out whatever words spilt out, "I want to apologize for the other night."

Chloe put up her palm. "I don't want to hear it. I was just trying to be nice to you, and you completely blew up in my face."

"I know, I was a real jerk," he said. "I've been under extreme stress lately, but even that doesn't excuse it."

"Stress over what?" she asked.

"I-I've been separated from my daughter."

Chloe pushed the door further open ever so slightly. "Go on."

"I don't even know where to begin," he stuttered. "I feel like I've been separated from her for so long."

"Start at the beginning," she told him gently.

"Well, my daughter was a teenage pregnancy."

"Wow, that really is the beginning."

Her faint smile told him that he should go on.

"Her mother and I got married too young, and I was never there for them from the beginning. The only thing that mattered to me was passing the police force entrance exams and becoming a homicide detective like my father. When I finally did, I rushed straight to my father's house before even calling my wife and daughter, but he was gone. My mother told me he had packed a suitcase and disappeared in the middle of the night, and we never heard from him again. I neglected my own family to please a father who didn't even give a shit about me. After that, I wanted to be a better detective than he ever was. I wanted my daughter to be proud of me. But I was never home. Along the way, I forgot that I didn't need to save people to be my daughter's hero. All she wanted was for me to be there for her, to spend time with her, and to tell her I love her."

"Then why don't you go and tell her?" Chloe asked. "Did your wife take her?"

Gregg shook his head. "No, she tried to during the divorce, but we worked things out. There was a time, though, when I almost deserved to lose my daughter. During the custody battle with my wife, I acted in ways that I shouldn't have. She eventually agreed not to move out of state with our daughter, but, when we split, my wife initially wanted to take Silvia to her boyfriend's hometown in Tennessee. When I found out, I was drunk, but still thought it was a good idea to confront them both at their home. I yelled like a crazy person, got into a fight with her boyfriend, and even accused my daughter of not loving me to her face. I was angry that Silvia chose to live with her mother despite what her mother had done to me. It was traumatic for Silvia, and the cops had to remove me from the house. It was likely the final straw that led to me losing my badge."

"Then I don't understand. Where is your daughter now?"

Gregg stepped forward. "That's why I'm here. I was terrible to you the other night because I was afraid of slipping some details that I couldn't allow to slip. But now, I realize I need help. So, if you'll listen, I want to tell you everything."

Chloe stood and drummed her fingers against the doorway, as if contemplating whether to let him in. Eventually, she opened the door fully.

Gregg followed her into her kitchen, where she poured them some coffee. As soon as she handed him his cup and sat down, he decided there was no point in dancing around it. "Over a week ago, some people came to me and blackmailed me into finding the body of Liam Watts and his killer."

Chloe slammed down her coffee. "Liam's *dead*?"

"That's what my employers seem to think."

"Wait, what do you mean you're being blackmailed?"

"These people—they kidnapped my daughter, and they're holding her. They won't give her back until I solve the case. If I don't, I won't ever see Silvia again. That's why this investigation means so much to me."

"Have you told the police?"

"No. I can't. And you can't either. They would kill my daughter if I contacted the police. These people are dangerous."

"What do you mean dangerous?" she asked.

"When they took my daughter, they killed my ex-wife and her boyfriend."

Chloe covered her mouth. "Oh my God!"

"That's not all. They murdered Shannon Alvie, the café owner. They shot her right in front of me."

Chloe stepped back, her eyes like a deer in headlights.

"All I can do is find Liam and his killer, and then maybe they'll give me my daughter and not hurt anyone else. And I could use your help."

"Of course. But who are these people? What do you know about them?"

"I don't know much," he admitted sadly. "I only ever have contact with the same woman. I think she's in charge, but I can't be sure of even that."

After a pause, Chloe said, "There's something I think you should know."

"What?"

"There's someone in town who's heavily invested in Liam being found."

"Who?"

"Bernard."

"What do you mean?"

"Well, even before you got here, Bernard was convinced Liam was dead. He's been searching the woods for Liam's body for months now."

"Why on Earth would Bernard be out looking for Liam's body?"

Chloe shrugged. "I don't know. But I do know he desperately wants Liam to be found. More than anything."

A detective once shone so bright,
But a divorce dimmed his inner light,
He lost his job, his life fell apart,
Yet he's determined to make a fresh start.

One day in public, he lost his cool,
His daughter watched, aghast at the fool,
He caused a scene, made a terrible mess,
Ashamed, he wished for time to regress.

He knows he has a long way to go,
To let go of his past, and make things glow,
He'll keep trying to be a better man,
And show his daughter that he can.

26

GREGG TURNED OVER IN THE UNFAMILIAR BED, ONLY TO FIND himself staring at the back of Chloe's head. They hadn't done anything last night, but it was late by the time they finished talking, and just the mere feeling of a warm body beside him gave him comfort.

He had struggled to sleep every night since arriving in Blackberry Cove. After all, a woman was dead because of him. Rachel shot her right in front of him. The image of blood spurting from her stomach and her collapsing to the café floor flashed through his head. Again, he felt like he was going to be sick. More than that, his ex-wife was gone. If Gregg had accepted the job to begin with, she'd still be alive, and Silvia would still have her family and home.

"Morning." Chloe sat up and turned to face him.

"Hi. Have you been awake long?"

Chloe nodded. "I've been thinking about your daughter."

Gregg sat up. "What about her?"

Chloe played with strands of hair. "Well, I figured, why don't you just tell this woman you've found Liam's body, and then she'll bring your daughter to town, and we can take her by force?"

Gregg shook his head. "Chloe, I appreciate the sentiment, but that is the worst plan I have ever heard in my entire life."

"How do you know it won't work? We at least have to try."

"There is too much at stake if it was to go wrong. My daughter's life is on the line. I have to stay completely compliant to this woman." He fumbled as he tried to button his shirt.

"But what if it doesn't go wrong? What if this is your only chance to get Silvia back?"

"What do you mean?" he asked.

"Well, what if you *never* find Liam's body? You could be on some wild goose chase, and never get your daughter back."

Gregg sighed. "You may be right. Still, I can't underestimate Rachel. If I ran away with Silvia, she would find me. I know it."

Chloe placed her hand on Gregg's. "But what if she doesn't? Isn't there someone from the force in Boston you could call? Someone you trust?"

"My old partner, Jim," he said. "I trust him more than anyone."

"Call him," she urged. "Tell him where you're meeting with Rachel, and then he'll see for himself that she has your daughter hostage."

"I don't think I should get anyone else involved. I've already seen these people kill."

"That's all the more reason to take your daughter back by force. If you've seen these people kill, do you really think they're going to let you walk away after you've solved the case?"

It was a thought he had tried desperately not to consider. "Probably not," he admitted, as much to himself as to Chloe. "I can't call Jim from my phone, though. They might be monitoring it."

Chloe reached over to her bedside unit and handed him her cell phone. "Use mine."

He punched in the numbers before giving himself a chance to talk himself out of it.

"Hello?" Jim said almost immediately. "Who is this?"

"Jim, it's Gregg."

"Holy fuck!" he exclaimed, spitting a thousand words a second. "Gregg, is that really you? I knew something was wrong. My daughter hasn't heard from Silvia, and I haven't been able to reach you. Where are you?"

"Jim, I'm in Vermont."

"Vermont? What you doin' there?"

"Any chance you can get here by the end of the day?"

"Sure, I can bring the family, though my kid will be disappointed about missing trick-or-treating," Jim replied, always willing to help before even knowing the situation.

Gregg sat straight. "Jim, I'm in a town called Blackberry Cove, and I'm in a lot of trouble, like you have no idea. These people kidnapped Silvia. They killed Sarah and Noah."

"What people? What are you talking about?"

"I'll explain everything later. Right now, I need you to promise you won't call the authorities until I say so. These people will kill my little girl, Jim, if they get even the slightest sniff of the cops."

"Look, Gregg, if you had a slip and accidently did something you shouldn't have, I'll understand. But you need to tell me so we can go to the authorities together and I can help you. I know how badly you wanted Silvia back, and I know how difficult Sarah was making things for you."

"No, it's not like that, Jim. People kidnapped my daughter."

"Then we need to call the FBI," he argued.

"Not yet, Jim. I need you to trust me."

There was a brief silence. Then: "Okay. Just tell me how to help."

"I'll call back soon," Gregg said.

Gregg hung up the call, then dialed Rachel's number from his own phone.

Rachel answered on the other side. "News, Hunter?"

"Yes, I have found the body of Liam Watts. He was in the freezer of the therapist's house, down in the basement. Gunshot to the head. No one knows I've found the body. You said to call before alerting the authorities or making a scene."

"Well, great!" Rachel exclaimed, sounding flabbergasted. After a pause, she asked, "How is the body?"

"What do you mean?"

"Is the body all in one piece?"

"Eh, yes."

Gregg could hear Rachel sighing with relief. She ordered, "Grab it without the therapist noticing and bring it to us."

"I'll meet you at five on the road from the other day. Bring Silvia."

He hung up.

27

RACHEL WAS DETERMINED FOR THIS TO GO DIFFERENTLY THAN HER first operation. In Pennsylvania, a few years ago, a boy a little younger than Silvia Hunter asked her if he was really going to be let go. Rachel needed for the boy's father to sell his business, and she had held the boy and his mother as leverage. All the father had to do was sell his business to the people she instructed him to, then meet her, and he'd get his family back. He sold the business, but he didn't meet her. It hadn't occurred to Rachel that she was actually doing this man a favor, and that he had been wanting to get rid of his family for some time.

Obviously, things hadn't ended well after the father didn't show up. Rachel shot the boy and his mother, tracked down the father, and put a bullet in his head too. It had ended that way even after Rachel promised the little boy that everything would be okay, all because Rachel had misjudged the father's motives. She would never make the same mistake again.

Gregg Hunter loved his daughter; she had made sure to be certain about it this time. As long as he had solved the case of Liam Watts, without any tricks, this could go much better than her operation in Pennsylvania.

The black van rumbled along the forest road outside Blackberry Cove and finally came to a halt. Rachel stepped out of the front passenger seat and opened the back. Silvia was bound inside with one of the men keeping watch over her.

"Are you really going to let me go?" she asked, just as the little boy had.

This time, Rachel didn't want to make any promises. She turned away and glanced down at her watch—five o'clock. *Hunter should be here by now.* Rachel pulled out her phone and dialed Gregg's number, but he didn't answer. She put the phone back in her pocket, glaring—something wasn't right—he wouldn't be late.

"Miss Milgram," the driver called. "We have an observer."

Rachel marched towards the driver's open window and took the binoculars from him. She followed his pointing finger up to a hill where a young woman was hiding in the bushes, watching them. It was Chloe Mason.

Rachel frowned and lowered the binoculars. "Lock the girl up!"

The man in the back of the van pulled Silvia inside. He cut off her screams by gagging her mouth with a neckerchief. He slammed the back door of the van. Rachel got in the passenger seat and told the driver to start the vehicle.

Gregg's car was soon visible behind them. He was racing towards them, and Rachel told the driver to put his foot right down. The van took off, skidding around a bend, but Gregg managed to follow. They knocked down a metal gate and barreled into what seemed to be an abandoned construction site or quarry.

Rachel glanced at her side mirror to see if they had lost Gregg, but to her dismay, he was still following them. The driver also must have been too busy looking at Gregg because when she looked back up, they were heading straight for a heap of rocks dug from the quarry.

"Look out!"

The driver turned his eyes back to the road and slammed down on the brakes. But it was too late. The van soared over the mound and crashed to a stop, turning over on its side. Rachel's head jerked forward, striking the dashboard and knocking her unconscious.

28

GREGG'S CAR RACED ACROSS THE MUDDY TERRAIN OF THE QUARRY'S crater, speeding round the heap of rocks to avoid colliding as well.

The driver crawled through his window and ran around the crashed vehicle to aid Rachel. Meanwhile, the other man stepped out of the back of the van, pulling Silvia with him. He lifted his gun and shot at Gregg's windshield.

Gregg slammed on the brakes and his car came to a stop. He jumped out and held up his gun as he marched towards the crashed van.

The man holding Silvia turned away with her. They ran towards a portable office at the edge of the construction site. The driver went for his gun, but before he could do anything, Gregg shot him in the chest.

Inside the vehicle, Gregg could see Rachel's eyes open in the side mirror. Her lip was bleeding. She grabbed her aching head, trying to keep it still, and blinked repeatedly, as if trying to regain her vision. She spotted him approaching the van, and her hand went for the gun on her belt.

Gregg burst the window with his elbow before she could grab it. She shielded her head from the flying shards. Gregg grabbed her by the hair and slammed her face into the dash-board, bursting her nose. He opened the door and dragged her out. Rachel reached out her hands and clawed into the earth, dragging herself forward. Gregg stopped her, kneeling on her back, and pressed his gun against the back of her skull.

"Where did they go?" Gregg demanded. "Where's my daughter?"

Rachel's eyes flickered towards the construction site trailer, and without hesitation, Gregg grabbed her by the back of her jacket, his gun still trained on her. He dragged her towards the trailer, his grip on the gun tightening in his sweaty palm. Despite his years of experience as a cop, he had never been in a situation quite like this, and his heart was pounding in his chest.

"You made a big mistake," Rachel said. "Now, you and your daughter are gonna die."

"Shut up!" Gregg kicked open the cheap door, and aimed his gun, his heart racing and his hands shaking.

From a corner of the office, Rachel's man stepped out, holding a gun to Silvia. "Let Miss Milgram go!"

Gregg aimed his gun at the man. "Let my daughter go first! Let her go now!"

"Daddy," Silvia called.

"Silvia, I'm going to get you home tonight, I swear," Gregg said.

"I wouldn't be so sure of that. I've been prepared for this moment, Hunter," Rachel uttered. "What about you? Are you prepared to lose everything?"

Gregg tried to hide his trembling. "Let her go!"

"Kill her," Rachel instructed him.

The guard pushed the gun harder against Silvia's skull. Gregg couldn't risk it and he lowered his gun, releasing his grip on Rachel. He howled in frustration and beat his fists against the wall.

Rachel wiped the blood from her nose with her glove. "You failed, Hunter."

"This can still work. Give me another chance," Gregg pleaded.

"Another chance to fuck me over? I don't think so!"

"I will solve the case!"

Rachel held a blank stare. She turned to her subordinate. "Take the girl to the car."

The man stepped around Gregg, dragging Silvia outside. Rachel took the gun from Gregg's hand and backed away. Gregg followed.

Outside, the man threw Silvia into the trunk of Gregg's car. He dragged the body of the driver, throwing him into the trunk as well, then slammed it shut. Rachel walked to the driver's seat. Once the man was inside, she drove away.

Gregg watched as the car disappeared down the road. He slid out his cell phone and with a sad sigh, phoned Chloe.

"Well?" she asked.

"I didn't get Silvia back," he replied. "But Rachel took the car, with the attached tracking device like you suggested. The plan worked."

"Great. Now what?"

"Jim is on standby to follow the signal, then contact the FBI when he finds their location."

"Maybe we should call them now."

"Then we risk Rachel making a run for it," Gregg said. "If she manages to disappear, she'll kill my daughter for sure."

29

ANDREW SAT IN A PATROL CAR, PARKED RIGHT BEFORE THE SIGN TO
Blackberry Cove. He had paid a local pig to borrow the car and
uniform. Luckily, there was only one road in and out of the
town. Gregg had been too smart to use his own phone to call for
help. Sadly for him, Rachel already anticipated this, and she'd
placed a bug within the upper pocket of Gregg's coat.

Andrew knew he should feel some respect for Rachel being
good at her job, but he felt nothing for her. Maybe it was because
she was too young for them to have anything in common, or
perhaps it was just that they spent too much time together. Eventually, when you spend all of your time with someone, every
little thing they do becomes annoying. It got under his skin how
much she talked during their long car rides, even though she
knew he preferred to sit in silence. It pissed him off how she put
her feet up on the dashboard when going to sleep. Even the
smell of her shampoo was beginning to bother him.

Most likely, he would get rid of Rachel once the operation
was over. It wouldn't be the first time he retired a colleague for
getting on his nerves. Was colleague even the right word? It
didn't seem to be considering their line of work. More accurately,

they were temporary partners, and both knew it wouldn't last forever.

Rachel was an orphan, like most of Andrew's previous partners. Some he even rescued from the street, and they were nearly always young and female. It was better that way; it meant they had no families and were usually more submissive. If they were also hungry, it made it even easier to convince them. Rachel, though, was more disagreeable than most. Blackberry Cove had even been her idea. It was unlike his partners to choose cases for themselves.

Andrew had even dispatched partners he got along with for one reason or another. For example, if they decided this line of work was no longer for them and wanted out. That was a no-no. Once you started this work, there was no going back. Everyone knew that. It wasn't something that had to be said. It was like an unwritten agreement, and anyone who broke it was aware of the consequences and would have to pay the price. If there was one thing Andrew hated most in this world it was actions being carried out without consequences.

In this world, everything has a cause and effect. One action causes another. Eventually, we all have to answer for the actions we've caused. Don't complain about cancer if you smoke five a day, and don't whine about cavities if you forget to brush your teeth. Andrew knew perfectly well the events he'd brought about, and he was ready to be held accountable for them. One day, he would meet his end, and it most likely wouldn't be pretty.

That's why he wasn't troubled by what was about to happen to Gregg's ex-partner and his family. The fucker had answered Gregg's call and dove at the first chance to help, without even knowing what he was getting himself in for. Worse than that, he freely decided to bring his family into the mess. Now the idiot would watch his wife and daughter die before he too would have his ticket punched.

Almost on cue, Jim's car came into sight. Andrew activated

the patrol car's sirens and pulled him over. By the time Andrew got to the car, Jim was ready with his window down and detective badge on show. "I'm a detective from Boston. Here on police business. What seems to be the problem, Officer?"

Andrew glanced at the wife in the passenger seat and the teenage girl in the back before turning his attention back to Jim. "Do you always bring your family on police business, Detective?"

Jim let out an exasperated sigh. "Look, I don't have time for this. Could you just tell me why you pulled me over? I wasn't speeding."

"I'll get to that when I'm ready," Andrew replied, leaving no doubt from his tone that he was in control of the situation.

Jim raised his eyebrows, perhaps surprised that a mere officer would talk to him in such a way. Andrew would make him scream twice as loud for his arrogance.

"What's your name, Officer?" Jim asked.

"Officer Fury."

The forest was Bernard's sanctuary.

It was the one place he felt free. He could walk forever and never come across another person. It was a world separated from the one with daily anxieties and worries. As he wandered deep into the woods, the trees enveloping him, he felt his mind become clear.

The trail of dried blood he found the previous week was gone. The recent rainfall hadn't been heavy enough to wash it away, so he assumed that animals must have taken care of it. Perhaps the new family of coyotes he had spotted on his hikes had been responsible.

He stopped abruptly in his tracks, spotting a figure standing between the trees. It was his wife, Flora, and he felt a chill run down his spine. She had been following him again.

He fell to his knees and looked up at her, trembling. "What do you want from me?"

The vision stood still, eyes darting through him. "You have forgotten why you're here."

"No, I remember every day, every second of every damn day! But I need him to find the body first! I need Liam Watts to be found!"

Bernard clutched his head, feeling his vision blur and his heart race. He was so lightheaded that he thought he might collapse.

His wife would never leave him, and he wouldn't let himself move on from her until he finished his task. But finding Liam's body remained an impermeable wall in his path.

Then, he noticed something wasn't right.

The shrubs he knelt beside were distorted, as if they had been crushed by something heavy. Further ahead, he saw more bushes and small trees that looked the same. A vehicle had driven off-road, between the trees.

He examined the small bush, seeing how high it had grown. It had been flattened to the ground by wheels—*not recently, but some months ago. Maybe about the time Clementine and Liam were killed.*

Someone had driven out here into the woods, and then left a trail of blood from their car.

Bernard took out his cellphone and prepared to make an anonymous call to the sheriff. It would only be a matter of time now before the body was found, and this would all be over. Finally, he could move on.

———

Gregg drove Chloe's car along Blackberry Cove's country road in the dark, worried that he hadn't heard anything yet from Jim, who wasn't answering his calls. One hand was on the steering wheel, while the other held his phone, which displayed directions to the tracing device he had planted under his car.

Eventually, he pulled over to the side of the road, his phone indicating that he had reached the location of the tracking device.

Gregg stepped out of the car and glanced around, but he didn't see any sign of his car. His foot hit something as he walked. He realized it was the tiny metal tracking device, now detached from the car. Someone had removed it. Just as he picked it up, his cell phone rang, and Rachel's voice came through on the other end.

"You should have known better than that, thinking I don't cover my tracks," she said.

Gregg felt a wave of fear wash over him. "You found it?"

"You really should know by now not to mess with me. I mean, honestly, it was such a crappy plan, I have a hard time believing you came up with it. Haven't been drawing ideas from the yokel town you're in, I hope?"

"I don't understand," he said. "Where's Jim?"

"Both Jim and his family are safe for now."

"You bitch," he spat. "Let them go. They have nothing to do with any of this."

"You made them part of this. The only way out of this for you is to solve the case. Now, to avoid any further incidents like today, I've decided to give you a little reminder of how serious I am."

"What reminder is that?"

"Take ten steps forward from where you picked up your tracker. And know to never try to fool me again."

She hung up the phone.

Gregg took ten paces onwards, coming to a tree. He noticed something had been placed down in front of it.

Whatever it was, it was wrapped in layers of cellophane. Picking it up, he unwrapped the levels of plastic.

His stomach churned at what he found: a finger, covered in blood, which had been crudely removed.

It was accompanied by a bloodstained note which read: *Next time, it'll be her whole hand.* Gregg fell to his knees, and cried, the severed finger of his daughter resting in his palms.

30

SOMEONE WAS WATCHING HER.

Chloe felt it every time she turned her back. It was like she was being followed, but whenever she turned around, there was no one there.

She made her way to the Swan Inn to try and get Gregg out. Since the horrific discovery of his daughter's finger, he had barricaded himself in his room and wouldn't come out. He had to get back to solving the case. It was the only way he'd see Silvia.

As she opened the door to the inn, she noticed something in the shrubbery outside—a pair of eyes watching her. Stunned, Chloe took a step back, breathing deeply as she tried to calm herself down. When she looked once more, there was nothing there. *Is it all in my head?* She walked up the stairs.

She entered Gregg's room during a phone call with his employer, Rachel Milgram, on loudspeaker.

"Now Hunter, I can only begin to imagine what you must be feeling since you received our little surprise," Rachel said on Gregg's cell. "But just know that wouldn't have happened if you hadn't defied us."

151

Gregg grunted in response.

"Bear in mind that I too feel bad. I've grown rather fond of having your lovely daughter around. Trust me, I took no pleasure in what I had to do."

"*You* did it?"

"Does that surprise you?" she asked.

"I thought it was one of your goons, but you actually held the knife?"

"I'm shocked you didn't recognize my handwriting. Though I detested causing harm to Silvia, don't think for a moment that I won't hesitate to remove her entire hand if you attempt to pull another stunt. Think of her the next time you consider it."

"All I'm doing is thinking of Silvia!"

"Exactly. You're neglecting what's necessary to get her back, which is working on the case. Find Liam Watts and make some progress, will you?"

Gregg wrung his hands together. "I'm trying."

"Not hard enough." After a pause, she continued, her voice utterly calm. "Investigate your new neighbors a little further. Find out what they were doing on the night in question. You're supposed to be a genius, I'm sure you'll think of something."

"What if I don't?" he asked. "Maybe I'm not a genius. When you first came to see me, you brought an article that impressed you—the one that said I saved a little girl. But the truth is, I just got lucky on that case. There's nothing about me that's impressive. You picked the wrong person for this job!"

"You're not doing yourself any favors, Hunter. You need to prove your worth to me by solving this case."

"Rachel, why is Liam Watts and his killer so important to you? Maybe, if you tell me more, I'll be more likely to solve this."

"Hunter, the less you know, the better off you'll be when this is over. Just focus on solving the damn case."

She hung up. Gregg dropped his phone and collapsed onto the bed with a heavy sigh. Chloe sat beside him and put a hand on his shoulder.

"She's really mad about what we did," he said. "I have to get a serious move on."

"You need to get everyone together and question them all. Luckily, the Holst family is hosting a poker night tonight at their place. Loads of people are invited, including me. I'm sure you could tag along."

"Really? That's fantastic!" Gregg said, hugging her.

The two of them headed downstairs for breakfast, Chloe asking, "If you get the chance, will you kill Rachel? No one could blame you after what she's done to your daughter."

"I'm not thinking about revenge," Gregg said. "All I want is my daughter back."

"But would you if you had to?"

"Absolutely."

They sat down and ordered some eggs from Hannah. "You've endured a lot. How do you cope with the stress?" Chloe then said.

"Even as a boy, I used to write a lot. I kept a journal, of poetry mostly. Whenever I'm feeling overwhelmed, I turn to that and it helps to focus my attention on something else."

"Do you still keep a journal?"

Gregg nodded. "I've had a lot of material to write about during this case. It helps me unwind and stops me spiraling to jot down my thoughts as a poem or something silly."

"You'll have to show me something you've written some time," Chloe said with a smile.

They moved onto discussing potential questions to ask that night. However, even while talking with Gregg, Chloe's eyes continuously darted to the windows, her mind preoccupied with the possibility of someone watching them.

Though her ex's fate was unknown,
Chloe's strength had clearly shown,
She kept moving forward with grace,
Her smile always lighting up the place,
And her spirit continued to be grown.

Her eyes are like diamonds so bright,
And her skin is as smooth as moonlight,
With her kindness that's truly so rare,
And a beauty that's simply beyond compare,
She makes everything seem all right.

31

G REGG SAT WITH THE OTHER GUESTS THAT NIGHT WHILE T IMOTHY
poured them wine, and Elaine cleared the poker table. While the
mayor inquired about Chloe's father in Gregg's right ear, the
mayor's secretary asked the innkeepers about their business on
Gregg's other side. Elaine was arranging the cards and chips on
the table, as they all sat in anticipation of the game to come.

"Excuse me, everyone," Gregg called, facing all the bodies in
the room. "Thank you for having me here tonight. While Mrs.
Holst finishes setting the table, I was hoping I could briefly ask
you all about July eighteenth, the night Liam Watts went missing. It would help a lot with my investigation and could result in
getting a killer off your streets."

There were some sighs and groans, but everyone kept their
attention on him. He took out his notepad and flicked through to
his notes on the day of the murder.

"As far as I'm aware, only two people remember encoun-
tering Liam Watts that day. Miss Mason saw him about five in
the afternoon in the park. Is that correct?" He turned to Chloe.

She nodded. "Yes, then I went home."

"And, Dr. Holst saw him in the evening before ten for drinks
at the inn. Is that right?"

"Yes, I believe so." Timothy nodded unsurely.

Gregg turned to the innkeepers. "Mr. and Mrs. O'Doyle, do you remember seeing Liam that day?"

Hannah shook her head. "No, I don't. And, I'm sorry, Dr. Holst, but I don't remember seeing you there that night either. I've thought about that evening a lot. The day after, the sheriff questioned me extensively about who had been present the previous night."

"Oh, I must have made a mistake," Timothy replied, a little too quickly. "It must have been the night before that Liam and I went for drinks. Yes, I remember now. It was a Monday night, so it must have been July seventeenth, the night before."

"So, you didn't see Liam on the eighteenth?" Gregg asked.

Timothy shook his head. "No, I did not."

"When did you first realize Liam was missing, Dr. Holst?"

"The day after Clementine's murder, the sheriff came knocking on doors to ask where people had been. He didn't find Liam at home. I told him Liam had probably gone hiking, but he never answered any of my calls. By the end of the week, I knew he wasn't coming back."

Bernard entered the room, the last of the guests to arrive. "What's going on?"

"Mr. Hunter has decided to hijack our evening for investigative purposes," the mayor replied with a heavy sigh.

Gregg faced Bernard. "Mr. Neumann, do you remember what you were doing on the evening of July eighteenth?"

"I was stargazing all evening atop the mountains," Bernard replied. "Venus and Saturn were both in the sky that night. Then, at about nine they were joined by Jupiter and by a beautiful crescent moon. It was truly a breathtaking sight."

"You were alone?" Gregg asked.

Bernard nodded.

The mayor rose from his seat. "Enough of this, Mr. Hunter, please. This is meant to be a fun night."

"Yes, and I've finished setting the poker table now," Elaine called over.

"Please, everybody, I'll just be a few moments more," Gregg announced.

Elaine's face had turned absolutely crimson. "He's ruining my party," she hissed in Timothy's ear. "Do something."

Timothy simply sank back into his armchair, as if pretending not to exist.

Gregg focused his attention on the mayor, who was still standing. "Mr. Mayor, where were you that night?"

"None of your fucking business," the mayor spat. "Now, this is my only night off all week, and I'm not about to have you ruin it. We are all going to play some poker. You can play or not. Makes no difference to me."

"Am I to assume that you were at home with your family, being a devoted husband and father?" Gregg quipped, a smug grin on his face to make sure the mayor caught on to the insinuation.

The mayor squared his shoulders and folded his arms, refusing to be intimidated. "Watch your step, Mr. Hunter."

Gregg wasn't willing to back down. "I apologize. If, instead of being at home, you were out fucking your secretary, just let me know and I'll add it to my notes."

The townspeople all looked at one another shocked, and Nathan went even more crimson than Elaine. He tightened his fists. "How dare—"

"Oh, please, everyone knows."

Everyone turned to Isabella, who had gone pink and lowered her head in shame.

"Or at least they do now," Gregg added.

"You call yourself a detective?" Nathan asked. "You couldn't find your own fucking footprints in the snow! Now, stop making accusations that aren't true."

Gregg could feel his façade falling, but he couldn't let the others know he was out of his depth. Though his entire life he had tried to seem tougher and smarter than he was, this wasn't the time for honesty. "I haven't made any accusations that aren't true," he said, head high.

Nathan stepped forward, looking about ready to punch him in the throat.

"It's true!" Isabella exclaimed.

The townspeople were so overrun with good gossip that they found themselves incapable of gasping.

Isabella stood and wiped away some tears. "There's no point in denying it. I love Nathan, and he loves me. We've loved each other for some time now, and there's nothing wrong with that. It has nothing to do with the investigations."

"How can we be so sure of that?" Gregg asked.

"We'd have no reason to harm anyone in town because we were planning on running away that night. Our bags were already packed when we got the call at the office, saying Clementine hadn't returned home from her run."

Now Hannah stood up. "What?" she shouted. "How could you have done that to Clementine?"

The townspeople began bickering among themselves when Gregg noticed Chloe walk over to the window, looking out as if searching for something.

Gregg went over to join her, leaving behind the mess he had just started. "What's wrong?" he asked. "What are you looking at?"

"I didn't want to tell you," she replied.

"Tell me what?"

"I've noticed someone following me lately."

"What do you mean?" He looked out the window but saw nothing.

"I don't know, just someone following me when I'm out at night."

"Why didn't you say anything?"

"You have too much to deal with. Your attention should be on your daughter. I've already distracted you more than I should have." She gave a smile, but Gregg could tell it was forced.

Gregg nodded, deciding to come back to this subject later. She was right; his attention had to be on his daughter and the investigation. "Are there any more details you can think of about July eighteenth?" he asked.

"I had asked if Liam wanted us to live together," she replied. "He seemed to get really mad at the idea of settling in this town. He said he wasn't going to live in this shithole forever, and he wasn't like the other hicks in town. He said he was going to make something of himself. 'Like your try at film school?' I asked. Then, he went red and shouted that it had been a waste of time and they had never appreciated his talent. I said maybe he should just be happy with what he had right now—meaning me —but he said it wasn't enough. He said I was nothing more than a *dumb bitch*."

"I'm sorry," Gregg said.

"Then, he threw my anniversary present to the ground and stormed off." She looked away and shuffled her feet against the wooden flooring. "I hated him for treating me that way. But I didn't kill him. You know that, right, Gregg?"

Gregg lifted her head to meet her gaze. "I do know that."

"Why are we even still here?" He then heard the mayor shout. "This was supposed to be a fun night, but Mr. Hunter has turned into a fucking inquiry. Except he's not even doing any inquiring."

Gregg turned back to face the guests. "Forgive me, but I just have a couple of last questions. I would like to know what people thought of Liam Watts."

"Oh, for God's sake," Nathan groaned. "I've already told you that I had no relationship whatsoever with Liam Watts."

"What about you, Miss Blake?" He turned to the mayor's secretary.

"I never really knew Liam," she replied, rubbing her hands.

"Go on," he urged her.

"I like to think I know most people in town, being the mayor's secretary for the last four years, but Liam really liked to keep to himself. I never liked him."

"Why do you say that?"

"He was a creep."

"In what way?"

"I can't put my finger on it. Whenever I encountered him in shops or at the inn, he was always unpleasant. I attempted to engage him in conversation multiple times, but he never seemed interested in talking. I think he disliked people."

"I had a similar impression," Hannah chimed in. She turned to Timothy. "Dr. Holst, you and Liam were friends. What did you think about him?"

Timothy's head snapped up. "Wha-at do you want to know?"

"What kind of person was he?"

Timothy fidgeted with some poker cards. "He was, um, reserved, I guess. Most people didn't really understand him, but once you got to know him, he was really quite nice."

Gregg looked around for Bernard, realizing he hadn't heard from him in some time. "Mr. Neumann, what was your impression of Liam?"

"I didn't know him very well."

"Where did you move from?"

"Boston."

"You moved straight here from Boston?"

"More or less," Bernard replied. "I did some traveling after my wife died."

"Where did you travel?"

"Many places. Why does that matter?"

"Just curious." Gregg closed his notepad, realizing he didn't have much more to ask and also didn't want to risk alienating people more than he already had. He handed out some of his business cards in case they thought of anything else. "Thank you all very much for your cooperation. I'll let you continue with your game."

"It's about fucking time," Nathan grumbled, and he and the other guests went to the poker table.

Chloe walked him out and he offered to take her home, remembering her possible stalker situation.

"I can manage myself," she assured him. "There's something else I have to tell you." She didn't wait for him to ask. "The other night, I heard something coming from the mayor's house. I looked out my window and saw him pull a rolled-up carpet to his car and then drive off."

"What? Why didn't you tell me this before?"

"I never thought much of it. Then, when you were questioning Nathan, I began thinking about that. You think he could actually be involved in a murder?"

"I'm becoming more and more certain Liam killed Clementine," Gregg replied. "It seems reasonable that the mayor may have hired him, but I need evidence."

"But Isabella claimed that they were planning to run away together, so why would Nathan bother?"

"Power means too much to Nathan, so I find it hard to believe that he would be willing to abandon his position as mayor. Isabella might have thought they were going to leave town together, but that doesn't mean Nathan couldn't have hired Liam behind her back."

Chloe shook her head. "Nathan was always so sweet when I was a kid. But tonight, I realized how much he's changed."

He sighed, rubbing his hands through his beard.

"What's wrong?" she asked.

"I still have no idea what happened," he admitted. "My entire life, I have tried to look smarter than I am. Now, it's finally catching up with me. I'm not sure I can solve this case. I think Nathan has seen through my façade."

"Don't worry," she said, stroking his face gently. "You'll get there."

"I hope you're right."

They got to the end of the garden pathway, and Chloe reassured him that she was, and then she gave him a soft kiss on the lips. The two of them went their separate ways, and Gregg attempted to return to the inn with a smile. However, given the lack of progress he had made that night, he found it too difficult.

32

CHLOE KNEW LIAM'S SOUL WAS DARK, BUT THAT'S EXACTLY WHAT had first drawn her to him.

Back in school, he had been a quiet kid, and Chloe often wondered what thoughts lurked inside his head. Perhaps it was something ghastly that only she could understand. She wanted to know him, and for him to feel close enough to her that he'd open up. Chloe knew that was crazy, but he was the only slightly curious thing in the entire town.

He reminded her of the serial killers she read about in her book collection, who too had been turned against the world after years of abuse or of never fitting in. They were forced to retreat into their heads until their dark fantasies of power took over. She often wondered if these killers would have turned out differently had they had someone to confide in about their dark fantasies.

During her visit with Dr. Holst, she expressed her anger towards her father for the things he had done to her. The therapist warned her that suppressing her problems could lead to unpredictable consequences.

No matter how close she wanted to get to Liam though, even after five years of dating, he was still a complete stranger to her.

The day he broke up with her, it had filled her with a rage she hadn't known since before her father's paralysis.

On her way home, her phone vibrated. Bernard was calling.

"Hello," she answered.

"Has Gregg figured anything out yet?" he immediately asked.

"If you want Liam to be found, Gregg needs to be told the truth."

"You haven't told him everything," Bernard shot back. "You didn't mention that Liam was headed towards Richard and Hannah's house that night, and that you bumped into me because you were following him."

"You told Gregg that you were stargazing," she replied. "This is the problem. How can Gregg find Liam if everyone is lying to him?"

"Who's lying?"

"Richard and Hannah said they heard nothing. We know Liam was going to their house that night. We saw the light go on. They must have seen him."

"Everyone has something to hide," Bernard said. "We just need to steer Gregg in the right direction. Leave it to me."

He hung up and Chloe made her way home. She looked over her shoulder as she entered the house. There was no one there. She closed the door and peeked through the peephole. A figure stepped out of the shadows into the light of a streetlamp, facing her home.

She locked the door and shivered.

"I'm home, Dad," she called out as she entered the dark living room. She hadn't left the TV on or even a light. Her father sat motionless in his armchair. Chloe noticed the bag of urine at his side and went to replace it. She smiled to herself, knowing that her father had been rendered powerless, unable to hurt her again. Like Liam, he had paid the price for the things he had done.

33

THE DAY WAS SILVIA'S BIRTHDAY. IT PAINED GREGG KNOWING SHE would spend it alone, or even worse, in the company of monsters.

For her ninth birthday, he got her the violin she so badly wanted. How quickly she had excelled at it, playing in concerts at her school. She was such a clever girl, far smarter than he or her mother.

For her eleventh birthday, he bought her the Sherlock Holmes complete collection, because of how much she wanted to be like him and how joyful that made him feel.

Now for her sixteenth birthday—the one that should have been her best yet—the only gift he wanted to give her was her life.

Gregg made his way downstairs, ready for another day of sleuthing. He was going to walk out when he saw a young man in a deputy's outfit, sitting in the lounge having breakfast. Gregg sat down beside the deputy and introduced himself.

"I know who you are." The young man ignored his offer of a

165

handshake, too busy coating his scrambled eggs with ketchup. "I'm Deputy Marc Chips."

"Where have you been, Deputy?"

"On a fishing trip, but the sheriff has got me up to speed with your so-called progress."

"Any new developments?"

Marc mixed his scrambled eggs and ketchup together into a terrible-looking pink paste, and then took a forkful and ate it. He grinned.

"Deputy?" Gregg said, tapping his feet.

"The sheriff got an anonymous tip the other night," Marc said, squirting even more ketchup onto his plate.

"And?"

"Can't say. Not until we've fully followed up on it."

Gregg wasn't pleased with that response, but he didn't want to create another adversary. "Alright, but keep me informed once you do," he said, hoping the deputy's smile indicated agreement.

Gregg stood to leave but Marc put a hand on his shoulder. "How's Chloe? I hear you two have gotten pretty close."

"Who told you that?" Gregg asked.

"I heard it around."

Gregg shrugged. "I don't know what you're talking about."

"Right. Just be careful, Mr. Hunter, about getting too close to a suspect."

"I don't think of Chloe as a suspect," Gregg replied.

There was that grin again. He continued shoveling in his eggs. Gregg departed, feeling uneasy about the anonymous tip that had been received.

"Happy birthday," Rachel called.

The girl's bleak room was windowless and had concrete walls. It was lit only by a small ceiling light.

"I think you've had enough pizza. Hope you like grilled

cheese." Rachel's footsteps echoed against the metal flooring as she planted a tray of food on the small table.

Silvia curled up in the fetal position and buried her face. Rachel realized the girl looked a lot like Rachel once did when she was similarly trapped.

"Oh, don't be like that." Rachel approached the bed and sat down beside her. She placed her hand on the girl's back, but Silvia juddered her away, tears in her eyes. "I know this isn't an ideal birthday, but you'll be home soon enough."

"How can you say that?" Silvia lifted her right hand to reveal the finger that was missing.

Rachel crossed her arms. "Yes, I know my last visit involved a rather large knife, but it wasn't entirely my fault."

"How'd you figure that?"

"Well, your father shouldn't have tricked me."

"Well, you shouldn't have kidnapped and locked me up."

"Again." Rachel gritted her teeth. "Not my fault."

Silvia returned to her fetal position and refused to speak any further, causing Rachel to feel a pang of sadness. Just then, the metal door opened, and Fury walked in.

"Milgram," he said. "We have something to discuss. Please stop engaging the prisoner in conversation. That's not what it's here for."

"I'll try and slip in another visit later," she whispered to Silvia.

"Please don't," the girl pleaded.

"Next time, not only will I bring a knife, but I'll also bring a fork and some birthday cake to go with it."

"I'd rather go hungry."

"Suit yourself," Rachel said with a shrug.

Rachel followed Fury from the storage facility outside, and they stood in a quiet area of the deep forest.

"What is it, Fury?"

"We need to discuss the Boston cop."

"Once the case is over, we'll let him and his family go."

"That's not happening."

"But after the case is over, we'll disappear. It won't matter anymore."

"The cop dies. And his family. No more loose ends."

"More bodies means more loose ends." She went to walk away, but Fury grabbed her by the throat and pinned her against the wall. He held his gun under her chin with his other hand.

"I don't think you're properly focused, Milgram."

"Of course I am! You know how important this case is to me." She bit her lip to calm herself, aware that any small move on her part and Fury wouldn't hesitate to pull the trigger. He may be a hitman, but he wasn't like the ones on TV who become criminals for money; Fury became a hitman because he was already looking for a reason to kill.

"Don't get soft. We'll frame Hunter for the murders using the same gun we used to kill his ex-wife and her partner. We'll make it look like the Boston cop went after Hunter, suspecting him of killing his ex-wife, and Hunter killed him to escape with his daughter. No loose ends. Can you handle that?"

Rachel knew she couldn't hesitate. "Whatever it takes to get the job done."

34

Isabella never imagined she'd be doing something as normal as packing a picnic, but she never had a family to do such things with. Doing things with Nathan and Raymond was the life she used to dream of as a child.

But it wasn't really her dream to be living. It was supposed to be Clementine here, packing a lunch for her husband and son. Clementine would also have been better at it, preparing something a little more creative than peanut butter and jelly sandwiches.

Raymond excitedly watched her pack the picnic. "Is Isabella coming too, Dad?"

"She is."

Isabella smiled as Raymond swung his arms and danced on the spot.

"And," Isabella said, "we'll be picnicking by the lake, so if you want to go and pack your bathing suit, I'm sure your father won't mind."

"The water's cold this time of year," Nathan protested.

"We'll be out before it's dark and gets too cold." Isabella gave a wink to Raymond, filling him with further thrill. He ran upstairs, leaving the adults alone with each other.

"You know, I find it really nice how much he's come to like you," Nathan said, and Isabella felt touched.

Isabella hugged Nathan in a quick burst of joy. "Thank you."

"Thank you? For what?"

"For welcoming me into your family. The truth is I've never had a family before. Not a real one."

Nathan lifted her chin and gazed into her eyes. "You've never spoken about your childhood before."

"My past isn't important. This—today—that's what means everything to me."

They remained silent for a moment in each other's embrace. Nathan kissed Isabella's cheek, and as she looked over his shoulder, she noticed something odd. "When did you remove the carpet in the dining room?"

"Oh, almost a week ago. I've been meaning to buy another."

"Why would you take out the carpet without having a new one?"

"Because, Isabella, *it* wouldn't clean."

"What wouldn't?" she asked.

Nathan made sure Raymond hadn't returned from downstairs then leaned close. He replied in a hushed tone, "Clementine's blood."

She pulled herself away. "Why was Clementine's blood on the carpet?"

"It's nothing. I just-I had to get rid of the carpet in case people got the wrong idea, especially after that detective arrived. And it's a good thing I did because he's been here asking questions."

"Please tell me."

Nathan sighed. "She found out about us. She knew about the affair."

"What? When?"

"About a month before her murder. That's what urged me to finally agree to run away with you."

"Was she angry?"

Nathan's fists clenched as he spoke. "No, she was relieved. *I* was angry."

"Why?" she asked, confused.

"Because she thought it meant the marriage was over, and she was actually happy about it. She said the marriage had never been right, and we both only wanted to try it for Raymond. She thought it was best for us both if we got a divorce."

She shrugged. "So why didn't you?"

"Because I wasn't going to let it be her decision! I felt like a child again, wh-when, when..." He stopped talking, too pained to voice whatever memories he was recalling. However, Isabella knew he was referring to his mother abandoning him, something he never got over. After taking a breath, he continued, "Well, I was so angry, Isabella. So, I hit her. Hard."

She stepped back. "You hit her?"

His face was red, his fists clenched, and he was shaking, his voice getting louder. "Yes! I made it clear that our marriage wasn't over until I said it was over. She had no right to leave me. I gave her everything—money, a son. I warned her that if she left, she would get nothing!"

Isabella eyed him for a moment, and then she stepped forward and grabbed hold of his trembling hand. His shaking subsided. For the first time, Isabella began to feel quite sorry for Clementine; before her death, she had been truly trapped in a loveless marriage, unable to fulfill her own dreams, all so she could keep her son.

Nathan looked at her, smiling, and stroked her hair. The anger and redness seemed to drain away from his body. "Do you know it would make me very happy if you were to live here?"

Isabella pulled away again. "Live here? Isn't it too soon after what happened to Clementine?"

"But then we could be a real family, and everyone already knows about us now anyway. I want you to. I love you. And you love me."

"But Raymond—"

"—loves you too."

"I still think it's too soon. But I'll think about it."

"Great," Nathan said, smiling. He glanced at his watch and turned to the stairs. His smile deteriorated. "What is taking that damn boy so long? Raymond, we're waiting, hurry up!"

Nathan marched up the stairs, and Isabella wondered if she should be worried and for how much longer she could continue living Clementine's dream. Eventually, Isabella's fantasy too would come crashing down.

35

SILVIA SAT ON HER BED INSIDE THE CONCRETE ROOM, PLAYING solitaire for what felt like the millionth time. Rachel had given her books to read and paper to write on, but there was only so much she could read, and she never thought she had anything worth writing.

She glanced towards the door that she had to knock on anytime she needed the bathroom or wanted to wash. There was a toilet and shower room down the metal corridor, but the shower had no hot water. Silvia didn't know what this facility was, but she figured it was old and belonged to her kidnappers. She had been given a clean set of clothes by Rachel, but only the one set, and they were now beginning to get as dirty as her other clothes.

Fed up with playing, she turned away from her game of cards and sighed. *This must be what it's like to be in prison. No, this must be worse. At least prisoners get to go outside.* She hadn't been outside in days, not since the day that she had been told she was going home but had actually ended much less joyfully.

Silvia glanced at the door, and she thought about making a run for it the next time it opened, but she shook her head and decided against it. They would be certain to overpower her. She knew there were many of them down here. She had seen several men, as well as Rachel, whom she had devised was in charge. Plus, she wasn't even sure if the door exiting the hallway was unlocked. Her only chance was her father finding the body. She was confident he would; he was the best detective she knew.

Silvia heard footsteps on the metal flooring in the hallway. Someone was coming. As the door opened, Rachel strode in, bearing a tray of what appeared to be beef and potato stew in one hand, and a small chocolate cake in the other.

Rachel slammed the tray down in front of her. "Eat. Now."

Oh no, she's pissed. Silvia prayed her dad hadn't tried something stupid again, and that she wasn't about to lose another finger.

Rachel plonked herself down on the chair by the small table and propped up her boots on Silvia's bed. She then dug into the chocolate cake that Silvia had assumed was for her.

"You didn't want this, did you?" Rachel asked, expelling a few crumbs.

Silvia shook her head, not sure what else to do.

"Good." Rachel finished the small cake in a handful of bites.

Silvia took a spoonful of the beef and potato stew, trying not to let her distaste show on her face for fear of enraging Rachel further. "Any news from my dad?" she asked.

Rachel smeared away the stains of chocolate around her lips. "No, but he needs to hurry the fuck up."

"Why? Is something wrong?"

Rachel marched over to the bed and sat down beside her. "The only thing that's wrong is that I'm stuck here until your father gets the job done."

"*You* don't have to be here," Silvia retorted.

"Life's not so simple, kid." Rachel stooped over and breathed into her ear, "We're more alike than you realize."

Silvia shuddered, trying to conceal her discomfort. "How so?"

"I've been in this kind of work since I was about your age."

"Kidnapping people is a kind of work?" Silvia asked, talking now just to keep her happy.

Rachel looked as though she was suppressing a smile; she seemed to like it when Silvia sparred with her. "That's the least of what I do."

It had been three days since Bernard anonymously called the sheriff with the information he found in the woods, and still nothing had been done. He wondered what was taking them so long, worried he hadn't been specific enough about the location and the sheriff hadn't been able to find it. Bernard thought about taking Gregg or the sheriff out there to randomly come across the tire markings. However, that would be too suspicious.

He heard a knock on the door and peered through the window. Chloe was outside, glancing back over her shoulder. He welcomed her inside, and she immediately shut the door behind her.

"Everything okay?" he asked her.

"I think I'm being followed," she said.

Her too. Maybe I'm not crazy. Though he doubted his dead wife was also following her.

"Who do you think is following you?" he asked.

"I don't know," she replied. "I think someone knows what we did, Bernard. Maybe we should come clean. After all, we didn't do anything wrong."

"No one will believe us," he reminded her. "We need to be patient, Chloe. It will all be over soon, once Gregg uncovers the truth."

"What about the person following me?"

"No one is following you, it's all in your head. Trust me, I understand what it feels like. You're just being paranoid, I promise."

Chloe seemed to consider Bernard's response, nodding in

agreement, but Bernard wasn't sure she could be trusted with their secret any longer. As she left, his eyes darted for the revolver he kept in his safe.

36

THE DOOR TO THE INN RANG AS CHLOE STEPPED INSIDE. SHE greeted Richard and made her way to the dining area, where Gregg sat, awaiting breakfast.

"So, have you thought about the next plan?" she asked.

"Next plan?"

"To find Liam. The other night wasn't too successful."

"I can't keep executing plan after plan. I have to actually get to the bottom of this." He lowered his voice. "My daughter's in danger every minute I don't find Liam's killer."

"Which is why we need a new plan."

"Any ideas? Cause I'm drawing a blank. This isn't like any case I've ever worked on. There's not even a crime scene, let alone a body. There's no prime suspect to investigate."

"You could always dig up the woods."

"Where would I start?"

Chloe smiled, but before she could say anything more, Sheriff Johnston entered the room, closely followed by Deputy Chips. They advanced towards Chloe and Gregg, with Johnston seizing Chloe's arm and hoisting her onto her feet.

"What are you doing?" she cried.

He handcuffed her wrists behind her back.

Gregg jumped to his feet. "What the hell is going on?"

"Chloe Mason, you are under arrest for the suspected murder of Liam Watts. You have the right to remain silent. Anything you say now can and will be used against you in a court of law."

Chloe stood utterly stunned as the charges were read, as did Gregg.

"Johnston, you can't possibly believe—"

"Stay out of this, Hunter. This is town business," Johnston snapped before escorting Chloe out of the inn.

Marc's smug expression made Chloe feel particularly sick to her stomach. He followed behind her and Johnston and they headed for the sheriff's car. As Johnston shoved her into the vehicle and slammed the door, Marc gave her a wicked smirk. Chloe gazed through the window at Gregg, tears obscuring her vision of him.

"This has to be a mistake," he shouted. "I'll work something out. Don't worry."

She was taken to the sheriff's office by Marc and placed into a cell. He wouldn't tell her anything, no matter how much she begged. Fortunately, Gregg arrived just behind them and rushed to the opposite side of the cell.

"I didn't kill Liam, Gregg. You have to believe me," she immediately said.

He looked her in the eyes. "I do believe you, and I promise I will get you out of here."

"I should tell you; Deputy Chips and I have history." She lowered her head.

"What kind of history?" he asked.

"I think he's the one who's been stalking me."

"You what?"

"We were friends as kids but hung with different crowds in high school. He was always a little obsessed with me, asking me out repeatedly and showing up at parties uninvited, but he never took no for an answer. Marc was there that night in Albany when I first got together with Liam. He didn't take it too well. I don't think he's ever forgiven me."

Gregg's eyes narrowed at the deputy, who was sitting at his desk. He stormed over to Marc. "Deputy Chips! Have you been stalking the accused?"

Marc feigned shock at the accusation, covering his mouth with his hand in mock horror. "I was gathering evidence, building my case against Miss Mason."

"I would like to see this evidence," Gregg said.

"Well, I'm sorry Mr. Hunter, but that is confidential information. And you are not a cop here. In fact, you're not a cop at all." Marc sneered.

Gregg glared at him and marched to the door, adding he was going to see the sheriff.

Gregg found Sheriff Johnston sitting on a park bench in front of a duck pond. He had a loaf of bread beside him and lazily fed the ducks. Gregg marched through the park towards him, picked up the loaf of bread, and threw it into the water.

The sheriff leapt to his feet. "What the hell, Hunter?"

"How could you arrest Chloe? You *know* she didn't do it!"

"She had a motive. She was Liam's ex-girlfriend. They broke up the afternoon of his disappearance. She was angry. I thought you don't believe in coincidences?"

"Oh, don't give me that crap, you know perfectly well that—"

"I find it pretty appalling that a supposedly professional private investigator is messing with the case for a girl he wants to screw. Did you even know that Chloe was getting therapy for anger issues from Timothy?"

Gregg didn't say anything. He didn't know that.

"Well, she was," Johnston went on. "I've been speaking to her neighbors and old teachers. Apparently, as a child she was so

179

mad that one day she killed a cat. Isn't that part of the homicidal triad?"

Gregg tried not to show his discomfort at this news. He thought back to when they went to the park, and Chloe hadn't been able to control her rage when talking about Liam. It had been foolish of him to have put that to the back of his mind. "That's a dated model," he said at last.

"But still applicable in some cases," Johnston argued. "It was you who told me profiling can be effective, so I looked more into it. Just because you didn't see it doesn't mean she couldn't have killed Liam. Besides, I've decided to butt out of this case now and leave it to Deputy Chips."

"Why?"

"Because Marcus is going to be the sheriff someday, and this investigation will be great preparation for him."

Gregg stood tall. "Fine, then maybe I'll just go to the mayor over this."

"Be my guest. But he'll side with me. The mayor wants this taken care of more than anyone. After all, mayoral elections are coming up."

"But how can you charge *anyone* with Liam's murder when there's no body?" Gregg asked.

"We've had new evidence come to light that indicates Liam was indeed murdered. So now that it is a murder investigation, charges can be made."

"What is this new evidence I keep hearing about?"

"Why would I share that very crucial information with the lover of the prime suspect?"

"We're not lovers!"

"The neighbors saw you going into Miss Mason's house the other night and not leaving until the morning. I'm afraid you only have yourself to blame for being excluded from this investigation. You got too close."

The sheriff stormed off. In his anger, Gregg kicked a tree, immediately regretting it as he cradled his toe.

He made his way to the mayor's office and stormed in without knocking. Nathan was receiving a backrub from Isabella, who quickly stood up to look professional.

Nathan put on his jacket and gave an exasperated sigh. "What can I do for you, Mr. Hunter?"

"Let Chloe go. She didn't kill anyone."

Nathan rolled his eyes. "I assume you're referring to the arrest of Miss Mason in the Liam Watts case. I've been wondering when you'd arrive, to be honest. I've noticed how close you two seemed to have gotten. Now I see why the police department fired you. Always shack up with the suspects in a murder investigation, do you?"

"I'm not here to discuss my social life!"

"You're not here to *discuss* anything. It appears, Mr. Hunter, you're simply here to yell at me. I don't respond well to yelling. So, you can apologize, and maybe I'll be open to helping you. Or you can, to be frank, fuck off."

Gregg sighed and sat down across from Nathan.

The mayor remarked, "That's better."

"So, can you help me?"

Nathan smiled. "No."

Gregg felt his face flush red.

"I've decided to stay out of the Liam Watts case. The press has been all over my ass, so I want it solved and fast. It's not as though you've made any difference, except for the fact that since you've come to town, my affair has been exposed."

At this, Isabella, who had stood silent, frowned.

"I have already organized a town meeting for Monday morning," Nathan said, "to announce that we have the killer safely behind bars. Perhaps Miss Mason is the killer and you're simply too close to her to realize that?"

Gregg banged his fists on the desk, causing Isabella to jump. "Chloe didn't fucking do it!"

"Well, apparently, she did. I'd much sooner take the word of my men than you, an ex-detective whose services are no longer needed. I now suggest you crawl back to whatever sad sack hired you and tell them what a failure you are. Thank you for staying in Blackberry Cove. Please come again. Actually, scratch that last part."

Gregg stood swiftly, knocking his chair to the floor. "I'm not going to let Chloe take the fall for something she didn't do."

"It is in everyone's best interest if the matter is simply addressed no further."

"And how does that help Chloe?"

"Why would I want to help a murderer, Mr. Hunter?" A sick smirk appeared on the mayor's face.

Leaning over the table, Gregg said, "No matter what you say, I'll keep investigating this case. I'll uncover the truth eventually. What will you do when I prove Chloe's innocence and reveal that you were responsible for her arrest? It will destroy your career."

Nathan stared off silently, a bead of sweat visible on his forehead.

Isabella chimed in, "If you'd like to make an official appointment with Mayor Stannard, I'd be happy to arrange that. But for now, sir, please leave. The mayor's on break."

"My apologies," Gregg said. "Please continue fucking."

Gregg made his way out of the building. Outside, his phone vibrated. He had received a text from Bernard. It read: *Meet me at my house. I have essential information!*

Gregg looked at it quizzically and rushed down the street to Bernard's place. He pounded on the door.

"Bernard, what is it? What's the info?"

Bernard called from inside that it was open. Gregg opened the door and made his way into the living room. Bernard stood with one hand behind his back.

"So, what's this info?"

"You had one job." Bernard appeared ghostly in the dim light. "All you had to do was find Liam Watts, but you've let yourself get distracted. It's time to end this now, Gregg. It's time to find

Liam's body once and for all. Then we can all get what we want, can't we?"

"What are you talking about?" Gregg stared, his head swimming with questions.

Bernard took out an old revolver he had hidden behind his back and pointed it directly at Gregg's chest.

"I wouldn't run," Bernard said. "I should warn you I'm more than capable of operating a firearm."

Gregg put his hands up. "Bernard, what are you doing?"

"You're always talking to someone on your phone. You excused yourself to speak to them your very first night here, and you've called them every day since. I know it's your employer you're speaking to, so don't try to lie. Now call them."

"Bernard, I—"

"Call them," Bernard screamed, thumbing back the hammer of his gun.

37

"Call them," Bernard yelled again, pointing his old revolver at Gregg.

"Bernard, please," Gregg begged.

He softened his tone, but kept his gun firmly aimed. "I need them to come to town. Call them."

"I don't know what you're talking about!"

Bernard shook his head. "Don't lie, Gregg. I know who you work for."

"Why do you *want* to meet them?"

"That's my business. Just call them."

"You don't understand. They have my daughter. Another stunt like this, and she's dead."

"I won't let anything happen to your daughter."

"How can you be sure?" Gregg asked.

"Just call them."

"What do you want?"

Bernard sighed. "When you came to town to look for Liam Watts' killer, it sparked something in me. I had hope again that I could finally complete what I need to do."

"What is it that you need to complete?"

"Do you remember that story I told you in the woods, about

Steve Callahan?" Gregg probably thought he was crazy, but Bernard didn't care.

"Sure," Gregg said, trembling. "He was a real-life survival story. He was… bipolar, or something."

"Or something, yeah. He was adrift at sea, and only survived because he split his mind into two characters: a captain, to give the orders; and a crewman, to obey them."

"Right, and he'd have arguments with himself, and the captain would always win," Gregg remembered.

Bernard nodded, rather awkwardly he realized, as he attempted to be casual while aiming a gun at someone. "Do you remember what I said next?"

"You-you said your wife died," Gregg recalled, appearing to think rather hard, but his voice was still nervous. "And, that you weren't sure how you were going to survive, and then you found another part of yourself. And that's how you… dealt with it."

"Yes."

"And," Gregg wondered, "what exactly was this other side you unearthed?"

"A promise I made to my wife. Something I knew I had to complete before moving on."

"What would that be?"

"Revenge," Bernard stated, gun still in firm aim. "After my wife passed away, I was angry at everyone, including myself for not being there, the paramedics for not saving her, and most of all, the police. They were the incompetent ones who couldn't find out what happened."

Gregg frowned and studied him, perhaps having an inkling as to where this was going.

Bernard sat in his armchair and placed the gun on the armrest. "Please, have a seat," he said, gesturing towards the sofa opposite him.

Gregg sat down, still looking uneasy.

"I want you to think back to when you worked for the Boston Police Department," Bernard said. "Seven years ago, there was a case of a murdered woman—Flora Neumann, my wife. Do you remember her?"

"The BPD dealt with nearly one hundred murder cases that year. I can't remember them all."

Bernard's heart raced with anger. "You see, that's how important she was to you! You don't even remember her. She was my wife, my entire world, and I trusted you people to find her killer, but you got nowhere."

"I'm-I'm sorry," Gregg uttered. "Did we never find the killer?"

"No, you didn't. The BPD said she was probably killed by a professional, then they cleaned her blood off the parking garage's floor and moved on as if she never existed."

Gregg's eyes widened. "I *do* remember your wife's case, Bernard—the woman killed in the parking garage, with no leads. It was a difficult case, and it came at a difficult time for me. I lost my badge, went through a divorce, and nearly lost custody of my daughter soon after your wife's case opened. It wasn't even my case."

"Not at first. But, once the detectives admitted they were stumped, they handed it over to you and your partner, Jim. Then you took time off, lost your badge, and Jim was as useless as those other detectives. I read about you. I thought you were the best, that if anyone on the BPD could solve my wife's case, it was you. But you didn't even try!"

Gregg shuffled in his seat. "I took time off because I was in the middle of a divorce. My life was falling apart. Our worlds came to a stop at the same time, Bernard, and I'm sorry for that. But I can't change the past. What do you want from me *now*? How is this connected to my employers and my daughter?"

"It's all connected, Gregg. Even though my wife's case was of no importance to you, I stopped at nothing to find answers. What I found led me to this town and to your employers."

Gregg arched an eyebrow. "What do you mean?"

"One day, I went to the police station, demanding to know why they were making no progress. That was the first time I saw you. I slammed my fist against the reception's counter in fury, and all the officers behind looked over. You were standing among them, dressed in your detective's suit, and wearing your badge, but you paid no attention to the ruckus I was causing. The officer told me he understood what I was going through, and I just had to be patient. I told him he didn't understand at all. There was a man running free who killed my wife, and I had no idea why he did it. I didn't know who that man was, if I had ever seen him before, or if my wife or I did anything to wrong him. All I knew was someone had taken everything from me. I couldn't sleep, live, or move on until he was found. I owed that to my wife, and I still do. I promised her I will never live my life until her killer is behind bars.

"I asked what was taking so long and the officer took pity on me. He explained that the killer had cleaned up the crime scene well, like a professional, and left no DNA or witnesses. He told me that, honestly, my best hope was that if the killer strikes again, they make a mistake. That's when I knew I could no longer trust the police to find Flora's killer. I took matters into my own hands and did some investigating of my own. Looking through her call history, I discovered a call lasting over an hour from an unknown number, occurring only a couple of days before her death. I bought one of those cell phone trackers online to locate the caller. The phone was no longer active, but I managed to get the GPS coordinates of its last location."

"Let me guess," Gregg said. "The coordinates led you to Blackberry Cove."

"Exactly. I was unable to find the caller. No one here seemed to recognize the number. When I showed pictures of my wife, no one knew her either. After a couple of months of being in town, however, I saw someone I recognized driving down the road from Liam's cabin. He drove off before I could stop him, but I managed to get a picture."

Bernard took out the picture from his pocket and placed it on the coffee table. It was only the man's reflection from his rear-view mirror, but luckily Bernard took it with his professional camera and so the quality was crystal clear.

"This man came to my apartment in Boston the day before my wife died." Bernard tapped the picture. "They spoke in private for only a few minutes. When he left, my wife was upset. I asked what was wrong, but she didn't want to talk about it. When I asked who he was, she said he was somebody from work. I knew she was lying. I took his picture around her office after her death, and no one recognized him. That's when I knew this man had something to do with my wife's murder. This town also has something to do with her death. This man was here to meet Liam. His cabin is the only thing up that road. When I asked Liam, he said he didn't know who the man was. He gave me some bullshit about how the man must have been lost."

Gregg picked up the picture and studied it closer, then his eyes lit up.

"You know him, don't you?" Bernard asked. "He's your employer, isn't he? It's not just a coincidence that you came to town to investigate Liam's disappearance, and your employer is shrouded in mystery. You work for this man. "

"The employer I've been speaking to is a woman, but this is the man who kidnapped my daughter." Gregg placed the picture down. "The woman referred to him as Fury."

"Fury? That's the closest I've come to getting a name. After I took the picture, I showed it all over town, but no one recognized him. I then considered what the cop at your station said about my wife having been killed by a professional. If he was connected to my wife's death, maybe he was connected to other crimes. Maybe someone had seen him at some point and given a description to the police. So, I traveled to just about every police station in the northeast to show the officers my picture, hoping at least someone would say he matched a description. Eventually, I had some success. There were some police sketches from various open cases in multiple states that matched my picture. They were also professional cases. This man's a hitman. That means the woman you work for is most likely a professional killer as well."

"It sounds like you should be investigating this case," Gregg said. "It doesn't explain what they want with Liam, though."

"Or why they killed my wife, but I'm sure they did. It's time to end this. You no longer have to be a part of their game or face them alone. Just tell the truth and then I can help you."

Gregg whipped his head back and forth. "You don't actually know anything about these people. You think you do, but you don't. We can't stop them. Not you. Not me. They kidnapped my daughter. They are holding her as leverage."

"Phone your employer. I will get her to tell me where your daughter is. And get her to help with my own aim, of course. Everyone wins."

"Not Rachel." Gregg could barely keep from smirking.

"No, I suppose not."

"I get it now, by the way. Why you were so interested in the case."

"Yes, I've been waiting for this for a long time. Phone her, please. Trust me, I'll get her to listen to me."

Gregg sat silently, thinking.

"You weren't able to help me before, Gregg, because your life was falling apart. But you can help now. And in return, I will assist you in rebuilding your world by finding your daughter."

Gregg sat forward. "Please, I've already seen these people kill without hesitation. So, before I get you involved, you must promise not to do anything that will cause my daughter harm."

"You have my word," Bernard promised. "Phone this woman and tell her to meet with you. We'll go to her together. She'll talk to me, I promise, and I will get your daughter back."

Gregg pulled out his phone. "I'm trusting you."

38

THE SCREAMS OF JIM'S DAUGHTER ECHOED IN RACHEL'S EARS. Instead of shooting them before setting the car on fire, Fury preferred to burn them alive first. He shot the crisp bodies with the same gun used to kill Gregg Hunter's ex and her boyfriend, planning to put the blame on the former detective. Rachel knew she was a monster, but Fury frightened even her.

The bloodcurdling screams made Rachel sick to her stomach, and she excused herself. She was supposed to meet Hunter in the woods, so she decided to walk there alone. She'd call her men to collect her afterwards. When Fury asked why she was leaving so early, she blamed it on the smoke, said she could hardly breathe, which wasn't far from the truth.

It still amazed her that Fury could be so unaffected by what he did. It was as if he was dead inside. He could watch a young girl's hair and skin burn away and be as disinterested as if he were watching a reality show. He didn't laugh, smile, cry, or flinch in response as the girl screamed in agony. Maybe that made Rachel the bigger monster. Unlike Fury, she actually knew what she was doing was wrong and felt repulsed by it, but she ignored her feelings and followed orders anyway. This was her life. It was all she knew how to do.

She came to the clearing in the woods and waited for Hunter.

39

EVEN AFTER EVERYTHING HER FATHER HAD DONE TO HER WHEN SHE was a teenager, Chloe found herself consumed by thoughts of him as she sat in her jail cell. He was in need of constant care—someone to wash him, change his bag, and feed him through his tube. Chloe knew it was pointless to ask Marc for permission to see her father, so she waited for the sheriff to return.

She stood eagerly as the door opened, but it wasn't Sheriff Johnston who entered. Instead, the timid-looking therapist faltered inside. "Miss Mason, why did you ask me to come here?"

"Because you were my therapist." She pointed over to Marc, writing at his desk in the corner of the room. "Please tell the deputy that this is all a misunderstanding and that I am not capable of killing Liam."

Timothy's forehead puckered as if he was pondering what to do. "I'm sorry, Miss Mason," he said at last. "I can't do that."

Marc put down his pencil, paying heed to Timothy's words.

"I treated Chloe for years," Timothy went on, his attention now on the deputy. "I helped her through issues with her father. She has a lot of deep-seated anger, so it doesn't surprise me that she could be capable of this. She's a troubled young woman. Of course, I can't disclose any specifics."

Chloe's body went rigid with shock. "Timothy, I thought we were friends! You confided in me about your condition that night at the bar in Albany. I told you to believe in yourself. I thought you trusted me. I thought we trusted each other."

"Liam was my friend," Timothy said, showing her his back.

"I turned to you when I hated my father. You showed me how to channel that anger healthily. Because of you, I could never hurt anyone. If you believed that I was capable of killing Liam, why did you warn me when Gregg Hunter arrived in town?"

"I warned you precisely because I suspected you were guilty," Timothy replied, glancing back at her over his shoulder. "I do care about you, Chloe, but it was wrong and unprofessional of me to try and shield you from the consequences. You require more help than I can give. I'm sorry for failing you."

Marc stood from his desk. "Thank you for your help, Dr. Holst."

"I'm glad we finally caught my friend's killer," Timothy muttered as he shuffled out the door, his head down.

Chloe felt tears trickle down her cheeks. She brushed them away with the sleeve of her plaid shirt and leaned against the bars of her cell. "Please, Marc, let me go. You know I didn't do this!"

"Actually, I think you did."

"Why?"

"No one can go on being a victim forever."

She crossed her arms. "I'm not a victim."

"But you are. You have been a victim since your father beat you. You have always needed someone to rescue you. When you were a frightened little girl crying on your doorstep, I was the only one there for you. It was meant to be that way because we understood each other. My father beat me too, and that's why my dream has always been to become the town's sheriff, so I can protect kids from ever going through what we went through. I was always supposed to save you, but somewhere along the way, you forgot that. Instead, you took matters into your own hands."

"I don't need anyone to save me. I can take care of myself. My father will never come home drunk and beat me again. Never again will I live in fear."

The muscles in his face tightened. "Yeah, right. You couldn't save yourself from your father, could you? Thank God for his stroke, right?"

"You still don't understand why he beat me or why I didn't tell anyone. It's because I did something unforgivable to him, something that made him hate me. I deserved the beatings.

"No one deserves what we went through."

Chloe lowered her head and wiped away another tear. "I did. And that's why I must care for him now. After the fire, I was all he had."

Sheriff Johnston walked into the room, and Marc quickly stepped back from the bars. He told the deputy to continue writing his report and so Marc went back to his desk. Johnston settled into his chair and took out his book.

"Sheriff," she cried. "I need to see my father!"

"You're detained, Miss Mason." He flipped to the right page of his book without looking up. "Detainees don't get to make home visits. Marcus is finishing your report, then he'll send it off, along with the evidence to the prosecuting attorney. They'll decide what to do with you."

"I don't understand what evidence you could possibly have." She frowned. "I didn't do anything. Now, I want to see my father. He has no one to look after him. Sheriff, please, he can't answer my call. He needs to be fed and have his waste bag changed."

Johnston lowered his book and sighed. "You can call Dr. Taylor to do those things."

"Dr. Taylor is out of town on Saturdays. My father will be sitting in his own waste until tomorrow."

"You can call a friend to check on him. Call Gregg Hunter."

He lifted the phone from his desk and handed it to her through the bars. She dialed Gregg's number.

"Hey, how are you doing?" Gregg said.

"I'm still in jail and need someone to check on my father," she replied. "Could you do it for me, Gregg?"

"I'm sorry, but I'm really in the middle of something."

"Is it to do with your daughter?"

"I'm meeting with Rachel again," he said.

"Gregg, be careful. I was wrong to suggest you take her by force. These people are not to be underestimated, just like you said."

"I'll be careful, I promise."

Johnston tapped on his watch, and she told Gregg she had to go, wishing him luck. She handed the phone back to Johnston through the bars. "Gregg's busy. Sheriff, please, I need to check on my father."

Johnston stood with a sigh.

"Sir," Marc called from his desk.

"Continue with your papers, Deputy. That's an order."

Marc scowled and returned to his report.

Johnston took the cell keys off the hook on the wall behind him. He threw the handcuffs from his belt towards Chloe. "Put those on."

When she did, he opened the cell and led her out, telling the deputy they wouldn't be long.

Once they were inside the sheriff's car, Johnston exhaled and stared off. "Your father was a good friend," he said at last. "I really admire you for looking after him like you do. It can't be easy. I really should have continued to visit him after his stroke, but I was never sure what to do or say. I'm sorry about that. I guess I'm not a very good friend."

"I'm not sure he'd know if you visited or not."

"Oh, I'm sure he understands everything you do for him."

They continued to sit in silence for a moment. Chloe glanced at his book resting on the passenger's seat. "What are you reading?"

"*The Old Man and the Sea* by Hemingway."

"What's it about?"

"Fishing."

"Any good?"

Johnston shrugged. "Makes me want to go fishing." He took off his hat and ran his hand through his hair. "I don't think you're guilty, Chloe, and if that's the case, you have nothing to worry about."

"Then why not let me go?"

"You have to let the legal system run its course, and I'm trusting Marcus with that."

"Why?"

"Because Marcus needs to learn. He needs to learn to take charge and protect this town better than I ever could. It's time for me to go fishing."

"What do you mean, Sheriff?"

Johnston slumped his shoulders. "I was never good at this job. Do you know that Marcus' dad used to beat him when he was a kid?"

"Yeah, I did." Chloe averted her gaze.

"Well, I didn't. But, looking back, I don't know how I missed it, and I wonder if I didn't want to notice it. Maybe I was happy believing this was a town where people could leave their doors unlocked, where people said hello on the street, and shoveled each other's driveways. Now, suddenly, women are being killed by nail guns and men are going missing. I haven't been able to sleep since that night. I keep thinking of what happened to Mrs. Stannard. Can you imagine how terrifying her last minutes must have been? How could someone in our little town be capable of such horrors? Could someone we pass on the streets every day really have been harboring such evil?

"The world is a scary place if you can't even trust your neighbors. I never expected this. I never wanted to see people as capable of committing such evil. I failed this town. Now, a PI has had to come here to clean up my mess. My only hope of doing any good is by leaving behind a good sheriff to replace me, and that's Marcus."

"You didn't fail this town, Sheriff. You're a good person, and no one could have foreseen what was going to happen to Mrs. Stannard and Liam."

Johnston forced a smile. "I want to ask you something, Chloe."

"What is it, Sheriff?"

"I heard that Shannon's café has been closed since Saturday. People figured she went away for a couple of days. But I just spoke to the gardeners at the park, and they directed Gregg Hunter towards her on Saturday. No one has seen her since then. Do you know anything about that?"

Chloe nodded.

"You do?"

"There's some things you don't know, Sheriff."

"Regarding Gregg Hunter?"

She nodded again. If Gregg was meeting with Rachel, this could be her chance to help him. She could lead the sheriff right to Rachel, as long as Gregg was meeting her in the same place again. "His daughter has been kidnapped. Someone is forcing him to investigate this case, using his own daughter as a bargaining chip."

"Please don't make a fool of me, Chloe."

"It's the truth!"

"I'll take you right back to your cell."

"These people killed Shannon Alvie. They're dangerous. We need to call the FBI."

Johnston shook his head. "I thought we were treating each other with respect, but you really must think I'm a joke."

"Gregg is meeting with the kidnapper right now," she said. "I can take you there. I know where they're meeting." She clung on to hope.

"You have nothing to gain by pushing me away like this."

"Sheriff, you said all you wanted to do was help people. This is your chance. There's a little girl who desperately needs your help."

Johnston turned the ignition. "Okay. Tell me where to go. But after this is over and you've had your fun, I'm putting you right back in jail."

For her own sake, as well as Silvia's, Chloe hoped Gregg was meeting with Rachel in the same place as last time.

40

CHLOE DIRECTED THE SHERIFF TO THE COUNTRY ROAD WHERE GREGG previously arranged to meet with Rachel. The deep frown he displayed the whole way suggested he still didn't believe her. If Rachel wasn't there, Chloe knew she'd be getting no more sympathy from the sheriff.

As they drove, news came over Johnston's radio that state troopers had found a car ablaze in the woods, containing three bodies. Chloe was certain that Rachel's associates were involved and prayed that neither Gregg nor his daughter were among the deceased.

A little past the construction site, there was a clearing in the woods by the side of the road. A woman stood in the clearing alone, dressed all in black. Chloe told the sheriff to pull over, and as they got closer, Chloe recognized the woman from the van on the road.

"That's her," she said.

Johnston turned off the engine and put on his hat. "Are you sure about this?"

She nodded. "That's her. Don't believe anything she says."

He stepped out of the car and approached Rachel. Chloe

inched closer to the sheriff's open window so she could hear. "Good day, ma'am," Johnston said.

"Oh, hello. Can I help you?" Rachel appeared chillingly nonchalant.

"May I ask what you're doing out here?" Johnston turned his head from side to side, probably to check if she was alone. Chloe looked around from the back of the car too. There was no one else in sight.

"I'm waiting for my boyfriend. Don't suppose you've seen him? Tall. Blond hair. Little beard. Kind of a jackass."

"Gregg Hunter?"

Chloe could tell Rachel was trying to mask a smirk. Instead, she shook her head and shrugged. "I don't know that name. My boyfriend, Roy, and I have rented a cabin near Shaftesbury."

"What are you doing out here?" He looked her up and down. "You don't look dressed for hiking."

"We're looking for a maple syrup museum," she replied immediately. "Corny, I know. But I want to do all the touristy stuff."

Johnston sniffed the air. "You smell smoke?"

"Oh, must be my jacket." Rachel took a whiff of her leather coat. "I wore it next to our campfire last night. We roasted marshmallows under the stars."

"Where are you visiting from?"

"New York City."

Johnston spread out his arms at the scenery. "The peace and quiet must be a culture shock."

"Not so much. I'm originally from Arizona."

"I've never been. Is the Grand Canyon as red as it is in pictures?"

"It feels almost like you're interrogating me, Sheriff," Rachel said. "Is there something you need?"

"I was just making conversation." Johnston shrugged. "But now that you mention it, I came over because there's been a report of a missing girl in these parts. Haven't seen anything suspicious, have you?"

Rachel put her hands over her mouth. "Oh, that's awful. No, I haven't seen anything."

She could almost be an actress, Chloe thought, but Johnston didn't seem to be buying it. His eyes never lifted from her. "Maybe your boyfriend's seen something."

"I'll ask him when he comes back, and we can call you."

"Maybe I'll wait for him," Johnston said. "Where is he?"

"He's away looking for directions."

"For the maple syrup museum," Johnston said, almost mockingly. "Why did he drop you off on the side of the road?"

"I get carsick. He needs to come back this way anyway, so I thought I might as well get some fresh air."

Johnston nodded. "Well, I don't know anything about a maple syrup museum, but you should check out Blackberry Cove. It's a very charming little town. Perfect place for tourists."

"Thanks for the recommendation, Sheriff."

"I can give you directions." He pulled a map and pen from his pockets, drew something on the map, then handed it to her.

She thanked him again and placed the map in her back pocket. As she lifted her jacket, Chloe could see a gun attached to her belt. Johnston must have seen it too. His hand went for the gun on his hip.

Bang!

Chloe shrieked. Flocks of birds flew from the trees. Johnston fell to the forest floor before his hand could even reach his waist. Blood poured from his stomach after Rachel's rapid gunshot.

Rachel stepped towards him. She placed her foot on his chest to keep him from getting up. Her green eyes narrowed. He seemed scared and confused but not for long. With a swift movement, Rachel pressed the flat sole of her boot against his throat and rolled her foot over his neck, breaking it with a resounding crack.

She took her cell phone out and told someone on the other

end to come pick her up, giving them a location and telling them to prepare for a body.

Chloe lay down and smashed the glass of the window with a few kicks of her boots. She then grabbed the outside door handle, leaped out, and raced across the fallen leaves towards the road. Over her shoulder, she saw Rachel raise her gun. Chloe ducked down into the bushes. A bullet shot above her head.

Chloe crawled behind a nearby tree and kept her eyes fixed towards the road. She could hear Rachel's boots crunch against the broken leaves, drawing nearer. A car was approaching. She prayed it wasn't Rachel's men.

Thankfully, it wasn't. It was Bernard's car, carrying both him and Gregg. She waved her arms in the air, and Bernard's car came to a stop right beside her. The two men jumped out, with Bernard wielding a revolver.

When she turned around, Rachel had already jumped into the sheriff's car, and she took off towards the road. Bernard lifted his revolver and shot at the rear window, but the car soon disappeared.

There was a mayor with blond hair,
His vanity beyond compare,
His wives disappeared, one by one,
Leaving folks to wonder what he'd done,
And whispers of an affair with his secretary did declare.

He saw himself as number one,
And that his way was always done,
No one could care for the town like he,
In his eyes, that was plain to see,
His ego and arrogance shone like the sun.

41

Sometimes, Isabella found herself thinking back on her childhood doll. This day was one of those times. As a young girl, she would perch in front of her bedroom mirror, softly humming while delicately brushing the luscious locks of her beautiful doll. With her miniature comb, she would meticulously groom every strand of the doll's perfect brunette hair.

"You're so beautiful, Dolly," she'd say. "Every boy is going to love you. One day you're going to meet a prince. You'll have everything and you'll be so happy. He will hold you in his arms and tell you, 'Isabella, I love you so very much.'"

Then she'd hug her doll tightly, wrapping her arms around herself so she was hugging herself at the same time.

Isabella used to live in a dingy and cramped motel room with two single beds and a basic kitchen area all in the same room. Her mother, who worked the streets during the nights, used to leave her with bread to make toast for dinner.

She used to tell herself she'd never be like her mother, but after her mother's death from an STD, Isabella was only a teenager, and she found herself homeless on the streets of New

York with only her doll to comfort her. She would sleep with the other homeless during the nights on the beach, heated by lit trash cans, and would hope she scraped up enough that day to afford a sandwich. Eventually, she too started sleeping with men for money, just so she had enough to spend occasional nights in a motel and to fill her swollen stomach.

Even when working as a prostitute, she carried her childhood doll everywhere and never gave up hope of one day being discovered by someone who would see her for what she really was and who would love her.

One evening, as she was working the streets, a young man approached her. He seemed to be muttering to himself and shaking his hands erratically. There was nothing too unusual about strange men walking the late streets of New York. Everyone who worked the nights knew not to go with them unless you wanted to be found in pieces in the Hudson the next morning.

Unfortunately, he didn't take no for an answer. When she refused him, he jumped at her, tackling her to the ground and mercilessly beating her until the sound of people approaching frightened him away. Isabella was left battered and bruised on the street, her cherished childhood doll lying in a filthy puddle, equally shattered.

That night, she retreated to a seedy motel room, staring at her reflection in the worn dressing table mirror, with a gun laid out in front of her, contemplating suicide. The beating had been the last straw. She couldn't do that work anymore, waiting to die like her mother or even more violently. Isabella had to accept that love was never going to land on her doorstep, so there was no point in continuing to hope. No point in going on.

As a child, she told herself she'd be nothing like her mother, but looking at herself in the mirror that night, she realized she wouldn't be able to tell the difference between them. She wiped away her tears, smudging even more of her heavy makeup. A tear dripped onto her doll, which rested on her lap, making it look as though it was crying too.

With only five dollars remaining in her possession, Isabella decided to enter the bar next door for a final drink. She ordered a scotch from the bartender and was surprised when the man seated next to her offered to pay for it.

"I'll take care of that," he had said, gesturing to her drink.

Isabella turned to him and noticed that he was impeccably dressed in a fine suit, polished shoes, and a solid gold watch.

"If you don't mind?" he asked.

"Not at all," Isabella replied.

The man took out his wallet to pay for her drink and she saw the large amount of money inside. After that, it wasn't long before she took him back to her motel room. He undressed to nothing, and she cuffed him to the bed, telling him it was her kink. With a smile on his face, he begged her to join him, but instead, she snatched his trousers, took his wallet, and grabbed his watch. He attempted to break free from his restraints, but they would not break.

She had given to men so many times, but no more. Now, they were going to give to her. If they weren't going to give her everything, she'd make them.

After she finished taking his belongings, she picked up the lamp from the table and struck it against his chest. He shouted for her to stop, but she kept battering him with it. Her pain was his fault, and every other man; they had filled her with this rage by neglecting her. She screamed and threw the lamp to the wall, shattering it.

She slammed the door after her, leaving her doll inside. She would no longer need it.

Now, walking Raymond to school, Isabella knew it was only a matter of time before she would be found out as a con woman, especially with Gregg Hunter uncovering every rock in town. She knew the combination for Nathan's safe and should have already left with the contents. So far, she had only taken enough to buy herself the odd piece of expensive jewelry. Why hadn't she already left with it all?

"Why are you so glum?" Raymond asked her, snapping her out of her daydream.

She sighed, deciding to tell the child the truth. "Your dad has asked me to move in with him and you."

"That's amazing!"

"But I'm not sure if I want to," Isabella added, wiping away Raymond's massive grin.

"Why not? Don't you like my dad?"

"I like him very much, yes."

"Don't you like me?"

"Of course I do."

"Then why don't you wanna live with us? You're at our house all the time anyway."

"Yeah, I guess I am."

"I would love for you to be with us! You're like a part of our family," Raymond declared with enthusiasm.

Isabella couldn't help but smile. "I've never really had a family before."

"You do now."

"Yeah, I guess I do."

"I feel safer when you're home."

"Safer?"

The boy nodded. "I love my dad, but he can be scary some-times. It's tough with my mom not being there. You make it easier."

Isabella knelt down and embraced the young boy, who hugged her back tightly.

Nathan would probably understand, she told herself, if she explained she gave in to impulse and spent a couple thousand on jewelry and shoes; it wasn't that much to him. He loved her enough to forgive her. She would just leave out the part about her having intended to rob his entire fortune; that would prob-ably be a bit harder to pardon.

Isabella wasn't sure she wanted his fortune now. She genuinely loved him, and this was finally her chance to be part of a family.

The clock was running now, though, and she needed to make a decision. By tonight, she would either come clean to Nathan, or disappear forever with all the money she could carry.

42

IT WAS ALL HER FAULT FOR LETTING HERSELF GET SO ANGRY. Johnston and Marc must have known she followed Liam the night he died. Someone must have seen her. What other evidence could there be?

Chloe always wanted to see herself as a strong and independent woman, so why had she allowed herself to get so angry at men? Of course, she knew the answer: She still seethed like a kettle over the things her father did to her before his stroke. Still, when Liam broke up with her, she wished she had been able to move on, instead of feeling the need to get even.

Nevertheless, she was confident Gregg would get to the bottom of it all and clear her. He was the first good man in her life.

Chloe sat in her cell, tapping her foot against the floor. The boots on her feet were once her sister Victoria's. Chloe had been wearing them the night her father saved her from the fire.

In fact, they were the reason he had saved her. That night, Chloe and Victoria had swapped bedrooms because Chloe was afraid of the woods outside her window. Victoria was their father's favorite, so when the fire broke out, he rushed to Victoria's room first. He saw the boots sticking out from under Victoria's blanket, mistook Chloe for Victoria, and carried her out of the burning house. It was only when they were outside that he realized his mistake and wept.

It was after the fire her father's drinking got worse and the beatings started. Chloe endured because neither of them had anyone else.

She didn't know what was going to happen to her now that Johnston was gone, or who would look after her father if she went to prison. Marc sat at his deputy's desk, looking sadly at the sheriff's old badge in his hand.

"He was a good man," she found herself saying.

Marc turned to her, not saying a word.

"He always cared about the community," she went on. "He didn't deserve this."

Before Marc could respond, they turned their heads at the sound of someone entering the room. It was Mayor Stannard, accompanied by his secretary.

Nathan's dress shoes tip-tapped against the floor. "Tell me what happened."

Marc rose to his feet. "Sheriff Johnston was escorting Chloe Mason to her place of residence, then he was jumped by an unknown female. The suspect was armed with a gun and shot Sheriff Johnston before fleeing the scene. Bernard Neumann and Gregg Hunter found Chloe, who later turned herself in and provided a description of the suspect. We've shared the description with law enforcement agencies throughout the state."

"Do we have any leads on who this woman might be?" Isabella asked.

Marc shook his head.

"It's hard to believe that Sheriff Johnston had enemies," Nathan said. "It seems like the perpetrator must have been concerned about him getting too close to something."

"Meaning?" Marc asked.

"Meaning the killer of my wife or the killer of Liam Watts."

"The killer of Liam Watts is already in custody." Marc pointed over to Chloe.

"Well maybe it's time to admit you might have the wrong suspect. Why else would she hand herself back in, Sheriff?"

It took a moment for that to sink in for Marc. "Sheriff?"

Nathan picked Sheriff Johnston's badge up and pinned it onto Marc's collar. "Congratulations, the job is yours," he said with almost a bored look in his eye.

"But the sheriff has to be elected, sir."

"I can appoint an acting sheriff until that time. Besides, with my endorsement, no one will even run against you."

"Thank you, sir." Marc gripped onto his desk as if he was afraid he might collapse. "I won't disappoint you."

"Well, you can start by locating this suspect and getting these murder cases solved once and for all."

"Absolutely, sir."

Nathan turned away to leave with Isabella, and Chloe noticed the secretary looked even whiter than normal. She had acted like a Sunday School teacher ever since coming to town, shy and timid, dressed in sweaters and long trousers, always attending church and knitting groups. But now, with the revelation of her affair, Chloe realized it had all been an act. She couldn't help but wonder what other secrets Isabella was hiding.

Marc seemed glued to the spot for a moment. Eventually, he walked over and took out some keys from his pocket, unlocking her cell.

"What are you doing?" she asked.

"If I'm going to fill Sheriff Johnston's shoes, I have to do things right. Maybe arresting you wasn't right. I think I let personal feelings cloud my judgment, and I may have jumped the gun before having the right amount of evidence. I hope you can forgive me."

Chloe stepped out, wondering if this was a sick joke, but Marc looked genuinely remorseful. Chloe didn't say anything to comfort him. She simply walked out of the cell, leaving Marc behind.

43

"GREGG, I'M SORRY!" BERNARD DASHED DOWN THE STREET after him.

"I don't want to hear it." Gregg marched on to the sheriff's station. He had to check on Chloe and let her know he hadn't forgotten about her. He'd get her out, but for now he had to focus on his daughter.

Despite Gregg's quick pace, he could hear Bernard's footsteps following closely behind. Bernard quickly circled in front of him, not a break of sweat on the seasoned outdoorsman. "Gregg, please listen."

"There's nothing to talk about." He tried to step around, but Bernard blocked his path. "You held me hostage!"

"I thought you were involved with professional killers. Now that I know that's not true and you're just their pawn, you and I can be honest with each other. We can solve this together."

"You may have killed my daughter!"

"*May*?" Bernard asked. "So, you still haven't heard back from your employer?"

"No, I've been calling but had no answer. I don't know if I even want to hear back; she's probably killed Silvia."

"I'm sure she hasn't. She clearly needs this case solved and quickly, or she'd have killed you and your daughter already."

Oddly, Gregg didn't find much solace in Bernard's words. "I can't excuse what you did, and I don't trust you anymore. We're done talking."

Bernard lowered his head in shame. "I thought we could have ended it. But you're right, I was thinking about my own agenda. I'm sorry. However, you can still use my help."

Gregg's cell phone rang, and he looked at the caller ID. "It's Rachel."

Bernard stepped back. "I'll let you answer in private."

Gregg accepted a video call. "Hello, boss."

"Hello, Hunter." Rachel passed the phone to someone else to hold so Gregg could make out the whole room. Rachel was inside a metal and windowless bedroom. Silvia lay face down on a tarp. Two men held her down. She had been stripped down to her underwear and was whimpering and squirming to get free. Another man handed a silver kettle to Rachel, steam coming from the spout.

"Listen, I'm sorry about what happened."

"No need for apologies, Hunter."

"Really?"

Rachel poured the scalding water from the kettle onto Silvia's exposed back, causing her to scream in agony.

"Stop!"

Rachel dispensed more water, causing Silvia to scream even louder.

"Please, stop!"

Rachel emptied the rest of the kettle, this time down Silvia's legs.

"Stop it! Stop it! I can explain!"

"I care not for your explanations. I've warned you time and again not to mess with me—with *us*—and you refuse to listen. Unfortunately for you, your daughter's the one who must face the consequences. Trust me, I'd much rather be scalding you."

The man handed Rachel another kettle. She drained the hot water all over his girl, much more furiously. Silvia screamed out in agony, her reddened skin crackling and peeling. Rachel didn't stop until the kettle was empty.

"Dad, please," Silvia whispered meekly.

"What's that, girl?" Rachel approached Silvia and put the phone to her head. "Say it again."

"Dad, please, help me."

Rachel put the phone to her own ear. "Do you hear that? It's your daughter crying for your help. It's time to listen to her and get this all over with. I've had enough. Are you motivated yet?"

"What do you want?"

"Progress, Hunter, by the end of the day… or I swear to God she'll die."

44

ANYONE WHO THOUGHT THEY KNEW ISABELLA REALLY HADN'T A clue. *You would like to book an appointment with the mayor? That's no problem, please hold for a moment and I'll see what's available.* She learned long ago that people paid you less attention if you used words like please. People assumed you fit. Society was like a jigsaw puzzle, with everyone searching for the pieces that didn't quite fit.

She looked like one of them, but she wasn't. Lying was something she had perfected. Say the right things. Smile, be polite. Pretend to be someone you're not. Then you might get everything you want.

Every day, she dressed in dull colors and clothing that would be sure to turn no heads. Normal looking. That meant invisible. Today, she was wearing a navy-blue button-up shirt with long sleeves, a matching blue scarf, a gray silk skirt, and tights. No bare skin. That'd be too revealing. The only thing that might have made her stick out were her Christian Louboutin shoes, the only nice pair of footwear she had ever owned. A thousand dollars. But that wasn't something the hicks in this town would notice. If she had been back in New York, that'd be different. People there noticed stuff like that, but not in a town where people discussed the high school basketball team and the price of apples.

Maybe she didn't need to go on pretending much longer. She could go back to New York, or anywhere she wanted, along with all of Nathan's money, and buy as many Louboutin shoes as she wanted. After all, she had come to accept long ago that love was never going to happen. Eventually, Nathan would discover who she really was and kick her out. Then she'd be back to having nothing. It was decided then; she was going to run away with the money that night. But first, one more lie.

She knocked on Nathan's door.

"Isabella?"

"Remember you asked me to think about moving in?"

"Of course, it's all I've been thinking about."

Isabella smiled. "Well, I had a conversation with Raymond this morning about it, and I've decided to do it."

"That's great!" Nathan wrapped his arms around her.

"We can do what we finally planned. Be a family. Now we don't have to hurt anyone to make it happen. I can't believe we planned to run away."

"Well, now we don't need to do that. We can be a family *here*. Now, come, and I'll help you pack."

"Oh, no. You have Raymond to look after," she replied.

"He can help. He won't mind."

"That would be very boring for him. I'll do it myself, honestly, it's fine."

"Okay."

"Thank you," Isabella told him, "for everything."

She kissed him one last time, turned around, and headed back to her apartment. There, she zipped up a suitcase, having already fully packed, and took it with her as she walked out the door, along with another empty suitcase.

Isabella walked through the streets of Blackberry Cove one last time with her packed, wheel-along suitcase in one hand, and her empty suitcase in the other. Instead of going back to

Nathan's house, she went to the mayoral office building and entered with her spare key.

Once in Nathan's office, Isabella left her packed suitcase near the door and walked over to the portrait of Nathan's father with her empty suitcase. She refrained from turning on the light in case someone saw from outside.

A sheet of plastic crinkled beneath her Louboutins. Nathan must have been planning to have the room painted the following day. Odd, he hadn't told her.

Her footsteps crunched all the way over to the portrait, the plastic sheet covering the entire carpet. She removed the frame, revealing the safe behind it, and swiftly entered the combination to unlock it. She unzipped her empty suitcase and started stuffing wads of cash into it from the safe.

With the money in her hands, she began to think about what she might spend it on: another pair of expensive shoes; other frivolous clothes and jewelry; a holiday or a condo, where she'd be alone. She reminisced of her, Nathan, and Raymond at the lake, then stopped packing the money.

What was she doing? This time with Nathan and Raymond had been the happiest of her life. Why would she want to run away from that? She wasn't that person anymore, because of them.

Coming to that decision, she felt lighter than she ever had before. The anger and hatred for men she had carried for years dispersed from her soul, and she at last felt free to be happy.

As she placed the last of the money back into the safe, a light came on from behind. She spun her head around.

Nathan sat at his desk with the lamp turned on beside him. He rose from his seat, emerging from the shadows with a gun in his hand.

"Nathan," she gasped.

"A while back, Sheriff Johnston was looking through some bills and ledgers," he said, looking ghostly in the shadowy room. "Turns out, there was some money missing. Highly troubling, especially since it's your job to check such matters. At first, I thought maybe you had just been clumsy and made some mistakes. For a long time, I tried not to think about it. Even if you were stealing from me, you still loved me, I told myself, otherwise you wouldn't still be here, so I let it slide. Then today, when you came to my house and gave that awkward goodbye, I knew something was wrong."

"No, Nathan, you don't understand—"

"Oh, I understand completely. You were planning to run away with my money."

"I changed my mind. I realized I love you. That's why I stayed in town for so long. You just scared me when you asked me to move in with you. But I love you and Raymond. All I want is a family. I want—"

He slammed his foot into the desk. "Stop lying to me!"

Isabella flinched back in fright. His face flushed red, and his finger trembled on the trigger of the gun.

"I should have known." Nathan stepped across the plastic sheet. "No one has ever loved me. No one. Why would you be any different? I should kill you now. You're not the first whore I've killed for hurting me."

At this, she felt her body go cold. She looked at the plastic sheet, and her heart thrashed in her chest as she realized its purpose.

"Please, Nathan," Isabella cried.

He slammed the pistol against her cheek, smacking her to the floor with a scream. Tears and blood dripped from her face onto the plastic sheet beneath her. Nathan pocketed the gun and pinned her down.

"I love you," she said one last time.

"I can't ever believe that now, can I?" He clasped his hands around her throat, squeezing it shut.

Isabella wriggled against the plastic to get free, but he was too strong. She batted her fists against him, but it did nothing.

She thrashed her legs wildly, but she was trapped. One of her Louboutins flew off and hit the ceiling as she kicked into the air.

She was running out of air. Her head spun. Everything was going dark. This, she realized, was how she was going to die, at the hands of the man she loved. There'd be no one to mourn her. No one would even care; she'd simply disappear off the Earth as if she never existed. Her body went limp as she lost the will to fight back. It was all about to be over.

Instead of searching for a way to get free, she turned to look at Nathan. She stared him right into the eyes. He'd need to look right at her if he was going to kill her. He stared back and a tear dripped down his face onto her own.

She slowly felt the air make its way back into her lungs and could hear herself wheezing for breath. Then, Nathan released his grip completely. He collapsed onto his hands and knees and began to weep. She crawled out from under him and made her way to the door.

Over his sobs, he told her to leave. She rubbed her neck, put her shoe back on, and left the room. Isabella was no longer afraid for her life, only devastated. Everything she had ever wanted—a family—was out of reach again.

More than that, her deepest fears about Nathan had been confirmed.

45

It had been months since Richard slept without the aid of sleeping pills. Whenever he closed his eyes, he couldn't escape the blood. It occurred to him that he could escape the nightmares once and for all just by taking a few extra sleeping pills in the bathtub. The option became more and more tempting. Everything he had gone through, it had all been for Hannah, but they were drifting apart now because of what they each had done.

It was beginning to seem as though they had no future. No way of getting past what happened. Nothing to look forward to. They could never have children. That was something they had learned nearly a year ago. Hannah had been born with only one functioning ovary, the doctor said, and now her other ovary had begun a premature failure. No matter what the biology behind it was, getting pregnant would be nearly impossible for her. What other hope was there for them? What light might they find in their lives down the road? There was always adoption. That was the one thing that kept him going and gave him hope things might get better. They had spoken about it some months ago. But could they really bring a child into this mess they had made since then? No, first they had to get past what they had done.

He had gone for a session with Timothy, careful to avoid the specifics of his problem. All he wanted to know was how to move on from something that was haunting him.

"You need to let go of whatever it is you're trying to forget," Timothy had said.

"How do I let go?" he had asked.

"Visit the source. Say goodbye and receive closure."

Closure. That's what he needed. Following the therapist's advice, Richard took his truck up to the forest. There, he went for a wander, on the same path between the trees that he had walked on that terrible night. A vision of blood quickly flashed through his head. Redness all around. Blood. So much blood. It was everywhere. He couldn't get it off. *Help me.*

He couldn't take it anymore. Richard collapsed to his knees on the forest ground and then lay down. He rubbed the grass with his trembling hands and cried into the dirt. Richard wondered how deep into the soil his tears would trickle. Maybe they would reach the body that lay beneath.

46

ELAINE HOLST HAD MARRIED A MOUSE. A PITIFUL AND COWARDLY mouse that couldn't stand up to anyone, and that made every moment of her life ache with boredom. He hadn't always been so spineless. Not that he had ever been the most brash of men, and she never wanted him to be—getting her way most of the time was something she initially enjoyed—but he hadn't always been so afraid to voice his opinion or to cross her. His operation had changed everything. Ever since he hadn't been able to give her a child, it was as if he lived in her debt, always groveling over any little mistake he made and only speaking when spoken to.

It made her sick how little of a man he had become, and she decided enough was enough. She hired a lawyer to begin the divorce proceedings in secret and a private investigator to look for anything she might be able to hold against her husband. Not that she expected him to put up much of a fight during the divorce. He'd probably bend over and let her take whatever she wanted. What could he even fight for? Juliet would never want to stay with him, not even for a weekend, and most items in the house were her family's belongings. As an only child, her parents left everything to her when they died. Still, she hired the private investigator to be on the safe side. She wasn't going to let that cowardly mouse anywhere near anything that belonged to her.

Elaine sat across from her lawyer. He had a face that reminded her of her husband: a long, pointed nose, beady eyes, and a terrible comb-over. "Hi, Elaine. How are you doing?"

"Did the PI find anything?" These lawyers charged by the hour, so she wanted to get right to the point. She wasn't letting his greedy paws on a cent more than necessary.

He placed an envelope on the table and slid it towards her. She opened it up. It was multiple photographs of her garden. She'd recognize her rose bed anywhere, even though it was dark in the pictures. Why would the PI be taking pictures of her garden? Then, in the next picture, she saw her husband walking towards the camera, and suddenly it clicked.

The subsequent photographs revealed Timothy's disturbing actions. He was captured stopping by the flowerbeds, deliberately uprooting plants, kicking down small trees, and scattering soil everywhere. His face bore an unsettling, maniacal smile that Elaine couldn't recognize. She had never witnessed such twisted joy in him before.

Timothy's nightly walks were a ruse. He had been lying to her. She didn't think he had it in him. The attacks on her garden had only begun in the past few months, while his evening strolls had been a routine for years. She had never suspected a thing. After all, why would she suspect her own husband? Why would he engage in such juvenile and malicious acts? These were the actions of rebellious teenagers, not a grown man. Instead of facing her or choosing to leave, he resorted to sneaking around behind her back and venting his anger on the one thing she cherished the most. She had been wrong—he wasn't a mouse, but a rat. A deceitful, conniving, and contemptible rat.

"Your husband is clearly disturbed. He needs help," the lawyer said.

Elaine packed the pictures into the envelope and placed them in her handbag. "By the time I'm done with him, he won't be able to afford any help."

She stood, confident she now had sufficient grounds for fault-based divorce. She and Juliet would be free of that rat by the end of the day. Good riddance. She had no need for a husband in her life anyway, or for any man. Her entire life, they had caused her nothing but trouble.

The lawyer noticed she was making an exit and stood too. "I understand this must be daunting news and you probably need time to digest it. Shall we schedule another appointment for later in the week?" He rubbed his mitts together.

"Fuck off," she barked.

As Elaine left the grubby lawyer's office, she smiled at the thought of her husband no longer being in the house. However, her smile began to decline as she considered that maybe her husband wasn't actually as harmless as she had thought him to be. She would have never thought him capable of destroying her garden, so perhaps he was harboring other secrets. She had to keep her guard up and be ready for anything.

47

A<small>FTER FINISHING WORK</small>, T<small>IMOTHY USUALLY WENT TO THE</small> S<small>WAN</small> I<small>NN</small>
to read the paper and drink a coffee, before going home for
dinner. He wanted as much time away from the house as possible. Even the mundane local news announcing school bus sched-
ules and the latest person to accomplish the Long Trail offered
some escapism from his suffocating existence at home.

The Long Trail was a hiking path running the full length of
the state, and it was tradition for the local paper to report on the
latest wary achiever. He remembered Bernard had done it once
but refused to be written about in the paper. Timothy liked his
privacy too, but Bernard was on another level when it came to
strangeness and secretiveness. If Timothy was fit enough to do
something like that, he'd want his picture on the front page.

Timothy often imagined what it'd feel like to be in the papers.
Even if it was for something small, people would still be reading
his name. They may forget about him shortly after, but for those
moments he'd be all that was in their minds, and no one would
ever be able to take that away from him.

Today's article on the Long Trail was less uplifting than
normal. A middle-aged woman died while attempting the hike.

She had slipped off the cliffside and landed by the river. For once, Timothy didn't pretend he was reading about himself. Instead, he imagined he was reading about his wife. It would be a fitting death for her. He grinned as he pictured it—Elaine slipping off a cliff, falling below, knowing the whole time that she was going to die. She'd be screaming in terror. How long would the fall last? About four, five, six seconds? Ha. Fucking brilliant.

He snickered to himself, quite loudly, he realized, as people looked over. Timothy quickly cleared his throat.

"Something funny?" Hannah asked, handing him a slice of pumpkin cake he hadn't ordered. She told him they had made too much, and it would spoil if someone didn't eat it.

"Thank you. And I was just reading the funny pages." He took the cake and covered the page so she couldn't see.

Hannah offered him a smile and told him to enjoy. He thanked her and watched as she moseyed back to the counter. Timothy felt sorry for Richard and Hannah. They were both kind, but their marriage was probably irreparable. Even to look at them both, it was clear they had given up. Richard had visited him earlier, smelling ripe, with deep bags under his eyes, dressed in yesterday's red polo and jeans, and his beard and hair unwashed. Meanwhile, Hannah ambled carelessly around the inn, dressed in a stained pink shirt, torn jeans, and a pair of old tennis shoes.

Still, the innkeepers hadn't experienced a failed marriage until they lived under Timothy's roof. It wasn't that he hated Elaine, but that she made him hate himself. She filled him with such rage that Timothy couldn't understand. He loved his wife, yet she made him feel worthless and as though he had no voice.

Things will get better, he kept telling himself. He could even start by making her a nice dinner, instead of wasting the evening at the inn. Timothy paid for his coffee and left a tip for Hannah, then headed home. He felt a spring in his step already as he pictured Elaine's reaction to him revealing a pot roast for dinner, or one of her other favorites. That would help make her happy. Then she might stop snapping at him for every little thing. At least for tonight. Yes, everything was going to be fine tonight.

Timothy's smile dropped as he approached the house. There were two bulging suitcases sitting outside the door.

48

ONCE UPON A TIME, BEFORE SHE WAS A PROSTITUTE OR A CON woman, Isabella dreamed of marrying a prince and having a happy ending. Like how a prince scaled a tower to rescue Rapunzel, or how Prince Charming found Cinderella, she hoped a prince too would come along and save her from her miserable existence.

The first time she liked a boy was in fourth grade. Isabella barely noticed him, or any boy for that matter, until he passed her a note during class one day, telling her that he thought she was pretty. It made her feel like the most important person in the world. All her friends were jealous. He was the cutest boy in class, they kept telling her, and he liked her, no one else. After that, she'd wait for him to walk home, before leaving school, so she could watch him without interruption until he reached his house. Then, she'd walk to her mother's motel room, where she'd spend the entire night thinking about him, imagining their life together.

If only Isabella had the courage to speak to him. Whenever he talked to her, she'd just smile or give a one-word answer. She was too afraid he would think she was dull or uninteresting. Or worse, she was terrified of revealing how much she loved him, that she spent her nights dreaming about them holding hands together and kissing like in the movies, which might have scared him away.

Eventually though, he got bored with her—someone told her he had kissed another girl during recess. Isabella couldn't remember the girl's name, only that she had blonde pigtails. After class that day, Isabella had followed her from class to the top of the stairs. There, she tripped the girl on purpose and she had tumbled down the stairs. She survived without much injury, but Isabella had been expelled shortly after that.

Once in high school, Isabella dated many boys that she thought might be her Prince Charming, but they all just seemed to be after only one thing. Eventually, she came to hate men and completely gave up on her search for Prince Charming; that's when she became a con woman.

For a while at least, Nathan had her believe in love again, but now she realized he wouldn't be her savior either. In a way, he was worse than all the men before him because he had filled her with false hope.

Isabella's bags were packed, but before leaving, she was going to make sure Nathan's life was in as much ruin as her own. She picked up one of the cards Gregg Hunter had given out at Elaine's poker night and called the number on the back.

"Hello, Mr. Hunter. It's Isabella Blake."

"Miss Blake, I'm extremely busy." He seemed agitated.

"I'm calling to say goodbye," she said. "Nathan and I have separated, so I'm leaving town today."

"Where will you go?"

"Probably back to New York. I always wanted to be discovered there, so perhaps I'll continue that dream."

"Discovered?" His voice perked up with interest.

"Yes, I always wanted to be a film star."

"Did you know Liam before moving to Blackberry Cove?" he asked. "Liam wanted to be a film producer. You must have known that."

She paused briefly. "Nathan doesn't like me talking about these things."

"Why do you care what he thinks now?"

He was right, she didn't. That's why she was calling Gregg in the first place. "I knew Richard O'Doyle back in New York. After he moved to Blackberry Cove, he got in touch to say someone in his town was putting together a small film project and was looking for actresses. When I arrived, Liam was still raising money for the project. Eventually, I realized he was never going to get the funds. Luckily, by then, I had already met Nathan. He was nice to me and gave me a job as his secretary. He was like my knight in shining armor."

"When you said you knew Richard O'Doyle in New York, did his wife know about your relationship?"

"Richard never cheated on his wife with me, if that's what you're insinuating. He loves his wife, but he did lie to her. He told her he stopped smoking marijuana back in Ireland, but he bought it from me a few times in New York. Eventually, he did stop using."

"You're telling me that you were his dealer?" Gregg said.

"Just a bit of weed. Are you going to arrest me for that?"

There was another pause. "Why did you call me, Miss Blake?"

"I have information about the case I wanted to share before leaving."

"What information?"

"They're lying to you, Mr. Hunter."

"Who?"

"Everyone."

"Why?"

"I don't know, but the night Clementine died, and Liam went missing, I heard a gunshot as I was walking back from the mayor's office."

"What time was this?"

"Just before ten," she said. "Later that night, I looked out my window and saw Richard O'Doyle returning home, wet and covered in blood."

"Why didn't you say anything before?" Gregg asked.

"I didn't want everyone in town to know my history, but that doesn't matter now. I'm sorry I didn't disclose everything sooner."

"Is there anything else?"

"Nathan is a violent man," she said after a pause. "I need you to know that."

"What do you mean?"

"He almost killed me earlier tonight, when he realized I might be leaving him."

"Maybe I should call the sheriff."

"Don't bother. I won't press charges. I want to disappear tonight. I'm only telling you so you look at him more closely. He's not the gentleman he appears to be. He hit Clementine. When she suggested they get a divorce, he struck her across the face and made her bleed. He removed his carpet so no one would find the blood. Nathan didn't even love her. He just didn't want her to leave him. Isn't that sick?"

"How do—"

"There's more," she said. "The disappearance of Nathan's first wife is something that has always nagged at me. He never talks about her. Whenever someone mentions her, he puts his guard up."

"I've noticed that too," Gregg replied. "He's evaded all of my questions about his first wife. What was her name again? Anna?"

"Yes, Anna. According to Nathan, she was an unhappy single mother who thought he could be the answer to her problems. In a way she was right; she abandoned her child with him and left during the night. She was never seen or heard from again. Somehow, I think she's key to all of this."

"I agree."

"You do?" she asked.

"Yes, it just doesn't seem reasonable that Nathan could be

connected to both cases without a direct association between them. Do you know if there was any connection between Anna and Liam?"

"No," she replied. "Liam would have been just a child when Anna was in town. However, her daughter would have been around Liam's age."

"What happened to the girl?"

"She went to live with her father in Boston. I don't think Nathan ever kept in touch with her, except to send her the life insurance money once Anna was declared dead."

"Was it a large life insurance policy, do you know?"

"I don't, but Nathan told me once that he gave all of it to the daughter."

"What was the girl's name?"

"Emilie."

"Emilie?" Gregg's voice went shaky, as though he was in disbelief. "Are you sure?"

"Yes, of course."

"What was her last name?"

"Jones," she said. "Emilie Jones."

Just then, Isabella heard the phone go dead; Gregg was gone.

49

THEY'RE LYING TO YOU. GREGG KEPT REPEATING THE WORDS IN HIS head as he dashed to Nathan's mansion. His mind was going a million miles an hour. Rachel was going to kill his daughter if he didn't make progress by the end of the day. But if he was going to make any progress, he had to keep calm and think clearly. It was time he started thinking outside the box. If the suspects had all been lying to him, then what could that mean? *Suspects.* Of what? He still didn't even have proof that Liam had been killed. The sheriff apparently did before he arrested Chloe, and Rachel seemed dead certain on the notion. So, who were the suspects?

The mayor. He lied to Gregg about Clementine not knowing Liam. They dated, went to film school together, and then broke up. Liam had never gotten over it. He spied on her with binoculars at the park. Years later, Liam killed her. Gregg was certain about that. Liam killed her and filmed it. *Why now?* He didn't yet know the answer to that question. *What happened to the recording?* He didn't know that either. Would this give the mayor motive to kill Liam? No, the mayor didn't love his wife. *You're a fool if you think I cared about Clementine enough to do that.* That was maybe the one truthful thing the mayor had said. Unless the mayor had hired Liam to kill Clementine and then killed Liam to cover his tracks.

The therapist. Liam's one true friend. They went to Albany together on the weekends, chatted up women, and lied about where they had been. Timothy hadn't seen Liam the day he disappeared, or so he claimed. Earlier that day, he had yelled abuse at a female cashier for giving him the wrong change and she had to call the sheriff to calm him down. Other nights, he wrecked his wife's garden in secret. He was definitely unstable. But what motive would he have for killing Liam? Chloe. She understood him, as the therapist had said, and made him feel better about his condition—his impotence. Chloe chose to date his best friend, surely filling Timothy with rage and jealousy. It didn't quite fit though. Liam's death had to be connected to Clementine's, or it was too strange a coincidence, and there was no connection between Timothy and Clementine that Gregg could see.

The outdoorsman. Bernard had no alibi. He was stargazing atop the mountains all night. He spent years searching for his wife's killer, and his search had led him to Blackberry Cove, where Liam had possibly met with the man in the brown suit, Rachel's associate and a hitman. Fury had met with Bernard's wife the day before her murder, but the connection to Liam was unclear. There was no reason for Bernard to lie—he had been searching for Liam's body and was offering to help Gregg solve the murder. Still, he should ask around to see if anyone remembers seeing Bernard that night and to make sure he wasn't lying.

The ex-girlfriend. They had broken up the day Liam disappeared. Chloe had been honest about that, and about being angry. In fact, she had seemed completely earnest with just about everything. There was just one thing bothering him. The first time Gregg saw Chloe, she had been sitting with Bernard at the inn. He had seen her leave, and then found her lipstick on the rim of the glass at the table. Ever since that night, they had never spoken to each other in front of Gregg, or even made eye contact with each other. They were pretending to be strangers, but strangers don't meet for a drink.

The innkeepers. They were each other's alibi. If they were lying, it meant they were protecting each other. He still couldn't think of a motive for the couple, but he felt uneasy with the news that Richard invited Isabella, his former drug supplier, to Blackberry Cove for one of Liam's film projects. That brought him to the final suspect.

The secretary. The con woman. The mistress. If she was involved in the murders, she wouldn't have called tonight. When Isabella told him about Emilie Jones, Gregg felt his entire body freeze and thought he was going to collapse. He thought about how Rachel had brought a copy of Emilie's article when originally attempting to hire him. Emilie's case was connected to why he had been hired in the first place, but what else was there to make of it? He couldn't call Rachel yet. First, he had to make some progress.

He pounded on Nathan's door. Soon, the hallway light went on and the door opened.

"What the hell is this all about, Hunter?" Nathan yelled. He looked more disheveled than usual, with a loosened tie and reddened eyes.

Gregg slid past him, into the house, and headed straight to the living room.

"Hey, I didn't say you could come in!" Nathan followed him. "Get out right now or I'll force you out!"

Ignoring him, Gregg forced open a chest of drawers and began digging for family pictures.

"What do you think you're doing? That's it, I'm calling the sheriff!" Nathan's footsteps wandered off.

Finally, Gregg found what he was looking for—a photograph of a little girl, standing between a younger Nathan and a black-haired woman. There was no mistaking it—this was the girl Gregg had rescued from the trunk of a car nearly a decade ago.

50

WHEN HE WAS A BOY, MARC CHIPS HEARD ENDLESS GHOST STORIES about the woods that encircled Blackberry Cove. The Native Americans thought the land was cursed, and they only ever wandered into the forest to bury their dead. Hunters got disoriented and lost in the woods all the time. At school, the older children would tell him about spirits and beasts that lurked between the trees. Nowadays, he understood the fierce winds were probably what inspired the many supernatural tales, and why deer hunters would get so confused. Still, there were some stories that couldn't be discarded so easily.

In 1892, a sawmill worker from town killed one of his fellow employees and fled the state. He was later captured in Connecticut and committed to a mental asylum because of hearing voices in his head. He escaped the asylum by hiding in a railroad car and was never seen again.

Several years later, a stagecoach carrying tourists was making its way through the forest towards the town. As a storm raged on, the horses grew agitated and eventually had to halt due to the strong winds and heavy rain. The driver decided to investigate and discovered fresh footprints on the road ahead. Suddenly, an unknown force caused the entire stagecoach to overturn. The passengers frantically sought refuge in the woods. From the underbrush, they claimed to have seen a massive, hairy man, like Bigfoot. He was named the Bennington Monster, but some believed him to be the escaped mental patient, now a wild man who dwelled in the forests around his old town.

Over the next hundred years, there were dozens of unexplained disappearances within the woods. Children, in particular, seemed to vanish without a trace. Some say the Bennington Monster, or the Wild Man, still lurked, but he'd surely have died long ago. Other people reported sightings of UFOs and believed alien abductions were responsible for the countless missing persons cases. Some thought the area to be a window or vortex to another world. Then, the strangest explanation yet for the disappearances was that of a stone in the woods that swallowed human beings whole if stepped upon.

Marc wondered if the cases of Liam Watts and Clementine Stannard too would go down in history as unsolved cases; two more names on the list of a Wikipedia page. They'd be remembered only by ghost stories children told on the playground, forever two faceless victims in a long line of missing persons cases. Maybe the real reason there were so many unexplained cases was because the sheriffs who worked on the cases were all like Marc—naïve and inexperienced. He wanted so badly to be a great detective, and to solve multiple murder cases like Gregg Hunter, but maybe he wasn't smart enough. Truth was, Liam hadn't been abducted by aliens, slaughtered by a monster, or swallowed by a stone. He was most likely dead. If he was, a person killed him, and it was up to Marc to find that person.

Sheriff Johnston had always been Marc's role model when he needed one as a kid. His father was a waste of space, so he had no positive influence there. Sheriff Johnston was the man he respected, and the person he wanted to make proud. Now, Marc had to try and live up to his image.

Marc entered the interview room, where Gregg was being held for breaking into the mayor's mansion and causing a disturbance. "Sheriff, I don't have time for this. There's a killer out there. We need to get on with the case."

Marc took a seat. "Do you have information to share with me?"

"Isabella called me. Apparently, the mayor tried to kill her. She also told me that he hit Clementine when she suggested they get a divorce. That's why I went to his house. I wanted to know more about the situation. I'm sorry that I crossed a line."

"Obviously, I'll look into this." Marc opened his pad and made some notes. "Thank you for sharing. Is there anything else?"

"Yes, Isabella also told me that she heard a gunshot the night Liam went missing. Later, she saw Richard O'Doyle returning him, soaking wet and covered in blood."

"Why didn't she report this?"

"That doesn't matter right now. If Richard O'Doyle killed Liam, I want to hear it from him. It's time for the truth."

Marc shook his head. "There's no evidence. If we went to Richard with this, he'd slam the door in our faces, and he'd know we're on to him."

Gregg nodded. "You're right. Even if you got a warrant, the bloody clothes are probably long gone. We need something else."

"I have something to share with you," Marc said after a pause. "I think it's time I told you about the anonymous call the sheriff and I received before we arrested Chloe."

Gregg waited for him to say more.

Marc cleared his throat. "Someone found a trail of dried blood in the woods and anonymously called it in. The blood was gone by the time we got there—washed away by rain or animals —but we searched the surrounding area. We found a chainsaw in a small stream nearby, caught between some rocks. No prints, but there was still blood on the blade—Liam's blood."

"Any idea where the chainsaw came from or who it belonged to?"

"We figured it came from an old carpenter shed nearby. It

belonged to Liam's father. The only fingerprints we found there belonged to Liam."

"So, someone cut up Liam with his own chainsaw," Gregg said. "Find anything else in the shed?"

"There were some marijuana plants growing in a greenhouse Liam kept outside. Other than that, just a bunch of tools."

Gregg stood and headed for the door. "I think I know who made that call, Sheriff. If I'm right and find anything else against Richard O'Doyle, I'll inform you immediately and we'll get that warrant. You should talk to Isabella before she leaves town."

Isabella Blake, the con artist so sly,
Once schemed for the mayor's money to fly,
But then she fell in love, oh what a twist,
For a family and love, she longed and wished.

But the mayor's heart was not to be tamed,
His love for her waned and her heart was pained,
As she longed for nothing more than a family,
Her heart was broken by love's tyranny.

51

Gregg knocked on Bernard's door. He was desperate. There were only a few hours of the day left. He had to call Rachel with something soon, or he would never see his daughter again. Images of his daughter's boiling flesh and the sound of her screaming flashed through his mind, but he had to stay focused.

The door opened, and Bernard seemed both pleased and surprised to see him.

"If you want to help, take me to where you found the blood," Gregg said. "I know it was you who gave the anonymous tip, so don't try to lie."

"How did you know?"

"Chloe told me that you were searching for the body in the woods," Gregg replied. "You should have just told me from the beginning."

"I wanted to, but you didn't want to listen."

"I'm listening now," Gregg said. "So take me to where you found the blood."

Without hesitation, Bernard took Gregg to his car and drove him past Liam's cabin to the end of the small country road. Gregg updated Bernard on Isabella's news about Richard O'Doyle and on Rachel's deadline.

Bernard expressed both his sympathies in regard to Silvia and some doubts over Richard's motives. Gregg agreed that he couldn't see any obvious reason for Richard to have killed Liam, but sometimes there was no obvious motive. He had dealt with his fair share of cases where the perpetrator just snapped. Richard may have been protecting his wife; if Liam killed Clementine, he may also have tried to hurt Hannah, and Richard stopped him. Seemingly, good people doing bad things wasn't a foreign concept to any detective. Frankly, Gregg didn't care about the motive. All he needed was some proof that Richard was the killer, so he could find the body, and get his daughter back.

Despite his lingering mistrust of Bernard, Gregg decided that there was no point in holding back information. Bernard might have been friendly with him only to gather intel about the case, but he also appeared to have a genuine interest in solving it. Gregg just wanted his daughter back. Once the case was over, Gregg would never have to think about Bernard, and hopefully not Rachel, ever again.

Equipped with flashlights to illuminate their path, Gregg and Bernard trekked through the forest on foot, buffeted by the wailing wind that carried the scent of wood rot.

"Tell me about the markings you found in the woods," Gregg said.

"About a week or so ago, I found some dried blood in the forest."

"Why didn't you say anything before?" Gregg asked, his tone a little harsher than he intended.

"I was already under suspicion, and I wanted you to focus on finding the body, not wasting time investigating me. Plus, it didn't lead anywhere at the time. But a few days ago, I found tire tracks leading to the dried blood. You can't see the marks anymore, but you can see where the underbrush and saplings have been crushed by a car or truck."

"You think the tire marks belonged to Liam's killer, dropping off the body?" Gregg asked.

Bernard nodded.

"You could have given me this evidence another way, without implicating yourself."

"I tried," Bernard said. "I gave an anonymous call to the sheriff, but that only got Chloe falsely arrested."

"Deputy Chips was just looking for a reason to arrest her. Once he had evidence of a crime, he jumped at the chance."

"I felt awful, but I knew it would all be made right in the end."

In the distance, there was a work shed that looked tired and out of place next to a small stream. "That must be the carpenter shed. I wonder why Liam's father would have his shed so far from the house."

"Like father, like son, I suppose," Bernard replied. "They both liked to be alone."

By the door of the shed was a small greenhouse. It was now empty, but Gregg recalled what Marc had said about Liam growing marijuana.

"How did the killer even know about this shed?" Gregg asked.

"What do you mean?"

"It's far from the house. You and I couldn't find it. Yet the killer knew to come here. He came because he knew it was secluded, and then, according to Deputy Chips, the killer used one of Liam's chainsaws. He and the sheriff found the chainsaw in the river. Traces of Liam's blood were on the blades."

Bernard shrugged. "You got me. How did the killer know about the shed?"

Gregg pointed to the greenhouse. "He had been here before to buy pot from Liam. Isabella had dealt the drug to Richard in New York."

Inside the shed, Gregg found a great number of tools hanging on a pegboard: hammers, screwdrivers, and spanners of all sorts and sizes. Missing was a nail gun, in a place where one would fit perfectly. As if he needed any further proof Liam had killed Clementine. Also missing, he noted, was a chainsaw, just as the sheriff described. Before he could investigate further, Bernard called his name from outside.

He went out to find Bernard bent over the ground. "What's wrong?"

"There's fresh footprints here," Bernard said.

"What is it with killers and returning to the scene of the crime?"

"Why would they return now?"

"I have no idea."

"Maybe you should call Rachel and tell her what you have."

Gregg shone his light on the footprints in the mud. "I think she'll want some idea of who the footprints belong to."

"Well then, let's figure that out now."

Gregg flew his arms into the air. "I don't even know where to start!"

"On our first trip to Liam's cabin, you told me about the case of a missing girl, and how your FBI friend taught you about tracking."

Gregg shook his head. "I'm not a professional tracker."

Bernard shrugged his shoulders. "Just do what you can."

Sighing, Gregg placed his foot next to the footprint in the mud. Although people always commented on his large feet, his print was slightly smaller. He stretched his leg to place his other foot beside the next print, carefully noting the strides and pressure releases as he followed the trail.

"Well?" Bernard asked. "Don't keep me in suspense."

"Going by the size of the print, the suspect is most likely male. He has a long stride, and so is obviously quite tall."

"Stride?" Bernard asked.

"The distance between the toes of the second foot and the

heel of the first foot. If you're taller, you have a longer stride. I'm just about six feet, and this person is taller than I am."

Bernard nodded to signal his understanding.

"No two people walk exactly the same way. Some of us drag our heels, some of us walk on our sides, and most of us walk more on the front half of our foot than the back half. This guy is an exception. He walks more on his heels than most, probably because he's concerned about his posture. Taller individuals are more vulnerable to back pain, and he was probably told from a young age that good posture would ease that pain. He doesn't appear to have stumbled or to have looked around, so he knew exactly where he was going. He wasn't lost, and he maintained a steady pace. The depth of the indentation indicates he's not very skinny, but rather quite heavy, though not overweight, and he wasn't carrying anything or dragging anything."

"I didn't realize you could tell so much from a print in the mud," Bernard said.

Profiling a suspect from footprints in the mud wasn't Gregg's normal police work, but nothing about this case had been normal. When searching for Emilie Jones, Gregg and the FBI tracker found two sets of footprints leading across the school's playground—one set belonging to Emilie Jones, and the other belonging to her kidnapper. When the FBI agent pointed out how small the footprints were, that's when Gregg first came to suspect that the girl's aunt was the abductor rather than her uncle, the police's primary suspect.

Gregg's suspicions regarding Richard's involvement in Liam's murder only intensified. The footprints supported Gregg's theory that the seemingly gentle giant was actually the killer they were after.

"Does it help us identify our suspect?" Gregg wanted to hear if Bernard was thinking the same.

"Well, it doesn't contradict what we already suspected. After all, Richard O'Doyle is heavy and one of the few in town taller than you. If nothing else, it adds further weight to Richard being the killer."

"I agree."

"But is it enough for a warrant?"

"Let's just hope O'Doyle believes it is." Gregg took out his cell to tell Rachel the case was coming to a close.

52

As Nathan poured himself a drink of scotch, he couldn't help but wonder if he had made a mistake by pushing Isabella away. Her betrayal still made him shake with fury. The rage pulsed through his veins and welled in his chest. He thought he could have a heart attack, he was so mad.

His mother ran off when he was nine years old, leaving him behind nothing but a note and a copy of her favorite book, *Catcher in the Rye*. Now, Isabella was gone too, and again, he blamed himself. He should have heard her out, instead of pushing her away. But how could he have? She betrayed him, so to forgive her would be weak.

Once, not long after his mother left, Nathan had been in a fight at school. Being the son of the mayor, he was often targeted by the other kids, who resented his special treatment by the teachers. He had gone home, bruised and beaten, and when Kerwin, his father, saw him, he grabbed Nathan by the wrists and dragged him back to the schoolyard. There, he had Nathan point out the kid who had hit him. His father gave him two choices: beat the crap out of the kid, or don't come home for dinner, because he wouldn't sit across the dinner table from a disappointment of a son. He had gone to bed with an empty stomach that night, on top of a black eye.

From that day on, Nathan promised himself he'd never be a disappointment again. He didn't complain about his father not ever being around or about being raised by the nanny, because he knew Kerwin was an important man and needed to work. Instead, he wanted to be just like his father. He, Nathan always thought, wasn't dependent on others, rather he knew that the only person he could count on in life was himself.

When Nathan returned home from college, he was genuinely surprised by how excited Kerwin seemed to see him. Then, his father spoke about the upcoming campaign, and Nathan realized he wasn't happy to see him, but rather he was happy about Nathan becoming the next mayor. Finally, Nathan thought he had a way of making his father proud of him, by carrying on the family tradition, but when he had introduced him to his girl-friend from college, the girl he had knocked up, he saw again that look of disappointment. So, that's why he married Clemen-tine, a young woman he didn't love, just to please his father. It was a quick marriage, so everyone in town would think the pregnancy was planned.

Kerwin died alone in a nursing home. Nathan rarely had time to visit him, too busy with work, just like Kerwin had no time for him when Nathan was a kid. His father had always pushed everyone away, not even allowing Nathan to get too close, and Nathan often wondered if his father felt lonely in the end, if he regretted the decisions he made. Nathan prayed that wasn't the case, or it would probably be his fate too. The only woman Nathan had ever loved was now gone, just like his mother, Anna, and Clementine. He had to know that being mayor would be enough, and that passing that title onto Raymond would be his legacy. Power was everything, as his father would say, and no real man needed a woman to fulfill him.

There was one vast difference between Nathan and his father:

his father was an old-fashioned gentleman, and he would have been ashamed of Nathan's affair. Unfortunately, Nathan also wasn't quite as loveable in public as his father had been. He never enjoyed making small talk, and he hated hearing about people's petty problems. His family name could only get him so far, and so he had been lucky that few people had ever thought to run against his family for mayor. After all, if he didn't have power, what did he have?

Luckily, things would be different for Raymond. Thanks to Isabella's help, Nathan had shown his son that he loved him, and his son could depend on him. Indeed, as Nathan sat alone in his office, sipping his scotch, he knew the only thing he had to be thankful for was that his son would grow up to be a better man than he.

As mad as Nathan was over Isabella's betrayal, the idea of her being out there without him was worse. If she found another man to be with instead of him, he wouldn't be able to take it. So long as she was out there, he knew she would always be on his mind, and he'd never be at rest. He should have killed her while he had the chance. Then she'd always have been his. If only he didn't love her so much.

Timothy's clients sought his aid,
Yet his own issues never swayed,
Silent sorrows haunted him each day,
At night, his anger refused to sway.

Though his behavior may not be just,
His fury continued to combust,
He'd destroy his wife's garden with glee,
But no relief from his troubles came to be.

53

GREGG AND BERNARD MADE THEIR WAY TO THE INN AND ASKED Richard if they could speak to him alone outside. As they exited, the innkeeper glanced over his shoulder through the window, as if to make sure Hannah wasn't watching. The muscles of his pale face tightened, and his hands trembled at his waist.

"It's over," Gregg said immediately.

"What do you mean?" Richard ran his hand up his beard.

"We know you killed Liam Watts."

"Me? Why would I kill Liam?" Richard's knees shook. "And why do you think he's even dead? I just figured he left town, maybe after killing Clementine. He always did seem a bit off."

"The detective and I think he's dead," Bernard said. "We found his blood in the woods, along with your footprints."

"My footprints?" Richard's face broke out in relief as he realized that was all they had. "You can't possibly prove that."

"Just come out and show us where the body is."

Richard crossed his arms, his face more serious. "Sorry, but I need to get back to closing the inn, so unless you have a warrant, this conversation is over."

"If we tell the sheriff what we know, he'll easily obtain a warrant," Gregg told him. "Isabella heard a gunshot the night

Liam went missing, then she saw you returning home that same evening, covered in blood. That's probable cause. All the sheriff needs now is something to search your house for. The sheriff's department can get a team to take proper copies of the prints in the woods before it's too late, then get a warrant to search your house for footwear that matches."

Richard knitted his brows. "If that was true, why wouldn't you have told the sheriff already?"

"The choice is yours," Gregg went on. "You can show us the body now and maybe there's a way out of this for you, or we can call the sheriff to arrest you."

Richard dropped his arms by his sides.

Bernard stepped closer. "We've been friends since I moved here, Richard, and I know better than anyone how love can make us break the bounds of normalcy. It can make us do dark things. If you were protecting Hannah, I'll understand."

Richard shook his head. "Hannah had nothing to do with this. It was me. Leave her out of it, and I'll take you to the body."

"No tricks?" Gregg asked.

"To be honest, this is sort of a relief. I'm not sure how much more I could have handled. Every time I close my eyes, I see blood. Hannah keeps talking about adopting, and starting a family, but how can we bring a kid into this?"

"Alright," Gregg said. "Let's go."

Bernard presented a shovel from behind his back, and they all made their way to his car parked on the street.

They drove up to the woods, without anyone saying a word, and got out by the footprints Gregg and Bernard had discovered. From there, Richard led them to a clearing where a large section of grass looked newer than the rest.

Richard shakily pointed. "That's it."

Bernard handed him the shovel.

"Start digging," Gregg said.

"Couldn't you just do it yourself?" he asked.

"You put him there, you dig him up," Bernard said.

Richard fell silent and pierced into the earth with his shovel while Gregg and Bernard perched on rocks, watching closely.

"I know about your past in Ireland," Gregg said. "Before you met Hannah, you dropped out of college and sold drugs to make a living."

"How do you know about that?"

"I did my research."

"I managed to get clean when I moved to America with Hannah. I changed for her. She made me want to be a better person."

"Not right away. You got your drugs from Isabella in New York. You were the one who told her about Blackberry Cove. Then, you got bored and had a lapse. Liam provided for you. That's how you knew about the carpenter shed. What happened? Did Liam threaten to tell Hannah you were still using? Or did you get into a disagreement with him about money?"

"You're crazy." Richard scoffed. "I sold some drugs as a kid and I occasionally smoke pot, but that has nothing to do with any of this."

Soon enough, Richard's shovel hit something hard, causing a loud thud. Gregg and Bernard helped Richard heave a relatively small chest out of the ground and up to the surface.

"He's in here?" Gregg asked.

"How did he fit?" Bernard said.

"I made him fit." Richard looked away, his voice and eyes filled with shame.

Bernard and Gregg turned their eyes to the box and stood there staring at it for a moment.

"Would you like to do the honors?" Bernard eventually asked.

Gregg knelt and released the chest's bloodstained lid. A repulsive stench filled the air, causing Bernard to cover his nose and mouth, almost vomiting. Gregg didn't flinch. The sight and smell of chopped up remains wasn't new to him.

"God, I didn't know they smelled that bad!" Bernard exclaimed.

"Rookies always say that on their first body," Gregg uttered, more to himself than anyone else. He turned to Richard. "Tell me what really happened."

Richard fell to his knees, tears cascading down his cheeks. "I only did what I did to protect Hannah. I had no other choice."

"Explain, and maybe I'll believe you."

"The night of July eighteenth," Richard said, "Hannah and I were watching television. I got up to let Sparky outside. While I was out, the phone rang, and Hannah answered. It was Liam. He told her he had killed Clementine Stannard, and that he was coming for her next. At first, she thought he was playing a sick joke, but there was something about the tone of his voice that creeped her out. When I got back inside, Hannah had turned off all the lights so it would look like we weren't home, and she explained what had happened. I went to call the sheriff, but Hannah was too scared, so she ran right out the back door.

"I was about to press the dial button when I heard a gunshot outside. I dropped the phone and ran to our chest of drawers where we kept our handgun. It was missing. I rummaged through the rest of the drawers, praying I would find it, but I didn't. I dashed to the exit, switched on the light, and found Liam's body on the front lawn with a knife in his hand. Blood was welling through his clothes from a gunshot. He was dead. There was no sign of anyone, but I knew it had to have been Hannah."

"Then what did you do?" Gregg asked.

"I did what I had to do to protect her," he replied. "I shoved Liam's body into my truck and drove up to the woods. If I could make sure no one would find the body, no one would find the bullet from our gun, and no one would know what Hannah had done. Problem was, I knew Bernard walked through these woods in time to see the sunrise every morning, so I didn't have much time. I was worried that someone was going to see me, so I only dug a small hole, and I brought a chest with me to put the body in. It was too small, and the body wouldn't fit. I tried squeezing Liam inside, again, and again, but he wouldn't go in. The sky was getting brighter and brighter. I was running out of time. I had to get rid of the body.

"Then, I remembered the old carpenter's shed by the river, where Liam would sell me pot, and found the chainsaw inside. With it, I got to work. There was blood, blood, blood, and more blood! I sawed through flesh and bone. Blood splattered everywhere. I vomited all over the ground. The thought of Hannah was the only thing that kept me going. Once I finished, I put the pieces of the body into the chest, buried it, and washed up in the river. So long as I had buried the body deep enough, Hannah would be safe. Please, when you report this, tell them I killed Liam, not Hannah. I don't mind taking the fall. I just can't bear for her to be arrested."

Gregg took out his cell and speed dialed Rachel. As soon as she answered, he said, "I'm standing over the body of Liam Watts as we speak."

"No tricks this time, Hunter. Send me a picture," Rachel replied.

Using his cell, Gregg snapped a picture of the remains and sent it to Rachel.

"I'll be right there." Rachel hung up.

"Who was that?" Richard asked.

"My employers."

"Will they contact the sheriff? Will Hannah be arrested?"

"I wasn't hired to subdue Liam's killer, only to find the body. If you've told me the truth, I won't say anything to the sheriff. No body, no case."

"So, no one will be arrested?" Richard said.

Gregg nodded. "As long as you've told me the truth about Liam."

"I have, I swear."

"Prove it." Gregg handed him his cell. "Call Hannah and have her testify to it."

Richard reluctantly took the cell and phoned Hannah, telling her to drive past Liam's cabin until she saw Bernard's car parked in the woods. They all stood and waited for her to arrive. The entire time, Gregg thought about Rachel arriving with Silvia. Finally, he would be able to hold her in his arms again.

It all seemed to fit together a little too easily. Richard had the perfect excuse for killing Liam—he was protecting his wife from a psychopath who had just earlier killed Clementine Stannard, yet there was no evidence as to why Liam killed Clementine in the first place or as to why he was then going to kill Hannah. Thing was, Gregg didn't care. All he wanted was for it all to be over.

It was a strange feeling for Gregg to not feel the usual rush of excitement about making an arrest. Throughout his career, he had been driven by a deep-seated anger towards crime and injustice. He had often appeared at parole hearings to make sure that convicts didn't get released early. His dedication to getting criminals off the streets had once caused him to sacrifice time with his wife and daughter.

Gregg didn't even feel the need to get even with Rachel once this was all over. He simply hoped that there were no loose ends that could come back to haunt him. All he wanted was to get his daughter back and put this entire nightmare behind him.

Chloe was the one exception. For now, he had to focus on getting his daughter back, but once he had, he'd perhaps like to see Chloe again. He felt they may have something special, and he wanted to find out what that might be. Maybe that was insane. He barely knew anything about her. They were two strangers who met because of a murder investigation. He had never felt this way about someone before, though. He married his first ever girlfriend, and it had been more for Silvia's sake than anything else. Since his divorce, he had never been particularly interested in dating.

Maybe he could stay in Blackberry Cove when this was all over, get to know Chloe better, and get a job at the sheriff's station. Silvia always hated living in the city, always pestering him to take her camping and hiking; now he could finally do those things with her. For the first time in his life, Gregg too longed for a quieter life. Plus, there was nothing left for them in Boston. They needed a fresh start. Now he was being insane. He had to focus on the moment, get his daughter back, then he could worry about the future. Enough daydreaming.

Once Hannah arrived, she caught sight of Liam's remains and put her hands over her mouth, gasping in fright. She teared up and ran to Richard's arms. Hannah cried, "Oh, I knew it. I didn't want to believe it, but I knew it."

"I had to," Richard told her. "To protect you."

"I understand, Richard, and I still love you."

"I love you too." Richard wept.

Hannah turned to Gregg, struggling to hold back her tears, and pleaded, "Please, don't arrest him. You don't understand what Liam was planning to do."

Richard grabbed her by the arms with a sudden smile. "They're not going to arrest either of us."

Hannah furrowed her brow in confusion. "Why would they arrest me?"

"It's alright, I explained everything to them, and they understand," Richard replied. "Liam called and threatened to kill you. He was outside our house when you took the gun and shot him in self-defense. I found the body and tried to hide it."

Hannah shook her head. "That's not what happened. After I left the house, I jumped the fence of our backyard. I was afraid Liam was coming for me and had to escape. Then, I heard a gunshot coming from the front of the house. I turned and saw you had put the light on. Afterwards, I saw Liam's body on our front lawn, and you standing over him. I knew what you had done, Richard, and I understood. You were trying to protect me. Still, I freaked out, and ran off. When my head cleared, I came back home. Both you and the body were gone. Later that night, you returned, wet and bloodstained."

Richard dropped to his knees, turning green. "Are you telling me you didn't kill Liam?"

Hannah shook her head.

"I don't understand, the gun wasn't in the drawer. The next day I found it in our bedside cabinet."

"I put it there weeks before," Hannah said. "I figured you found it."

Richard buried his head into his hands and wept. "I did what I did for nothing."

Hannah fell to her knees also and grasped her husband's hands, looking into his eyes. "All this time, Richard, I thought I was married to a killer. I'm just thankful I'm not. It was tearing me up inside, but I couldn't bring myself to talk to you about it, because that would just make it too real."

"I only did what I did because I thought I was protecting you. You have no idea how horrible it was, Hannah. Thinking of you was all that got me through it."

The couple embraced each other, crying. Gregg and Bernard looked at one another, and Gregg asked the obvious question—if neither of them killed Liam, then who did?

54

A̲n̲y̲o̲n̲e̲ ̲w̲h̲o̲ ̲k̲n̲e̲w̲ C̲h̲l̲o̲e̲'s̲ ̲p̲a̲s̲t̲ ̲m̲i̲g̲h̲t̲ ̲t̲h̲i̲n̲k̲ ̲t̲h̲a̲t̲ ̲t̲h̲e̲ ̲d̲a̲y̲ ̲o̲f̲ her father's stroke was the happiest day of her life. In actuality, it was the second worst day of her life, following only the deaths of her mother and sister on the day of the fire. When her father had his stroke, she had to turn down her college scholarship, crushing her dreams of leaving the town behind. Chloe accepted that she would have to care for her father for the rest of his life, or else she would never forgive herself. More than that, if she abandoned him when he needed her most, how could she ever expect him to love her? It was a sad thing to admit that she desired the love of her abuser, but it was the truth; she wanted her father's love more than anything.

His stroke did mean, however, that she no longer had to live in fear. That's why, when she came home that day to find her father moving the corners of his mouth and the tips of his fingers, she felt a panic rise in her that she hadn't felt in years. She immediately called Dr. Taylor, who said her father was showing signs of neurological movement or something. There was no telling how better he could get, and he could even eventually be back up and running. She couldn't bear the thought of him ever touching her again.

She had tried calling Gregg, but both times it had been engaged. Of course, Chloe understood that Gregg had bigger things on his mind, like getting his daughter back, but she needed someone to talk to. She put on her gray woolly hat and red jacket, then headed to the inn to see if he was there.

As Chloe cut across the park, there was a rustling of leaves behind her. She quickly spun around and smiled when she saw it was only Timothy.

"Oh, Dr. Holst," she said. "You frightened me."

Timothy stared back blankly.

Her smile dropped. "Dr. Holst?"

He took a step towards her.

"Dr. Holst? What are you doing out here?"

He pulled a black baton from his pocket, decorated with dark blue markings, and swung it into the air. It was stained with something red. *Blood. It's stained with dried blood.*

Chloe took a step back. "Dr. Holst, what's wrong?"

He gave an eerie smile. "Don't scream this time, Elaine."

55

Even after talking about it for years, Timothy was unsure whether he was ready for the hunt. Not like Liam, who had a sparkle in his eye and was bumping his shoulders. It was unusual to see Liam quite so cheerful. If it wasn't for the same old paint-stained jeans and ginger stubble, he would almost have seemed like a different person.

The café owner, Shannon Alvie, sat their coffee on the table outside. Liam took out his binoculars and scanned across the park for their prey.

"What about her?" Liam pointed over to Isabella Blake, walking through the park with two to-go coffees in her hands, clearly on her way to the mayor's office.

Timothy didn't reply. He had a knot in his stomach. Fantasies were one thing, but to actually start planning was something else. They had talked about it over and over at the inn, and watched films online, but Timothy knew even all that couldn't prepare him for ending someone's life.

Liam clearly sensed his disinterest and placed the binoculars down. "Do you remember high school, Tim?"

"Of course." Timothy looked up. "Why?"

"I was bullied," Liam replied. "Relentlessly."

"Kids can be cruel."

"This was different." Liam shook his fist. "Boys pulled my pants down in the restroom, threw garbage at me when I walked home, and laughed at me in class. They thought they were better than me. For a long time, I believed them. One day, when no one was home, I tried to hang myself. My dad came home early and found me hanging by my tie from the ceiling fan. Paramedics saved my life."

"I'm sorry," Timothy said. "I remember walking home from school one day with some kids that were supposedly my friends, telling them about a girl I liked. They saw the girl coming towards us, so they lifted me up and put me in the trashcan. They thought it would be funny to humiliate me in front of her. When she saw me, she laughed. It broke my heart."

Liam sat forward. "Did you want to kill her?"

"What?" Timothy sputtered, nearly spilling his coffee. "No, of course not."

"Why not?" Liam shrugged. "She deserved to die. They all did. They had no right to think they were better than us."

"Oh, come on. They were just kids. Anything that happened when we were kids, for better or worse, made us who we are today."

"How could it have been for the better, Tim?"

"Maybe that's why I became a therapist," Timothy said. "Because of my own pain, I now want to help people."

"Helping people will get you nowhere." Liam sat back and slurped his coffee. "It's a dog-eat-dog world. The world is filled with people only looking out for themselves, just like those kids in school. They'll put anyone down to get ahead. It's time to prove ourselves to this world. In Greek mythology, Perseus wasn't glorified for being a good man. He was disrespected by King Polydectes until he came back with the head of Medusa.

Perseus had to show that he was powerful enough to slay a monster before he was shown respect."

"It's too late to fix those things," Timothy replied. "What's done is done. We can only move forward and accept who we are. My brother, Derek, lives in Manchester with his wife and daughter in a large suburban house with two cars. He's the CEO of a canning company. They supply cans to beer and tinned food companies all over the country. It sounds like a random field to become rich in, and that's because it is. Derek was never particularly smart, but he was always determined to get to the top of anything he could. He's successful because that's just who he is. He was on the baseball team at school and always had a girlfriend. Now, he has a beautiful wife who adores him and cooks all his meals. His daughter gets good grades, is well behaved, and is on the rowing team. They refuse to visit because Derek can't stand how Elaine speaks to me. He thinks I'm spineless, and he's right. Even as children, he always stood up to our father, while I couldn't. When I expressed interest in joining the dancing club, my dad told me to join the football club instead, and I did so even though I despised it. That's simply who I am."

"It's not too late to change that," Liam said. "We can be whoever we want to be. We just need to make a stand for it. In this world, if we don't stand up for ourselves, we wither away. Do you remember what made the bullies in school different from us? How did they know they were stronger?"

Timothy shrugged.

"They just sensed it, like animals knowing the dominant one of the herd. After we've been the deciders of life and death, everyone will sense that we too are powerful. Even Elaine will show you the respect you deserve."

Timothy wondered if he and Elaine could ever truly be happy again, like they were before his operation and impotency. Since then, she had resented him and made his life a misery. He had realized how worthless he was, and that everything those kids in school had said was true. They were the reason he couldn't stand up to his wife. Their words still bounced around in his head. Now, he had to decide if killing an innocent woman would change all that. Would another person's death really make him feel better about himself? It would certainly make him feel powerful.

Timothy nodded and Liam went back to peering through his binoculars. It was too late to turn back now, Timothy told himself. They had come too far.

"Choose who you want," he said. "It doesn't matter to me."

"You know exactly who I want," Liam said with a smile.

Timothy nodded, knowing exactly who Liam had in mind. He turned his gaze to the playground, where Clementine Stannard was pushing her son on the swings. Their target had been chosen, and they were now ready for the hunt.

NOVEMBER 5TH, 10:32 PM

As Chloe's eyes fluttered open, dizziness overtook her. She attempted to steady her head, but found her hands strapped tightly behind her back. Her surroundings slowly came into focus—a dimly lit basement that she recognized from the newspapers as the same one where Clementine Stannard had been found murdered. Blood that hadn't washed away still stained the stone floors.

A single light bulb hung lazily from the ceiling, illuminating specks of dust in the air and utter emptiness. Apart from the chair holding her captive, there was no other furniture in sight.

A figure paced around the edge of the light. Momentarily, a face materialized from the shadows, and Chloe recognized Timothy. She then remembered; he had struck her across the head with the bloody baton. He was mumbling something to himself, but she couldn't quite make it out. Uttering something about making someone—*her*—pay, and she thought she heard him say his wife's name. Suddenly, it all came back to her. She was crossing the park to get to the inn, to find Gregg, and tell him about her father recovering from his stroke. Then, Timothy had appeared, instructing her not to scream this time and calling her Elaine.

"Dr. Holst, what's going on?" she said.

Timothy halted in his tracks and turned to face her. He came under the light towards her, revealing his enlarged eyes and sweat beads dripping down his face. He appeared completely deranged, like the killer from a horror movie, rather than the friendly therapist she knew.

"We're finally going to sit down and talk about it," Timothy whispered.

"Talk about what?"

"You know what," he spat in pure fury. "We loved each other once, Elaine. I moved to this town for you. I gave up my practice for you. I want to talk about when and why you came to hate me so much. I'm sorry I couldn't give you a child, but I didn't deserve this. I didn't deserve to live this life. I was disappointed too, but even after we adopted Juliet, your resentment never stopped. I deserve so much more."

Chloe stared back at him, completely at a loss as to what to say.

He roared in her face like a demented animal. "Answer me!"

"Dr. Holst," she cried. "I'm not Elaine. It's me, Chloe!"

Timothy's eyes narrowed in on her, and he fell to his knees. "Miss Mason?"

"Yes!"

Timothy buried his head into his hands and started to cry. After wiping his face, he surveyed the basement as if seeing it for the first time, appearing as bewildered and frightened as she was.

"Dr. Holst, what's going on?"

"I'm so sorry, Miss Mason." The therapist went back to whispering. "You must be quiet, or he'll hear us."

56

MARC KNEW HE MIGHT NEVER EARN CHLOE'S FORGIVENESS. THEY had been childhood friends, and he had betrayed her trust and their friendship by putting her in a cell. He had thought it was her who had betrayed their friendship by allowing them to drift apart and by dating Liam when she knew how he felt about her, but what he did had been far worse. He hoped more than anything that they could be friends again, even if that was all they could ever be.

It was getting late, so Marc locked the sheriff's station. He needed to go home and get some sleep. He would call Gregg Hunter the following day and discuss avenues for investigating Richard O'Doyle.

However, before retiring for the night, Marc decided to pay a visit to Chloe's house to apologize again. He knocked on her door, but there was no response. He stepped back and scanned the windows. There were no lights on. Marc looked at his watch —10:43 PM. Chloe never went to bed this early. Even when they were kids, she was a night owl.

The inn would be closed by now, but maybe Chloe was spending the night with Hunter. He stared across the park towards the inn but could see no lights coming from that direction either.

By the side of the park, there was a light that caught his attention. It was from the empty home a few houses down, where Clementine Stannard was found murdered in the basement. The sitting room curtains were open, and a lamp was switched on.

Could it be Clementine's killer, back at the scene of the crime? Impossible. Everything pointed to Liam being the killer. Even Hunter had agreed with that. Some kids had probably broken in. Or maybe the real estate agent had been and forgot to switch the light off. Marc pushed Chloe from his mind for now and went to investigate the house. Maybe he was overreacting.

He opened the garden gate and walked across the lawn. The garden was brimming with flowers placed there in honor of the mayor's wife. No wonder the real estate agent hadn't been able to sell it.

He jolted in fright as his phone vibrated in his pocket. He shakily slid it out. "Hello?"

"Sheriff Chips," a woman's voice replied. "It's Elaine Holst."

"How can I help you, Mrs. Holst?"

"I'm calling because I'm worried about my husband."

Marc reached the front porch and peered into the window of the house. There was no one there. "Why is that, Mrs. Holst?"

"Well, I'm not sure if you've heard, but we separated this morning."

"I'm sorry to hear that."

"I just received some disturbing messages," she said. "He seems incredibly angry, and I'm afraid he might hurt me."

"Did he say he was going to hurt you, Mrs. Holst?" Marc's foot kicked something on the porch. He bent down and picked it up—a gray, wooly hat. It was Chloe's. He remembered her wearing it last winter at the inn's Christmas party.

"In the messages, he said I was going to *end up like that other bitch*."

"I don't understand," Marc replied. "Who do you think your husband was referring to?"

"These messages are so graphic. He talks about smashing faces over and over again. I see now I didn't really know my husband. There was a darkness inside him I never saw. When I evicted him from the house, something in him seemed to snap. He started screaming at me from our garden. It made me flash back to the night that Clementine Stannard was killed and think how strangely my husband was behaving back then. I'm beginning to consider something that I never would have imagined."

Marc dropped Chloe's hat to the ground and felt his heart flutter. "What's that, Mrs. Holst?"

"Sheriff, I think my husband is the killer you're looking for."

Marc hung up. He wanted to scream for Chloe but stopped himself. If she was inside, there was no time to waste. He drew the pistol from his holster and slowly turned the door's handle.

57

CHLOE KNEW SHE HAD TO KEEP CALM. THERE WAS A WAY OUT OF this, and she had to be smart enough to find it if she valued her life. Maybe Timothy could be reasoned with. He didn't seem to entirely know what he was doing.

If she antagonized Timothy, he might lash out. He might even have been the one who killed Clementine Stannard, but she tried not to think about that. She had to show him she was different from his wife.

Chloe took a deep breath. "Dr. Holst, what do you mean he'll hear us?"

"I meant the voice inside my head," Timothy cried. "I haven't been myself lately. My mind is falling apart. A violent side of me takes over, and I can't control it. All this anger I've bolted up explodes. I don't know what's happening to me. Ever since that awful thing, I've been going into dazes and losing all restraint. It started the day Clementine Stannard died. Then, I started destroying my wife's garden, and things have only got worse from there."

"What awful thing, Dr. Holst?" Chloe asked. "What did you do?"

Timothy stared at her, tears streaming down his face. He

struggled to get the words out as though they were stuck in his throat. "Liam came to me and asked me to help him kill Clementine Stannard," he whispered hoarsely. "I didn't want any part in it, but he was involved with some dangerous people that wanted him to kill someone. He wanted to prove he could do it. He wanted the power, and so did I. He knew exactly what to say to me. Liam attacked Mrs. Stannard when she was out on her run and dragged her back in the night to this very basement. He brought a bunch of tools from his father's carpenter shed and said we were going to kill her together. But I couldn't do it, so I left. I left her alone with him. I saw the nail gun in his hand, and I left her to die anyway."

"You need help, Dr. Holst," Chloe said, as gently as she possibly could, trying desperately to mask her fear.

"Yes, I know." Timothy sat on the ground and grabbed hold of his head, cradling it back and forth. "My stress only got worse once that private investigator arrived. I began to have a nervous breakdown."

Chloe realized she had to reason with him before he lost control of himself again. "You need to let me go. Please, Dr. Holst. We can go and get help together."

Timothy moved his hands away from his face and looked at her. "Will you really help me?"

"I won't leave your side until you get the help you need," she promised.

Timothy stood and untied the knots behind her back. Chloe felt the ropes loosen and slip away from her arms, falling to the ground.

"I'm so sorry, Miss Mason." He stood there, trembling. "I never meant to hurt you. Not you. Not ever."

Chloe stood and grabbed his shaking hand. "I know, Dr. Holst. I don't believe you could hurt anyone. You've helped so many people in this town, including me. When I was struggling with my anger towards my father, you were the only one who was there for me. You helped me cope and showed me I needed to find acceptance and belonging. But you need help. Just like I did."

Chloe wiped the tears from her therapist's eyes, and then led him to the basement's staircase.

"I'm so ashamed, Miss Mason," Timothy said. "I must have really scared you."

They stepped up the stairs together. "If you promise me you'll commit to getting help, I'll forgive you."

"I promise I will."

"Can I ask you something, Dr. Holst?"

"Of course," he said. "You can ask me anything."

"You were the only friend Liam ever had, so I wanted to know if he ever talked to you about me."

Timothy nodded.

"Did he love me?" she asked. "He dragged me along for years, and treated me so badly, but I put up with it all because I thought he loved me, and I need to know if he ever did."

"Liam didn't love anyone other than himself. I'm sorry, Miss Mason, but he was a narcissist who couldn't emotionally connect with anyone. However, the human mind is never textbook, and I believe Liam really did care for you in his own way."

"Thank you for telling me that, Dr. Holst."

"You're welcome."

Chloe creaked open the door at the top of the staircase, and they stepped into the sitting room. Marc was standing there. He aimed his gun towards them. His eyes firmly locked on Timothy.

"Step away from her!" Marc ordered.

"Marc, you don't understand," Chloe tried to explain.

"He brought you here." Marc didn't lower his gun an inch. "Just like he brought Clementine Stannard here before he killed her."

"That's not what happened," Chloe argued. "Liam killed Clementine, not Timothy."

"I may not be as smart as Gregg Hunter, but I can put these

pieces together, Chloe. Now, step back and let me make this arrest."

Chloe took a step back from the therapist.

"Put your arms in the air!" Marc stepped towards him.

Timothy did what he was told, and Marc reached for the handcuffs on his belt. His quaking hand struggled to unhook them. His eyes darted up and down, from the handcuffs to Timothy, until he eventually released the cuffs from his belt.

"Don't move." Marc grabbed Timothy by the arms and placed them behind his back. "My dad hit my mom, and it gave me problems. Chloe knows that too well. But hurting other people is taking your problems too far. There's no excuse for what you've done. No real man hurts women because he's too sick to deal with his own issues. You're no man."

Chloe saw something snap in Timothy's eyes. They enlarged. Timothy curled his mouth and went red. Before Marc could slide on the cuffs, Timothy spun around and kneed Marc in the gut. Marc gasped in pain and fell to his knees.

"Dr. Holst," Chloe screamed. "Stop!"

Timothy yanked the gun from Marc's grip, then violently smacked Marc across the head with it, knocking him cold.

Chloe made a desperate dash for the door, but then she heard the cocking of the gun and Timothy yelled for her to stop. She halted in her tracks. There was no convincing Timothy to let her go now, she realized, and she could no longer mask her fear, not when the tears streamed down her face.

58

In the second that Sheriff Chips told him he wasn't a man, Timothy's life flashed before his eyes. He remembered himself as a young boy, telling his father he wanted to start dance classes. Instead, his father insisted he join the football team, to which Timothy agreed.

Years later, he told his brother, Derek, about a girl he was dating from his apartment building. Elaine was his first serious girlfriend, but Derek told him to propose, because he might not meet another girl. After doing as his brother suggested, Elaine told him she wanted to move back to her hometown in Vermont, so Timothy closed his private practice in New Hampshire and moved to Blackberry Cove with her. There, he was told that there were complications with his prostate surgery, and he had been rendered impotent. When the doctor said those words, he felt his wife's hand slip away from his own. They were never the same again.

Standing across from Chloe Mason, Timothy could feel his blood boil and the pressure inside his head skyrocket. It was as though his insides wanted to explode. He wanted to scream to the heavens as loud as he could and let everything out. Instead, he held the gun up to Chloe's face and checked through the window to make sure Sheriff Chips had come alone. He closed the curtains once he saw no one else on the street.

"Please, Dr. Holst, there is still a way out of this," Chloe cried.

"No, there isn't." He shook his head. "Not after what I've done."

"I don't understand," Chloe said. "You told me Liam killed Clementine, and you ran off because you wanted no part in it."

"Liam shot at Mrs. Stannard with the nail gun, but he couldn't go through with killing her," Timothy explained. "He realized, after all his talk, that he just didn't have the stomach for murder. Not like me. One of the nails from his gun got stuck in her windpipe and she was choking on her own blood. The sight made him vomit. He was a coward. He chased me down the street and brought me back to the basement. He begged me to finish her off, and then left me alone with her. She was already dying, so I had no option but to put her out of her misery. I lifted the baton Liam had left behind. I pretended she was my wife. Once I pictured Elaine's face, killing her was easy. I beat her with the baton, again, and again, until there was nothing of her face left."

Chloe's own face turned pale. "Why would you do that, Dr. Holst?"

"I did it because I was the strong one, not Liam. No one has ever seen who I really am. My whole life, people have doubted me. They should have come to me and asked me to kill for them, not Liam."

"Who's them?" Chloe asked.

"I don't know," Dr. Holst replied. "But they thought Liam was strong and wanted him to do their dirty work. They should have come to me instead. After tonight, everyone will know what I'm capable of, and no one will ever see me as weak again."

"I never thought you were weak," Chloe said. "You helped me when no one else would. You were my hero."

She's lying. She's the same as the sheriff. Neither of them thinks I'm a man. They both think I'm weak, but I'll show them.

"I don't wanna hurt Miss Mason," he whispered.

No one will respect me until I stand up for myself.

Timothy grabbed his head. It was happening. He couldn't control it. "I don't want to hurt her."

I have to kill her.

"She doesn't deserve this."

She has to pay!

"Dr. Holst, who are you talking to?" Chloe asked.

"You think I'm weak," he said. "You're just like Elaine."

"No, that's not true. You're my friend."

"I want more than a friend," he yelled. "I want to feel like a man again."

"I don't understand," she said.

"I told you about my operation," he reminded her, "and that there were complications."

Chloe nodded. "I remember."

"The doctors said that, under the right circumstances and with enough time, I might regain feeling. I knew it would never happen with Elaine. During our sessions, I thought a lot about you, Miss Mason. As you lay on my couch and asked for my help, you made me feel powerful and good about myself. I wanted you in a way I never wanted Elaine."

Chloe stepped back, wrinkling her face in disgust. Timothy felt his chest tighten. Chloe was like the girl who had mocked him in high school, and like Elaine when she rejected him. They were all the same.

"They're going to lock me up," he said. "I've longed for you for so long, and now I want you before it's too late. I want to show you how much of a man I can be."

Chloe shook her head. "Please, don't do this, Dr. Holst."

Elaine was right. I'm weak.

"No!"

Pathetic.

"Shut up!"

Worthless.

Timothy slapped the sides of his head with his own palms. "Stop it! I said shut up! Shut the fuck up!"

"Dr. Holst, you're scaring me," Chloe cried.

She won't.

"She doesn't have to."

I'll never feel like a man again.

"I can't force her."

A true man would take what he wants.

"I am a man."

I'm not a man.

"I am a man!"

Then prove it!

Timothy pulled Chloe forward by the arm, causing her to squeal. He pressed the gun against her forehead. "Take your clothes off and get on the fucking couch."

59

ONCE GREGG WAS FINALLY REUNITED WITH HIS DAUGHTER, HE KNEW things would have to be different. Now that he was all she had, he would need to be there for her. Gregg always swore he'd be a better father than his own, but he hadn't been.

He had just spoken with Rachel about meeting to exchange the body for Silvia. A tear spilled from his eye at the thought of holding his daughter again. It seemed like he had cried more in the past few weeks than he had in his whole lifetime. Bernard must have noticed because he soon felt a pat on the shoulder. Gregg wiped his face and explained, "I'm fine. Just, the thought of finally seeing my daughter again is pretty overwhelming."

"I'm happy for you," Bernard said.

Gregg smiled. "I hope you get answers when this is all over. You deserve to get justice for your wife. This must have been torture for her family."

"Flora had no family. All we had was each other."

Gregg slid the cell into his pocket. "Rachel wants to meet us at the end of the road with the construction site. She's bringing Silvia with her."

Bernard nodded, deep in thought. He examined the chest

containing Liam's remains, then unbuttoned his plaid shirt to reveal a sweat-soaked gray undershirt.

"Are you alright?" Gregg asked.

"I'm just nervous." Bernard forked his hand through his wavy hair. "How are we going to get there from here? My car won't make it off-road through the woods, and it'll take hours to drive back to town and then back into the woods."

Hannah stepped forward, holding out her car keys and offering her truck. They wasted no time accepting her offer. Gregg and Bernard hauled the trunk into the back of the truck and then jumped into the backseats, while Hannah started the vehicle and Richard got into the passenger seat. They took off across the mud, with Hannah strategically avoiding the trees in their path.

"I didn't mean to eavesdrop," Hannah said, "but I didn't know you had a daughter. Richard and I have been wanting a child for so long. Now this mess is finally over, maybe we can finally focus on that."

"It'll be the best decision you ever make," Gregg told them. "I freaked out when I found out we were expecting. We were so young, so I was totally against it right from the start, convinced that this child would ruin my life. But from the moment the nurse put little Silvia in my arms, I was in love."

Hannah reached for Richard's hand and the two seemed to be holding back tears. "Thank you for sharing that," she said. "Once you get her back, I hope you come and visit. I'd love to meet her."

"He'll be back to visit Chloe Mason." Bernard smiled slyly at Gregg.

"I didn't realize you were seeing each other."

"We're not," Gregg said. "She's been helping me get my daughter back. It'll be nice for her and Silvia to finally meet."

"She's a special girl," Bernard remarked. "Take care of her."

"Are you both friends?" Gregg asked. "You were both having a drink together at the inn the night I came to town, but then I never saw you talking with each other again. Whenever I'm around, you both look as though you're trying to ignore each other. Why? Did something happen between you two?"

"We were never involved, but it bothered me when she was with Liam. She deserved better."

"You?"

Bernard stroked his wedding ring. "No, not me. I realized a long time ago that I don't love like most men. All my life I've been blind to all but one woman. I've been in a trance the past seven years, still in love with a dead woman. But Chloe knew herself that she deserved better than Liam. She was just so longing for acceptance. Who can blame her after what her father did?"

Gregg leaned forward. "What are you talking about?"

"Let's just say, she had a difficult childhood. I'm sure she'll tell you herself when the time is right."

Before anyone could say anything more, the truck suddenly jolted to a stop.

"What's wrong?" Gregg asked.

"We're stuck!" Hannah exclaimed.

They all exited the vehicle to find the tires completely fixed into wet mud. Hannah got back into the driver's seat and floored it, but it was no use.

"You guys okay with pushing?" Richard asked as though it was a joke.

Gregg and Bernard weren't laughing however, and they walked around to the back of the truck to do just that.

60

RACHEL GOT OUT OF THE VAN WITH HER FOUR ARMED SUBORDINATES, all sporting their usual black. At the back of the van, Silvia was gagged and bound. Rachel opened the door and gently slid the gag off her mouth and the rope off her blotched wrists and ankles.

"Is my dad here?" Silvia asked.

"Not yet," she replied. "Sorry, kiddo."

"You are sorry, aren't you?"

Rachel crossed her arms. "What are you talking about?"

"I mean that this is just a job for you," Silvia said, "and that you don't want to do the awful things you're doing."

Rachel smirked. "Don't try and get me, kid."

"I'm not. And I don't forgive you either. You cut off my finger, and you burned me, but you're working with some scary people, and they don't seem like the kind of people you cross."

"Sweetheart, I am one of those people," she reminded her.

"Are you?"

Rachel averted her gaze. "Think of a nice memory, kiddo. Hold onto it. This will all be over soon."

Silvia closed her eyes and appeared to think.

"You got one?"

The girl nodded. "When I was seven, my family and I went on our first vacation to Acadia National Park. I had never left Boston before then or been somewhere so quiet. It was so beautiful, and the stars were incredible. A little like here. The best part was just sitting around the fire or sleeping in the tent. It felt as though my dad, mom, and I were the only people in the whole world. I kept begging my dad for years to take me back there, but he was always too busy. Maybe, when we finally reunite, we could go back there."

"Now I get you," Rachel said. "You're someone who holds hope and dreams about the future."

"You don't?"

"I live for the moment. I don't think about the future, because in my work, there might not be one."

Her phone vibrated—a text from Gregg.

"Who is it?" Silvia asked.

"Your dad. He seems to be having some car trouble and wants me to meet him elsewhere."

"Are you going to take me with you?"

"No," Rachel replied after a pause. "You'll wait here."

She ordered one of her men to put the girl back in the van and keep a close eye on her. With the wind picking up, Rachel zipped up her biker jacket and led her other three subordinates into the woods. She dialed Fury's number on her cell phone to update him on the situation.

"Milgram?" he answered.

"I'm going to meet Hunter."

"This better not be another trick. It's Hunter's last chance when it comes to the case of Liam Watts. If he doesn't deliver, silence him and whatever witnesses are unfortunate enough to be around at the time. Understand? I'll go take care of the girl."

"And what if he does arrive with the body?"

"We leave no witnesses," he said, as cold as ever.

She knew she was wasting her breath in trying to reason with him, but she found herself attempting to do so anyway. "If we let

Hunter and his daughter live, he won't tell anyone about us. He just wants his daughter back."

"It's an unnecessary risk," Fury said. "He knows too much, and so does the girl. Don't be going soft, Milgram."

Rachel took a deep breath. "Never."

61

GREGG ATTEMPTED TO PUSH THE O'DOYLES' TRUCK FORWARD WITH Bernard and Richard as Hannah pressed down on the accelerator, but it wouldn't budge.

"Crap! Rachel is probably waiting!" Gregg exclaimed.

Bernard massaged his forehead with his trembling hands. "How far away are we from the road? We could take the chest and carry it to Rachel."

"Not far," Richard replied.

Gregg nodded in agreement. He hauled the trunk from the back of the truck. Something rattled inside and he opened the lid to investigate. There were some truck keys and a wallet inside. Gregg opened the wallet, finding photographs of Rachel and Fury outside Liam's cabin. They clearly didn't know they were being photographed in the pictures.

"I think he was one of them," Gregg said aloud.

"Who?" Richard came over.

"Liam. I think he worked for the people who hired me."

"Does that help you figure out who killed him?"

"I'm not sure yet," Gregg replied.

"There's another reason I thought Hannah was the killer that I forgot to mention earlier," Richard said.

"What is it?"

"I only just remembered; when I heard the gunshot outside the house, our dog was still out there. Sparky barks at almost everyone, but he was silent when I went outside."

"He didn't bark at the killer?" Gregg asked.

Richard shook his head. "It made me think it must have been Hannah out there, but I guess the dog was probably just too terrified to bark."

"Or maybe your dog knew the killer," Gregg said. "It might not have been you or Hannah, but it could have been someone who visits the inn every day. Always brings a dog biscuit."

Richard squinted his eyes. "Bernard?"

Gregg nodded and scanned around them, but it was only then that he noticed Bernard was missing. He called the outdoorsman's name, but there was no sign of him. Gregg reached for his phone, but it too was gone.

62

BERNARD HAD A KNACK FOR REMEMBERING CONVERSATIONS. IT didn't matter whether it happened yesterday or ten years ago, he could play them back in his head word for word. Like an actor learning a script, all he had to do was rehearse the lines to himself. Given his penchant for solitude, he had ample time to do so. He was lucky that way, because it meant he would never forget the conversations he had with his wife. It didn't matter whether it was a discussion about having a child or a conversation about their favorite movies, he remembered every single word and pause she ever made. However, the most important words he ever spoke to her were the ones he uttered after her death, promising to find her killer.

Dedicating the past seven years of his life to finding Flora's killer had not been a difficult commitment. All of his life he had been driven by obsession. When he discovered he loved hiking and the outdoors, he let it consume almost all of his identity. If he came across a topic he found interesting, he wanted to know everything about it. In his career, he had forced himself to be the best he could be. It was as if without obsession, he could not function.

Flora was always so dedicated to others, she deserved his

dedication to finding out who killed her. Though she had worked in an office, her dream had been to become a psychologist and to help others turn their lives around as she had once done for herself. When Bernard met her at college, she was paying her fees by working night shifts at a call center, without any scholarship or help from parents. The worst part was not knowing why she had been taken from the world. She was too caring and innocent to have enemies, and she lived a normal life. Flora had always said he was too good for her, but it was only because she was unable to fully see the best in herself.

Bernard tossed Gregg's phone to the ground and pulled the revolver from behind his back. Ahead was the car he had already parked, ready at the spot where he would meet Rachel. She was there, along with three of her goons, waiting for Gregg to arrive. Instead, she was about to meet him, finally.

Bernard took shelter behind a nearby tree and tossed a pebble back the way he'd come to lure them out. As he hoped, Rachel sent two of her men to investigate. Once they passed him, he raised his gun and swiftly shot them both in the back of their heads.

The last of Rachel's men came dashing over. He was quicker. Bernard dropped to the ground, barely avoiding a bullet that whizzed over his head. Bernard fired directly at the man's chest, aiming for his heart. Behind the fallen goon, Bernard locked eyes with Rachel. He aimed his revolver as she took cover behind the trunk of the car. She took out her own gun and pivoted around the car to shoot, but Bernard was faster and got her in the leg.

Bernard raced over and pinned Rachel to the ground before she could get back to her feet. He wrapped his arm around her neck.

"Did you have a part in killing her?" he asked in her ear.

Rachel hoarsely hissed from her chokehold, "What are you talking about? Who are you?"

Bernard pulled her own gun from her hand and placed it in

his pocket. "I know all about what you people do, so don't try denying it. Did you know Flora Neumann?"

"I don't know what you're talking about."

Bernard pressed his revolver against her skull. "Then you'll take me to someone who does."

63

As he raced through the forest, yelling Bernard's name, Gregg couldn't help but think back to the watch he stepped on underneath the mat at Liam's cabin. Bernard had placed it there. Not for Gregg, but for Rachel and Fury. Bernard had been waiting for them. He had killed Liam to lure them out, knowing they'd look into the death of one of their own. Unfortunately for him, Richard O'Doyle had hidden the body, making things much more difficult.

Fury, and maybe even Rachel, clearly had something to do with Flora's death, and Bernard would stop at nothing to get answers. Gregg needed Rachel if he was going to get his daughter back. More than that, if anything happened to her, the people she worked with might blame Gregg and come after him. He couldn't allow Bernard to do anything that might jeopardize his daughter's safety.

In a small clearing, there was a car parked ahead. Before that, three fresh corpses. Gregg guessed from their black outfits they were Rachel's goons. He had heard five gunshots, so Gregg kept his eyes peeled for more bodies.

Suddenly, Bernard's voice boomed, warning Gregg to reveal himself, or else he would shoot Rachel. Gregg cautiously emerged from the bushes, raising his hands in surrender. Bernard had his gun pointed at Rachel's head, while his other arm was wrapped tightly around her throat. Blood was oozing from a gunshot wound on her leg.

"Don't get in my way, Gregg."

"What are you doing?"

"She needs to take me to Fury. He killed my wife, I'm sure of it!"

Gregg took a step forward, his hands still raised. "If you harm her, they'll never give me my daughter back. I'm sorry about your wife, Bernard, but I can't let you choose revenge over my daughter's life."

"They were never going to let you or your daughter live once they had what they wanted," Bernard replied. "The only way for you to be free of these people is to kill them."

Gregg didn't say anything; he already feared that was probably true.

"After I saw Fury that day in Blackberry Cove, I kept close tabs on Liam. One night, I found him approaching the O'Doyles' home with a knife in his hand, so I confronted him. As it turned out, Fury had not long ago recruited him into his circle of professional killers."

Rachel attempted to wriggle free, but Bernard tightened his grasp and told her to stop, then continued, "Liam had the darkest of longings, but before joining, he had to prove himself by committing and getting away with murder. It's hard to imagine how anyone could accept such a job offer, isn't it? Liam didn't know anything about these people, but he wanted to join them because they were killers, just like he wanted to be. It's ironic; he was delusional enough to think that killing someone would make him feel powerful, but the very fact that he selected victims he didn't think would fight back shows what a coward he was."

"He was going to kill Hannah?" Gregg asked, and he noticed Rachel averting her gaze.

"Yes, he told me as much outside their house," Bernard said. "He was going to kill her to prove himself. I told him that I needed to get to these people, but he said he had no way of contacting them. They told him they'd be in touch only after he had killed his first victim. He suggested that if I wanted to get close, I should step aside, let him kill Hannah O'Doyle, and then wait for them to show up. I told him I had another idea."

"You shot him instead." Gregg already knew how the story ended. "Then you waited for them to investigate his death."

"They have been recruiting people from the small towns in these woods for decades. Once they're hired, they get a new alias and they're trained in the art of killing."

"You still haven't figured out anything, have you?" Rachel scoffed.

"What do you mean?" Gregg asked.

"Liam was asked specifically to murder Clementine Stannard."

"Why?"

"Nathan killed my mother. I wanted him to pay for it. Death would be too good for that bastard. I wanted him framed for his second wife's death so he would spend the rest of his life in prison. That's what Liam was meant to do, but he went totally off memo."

"Your mother?" But then Gregg realized. "*You're* Emilie Jones."

"Bingo," Rachel said. "Took you long enough to recognize me. So much for my case being so important to you. You never even checked on me."

"Is that why you kidnapped my daughter and hired me? You're angry I never checked on you?"

"You thought you saved me!" she yelled. "You were even promoted to a detective because of it. What a joke that was. After Nathan killed my mother, I was sent to live with a father who let his brother rape and abuse me. Then after you *saved* me from that hell, I went to foster care. One foster home after another. All my life I went from one monster to another, while you patted yourself on the back and called yourself my hero."

"I'm sorry," Gregg said. "I had no idea."

"Of course you didn't, because you never looked back. You only looked forward to the career you wanted so badly. I was only a stepping-stone for you, and a story you could tell. Fury offered me a true family. An alliance."

"Fury hired you from the foster home?"

Rachel nodded. "Fury has a talent for locating lost souls. He offered me a thousand dollars for my first kill. What job do you know when you get a thousand dollars for one day's work? And without an education, what job was I going to get anyway? Liam wanted to join us, but he failed."

"Then why did finding his body matter so much?"

"We needed to know who killed him."

"And if Nathan had killed him for killing his wife, you might still have been able to send him to prison," Gregg said, things finally making sense.

"Enough of this," Bernard said. "I want to know why my wife was killed. Take me to Fury."

"That'll never happen." Rachel slammed her elbow into Bernard's ribs and wriggled free from his grasp. With her good leg, she kicked him to the ground, then turned and ran. You would never guess she had a bullet in her leg.

Bernard stood and aimed his gun but lowered it once Rachel trailed off the road and startled to hobble. Apparently, there was only so much pain even she could take.

"I'll get her," Bernard said, stepping forward.

"What about my daughter?"

Bernard tossed him Rachel's gun. "She's in a van further down the road. Let's go get her back."

64

CHLOE COULD NOT TAKE HER EYES AWAY FROM THE THERAPIST. SHE felt if she broke that connection, she might die. The pulsing in her ears was so loud she could barely hear her own breathing. Her leg muscles tightened, ready to run the second he lowered his gun. It was the only way she was getting out of this unharmed. The sheriff lay unconscious at her feet. Beneath her was the basement where Timothy had beaten Clementine to death. Chloe could not stop her mind from thinking about those things anymore. It was suddenly all too real that she was probably going to die that night.

He wasn't going to touch her, she kept telling herself. She wouldn't allow it. She'd go down screaming and kicking, and he'd have to kill her to keep her quiet. That was preferable to him doing anything else to her. After her father's stroke, she promised herself no one would ever lay a hand on her again, and she intended to honor that promise no matter what.

"Why are you doing this, Dr. Holst?" She could feel the dryness in her throat as she spoke. "Why are you so angry?"

"My entire life, I did everything right," Timothy said. "I did well in school and when bullies hit me, I didn't hit them back. I suppressed. I respected my father and followed all his rules, even when he was wrong. I've been polite and kind my whole life and devoted myself to helping others. Whenever people bumped into me on the street, cut me off on the road, or made jokes about my height and balding hair in the back of the grocery line, I just let it slide. I suppressed. I was a devoted husband and father, providing everything I could for my family, yet they gave me nothing in return. And still, I suppressed."

"I'm sure it's not too late to get your family back."

"I don't want them back," Timothy yelled. "My life was miserable. I was trapped in darkness and never appreciated. All I want is to feel powerful and respected. When Clementine looked into my eyes in her final moments, she knew that I held her life in my hands. For those few seconds, nothing was more important than me. It felt so good to have that power, to feel the blood pumping through my veins. I want you to look into my eyes and feel the same. I want you to obey my every command."

"This isn't the real you." Chloe shook her head and sprayed her tears. "This is the violent side that you spoke of. But you can still fight it, Dr. Holst."

Timothy stepped towards her, his eyes ice cold. "When I was little, my father told me a story about a fisherman who took his bagpipes to the river and played, hoping the fish would dance in response to his music. The fish did not dance. They ignored his orders. So, he cast his net and drew out the fish from the water. Then, with the fish as his prisoners, the fisherman played his bagpipes. Within the net, they flopped and flopped in tune with the melody. 'They dance now when I play,' the fisherman declared happily. The fish danced finally, because when you are in a man's power, you do as he bids."

Chloe backed against the wall, sobbing uncontrollably. She wanted to scream and beg him not to touch her, but she felt frozen. Her throat was so dry that nothing came out. Timothy leaned in close, taking a deep breath to inhale her scent. Chloe felt sick to her stomach.

Timothy pocketed his gun and removed her gloves, then slid

off her jacket and dropped it to the ground. He seized her flannel shirt and tore off the buttons, sending them flying across the room.

Chloe let out a terrified shriek. "Please, Dr. Holst, don't do this."

"Pull your pants down," he ordered in a deep whisper.

She tried so hard to shake her head but in fear of defying him, she found herself unable to move.

"Pull your fucking pants down," he roared. Timothy removed his own buttoned shirt and unbuckled his belt, allowing his slacks to drop to his ankles.

Chloe cried and slid down her jeans to the boots below her knees. She gasped for breath as he grabbed her from behind and pushed their bodies together. He ran his hands across her back, unhooking her bra.

"I'm in control now, aren't I?" he asked.

"Dr. Holst…"

"Answer me!"

She nodded, disgusted with herself for agreeing.

Timothy caressed her face, his breath hot against her skin. "This is how it's supposed to be. I give the orders and they're obeyed. Now it's time for what's owed to me."

He pulled her from the wall and threw her down onto the couch. She shrieked in fright, but quickly controlled herself, not wishing to fuel his rage. Timothy crawled onto the couch after her, and his face hovered above. Chloe turned away and looked at the glass coffee table at the side of the couch. There was a way out of this. She had to be smart and find a way. She needed something heavy to hit him with, but there was nothing atop the table.

Timothy grabbed her chin and straightened her face, then kissed her. His eyes alighted with passion, and she could feel the bulge in his underwear.

Timothy grinned at her. "I feel something."

Chloe kneed him heavily in the groin and the therapist

gasped in pain. She tossed him off and flipped him from the couch, sending him crashing through the glass coffee table, which shattered into pieces.

As Timothy struggled to get up, groaning in agony from the shards of glass embedded in his skin, Chloe quickly pulled up her jeans and sprinted towards the nearby basement door. Timothy roared in frustration and limped after her, with a sharp piece of glass still lodged in his right leg.

As he followed her through the basement door, Chloe crouched around the corner, extending her foot to trip him. He stumbled and hurtled forward, rolling down the staircase. With a sickening snap, his leg broke upon impact with the concrete floor at the bottom, eliciting a piercing scream that echoed against the stone walls. His gun tumbled from his pocket and skidded across the floor as he writhed in agony. He started crawling towards it, but soon gave up. Instead, he cradled his broken leg and moaned in pain.

"I'm going to wake the sheriff," she said.

"You dumb bitch," Timothy muttered under his breath, and she halted in her tracks.

Chloe stepped down the staircase and loomed over the helpless therapist. "What did you call me?"

Timothy stared back and tried to disguise his fear and anger, but he just couldn't. Instead, he stammered like a broken coffee machine.

Chloe shouted through gritted teeth, "What did you call me?"

Before he could say anything more, she ripped the shard of glass from his leg, producing a chilling scream. She held it against his neck.

"Do you know how Liam died?" she asked.

Timothy shook his head.

"Liam was going to murder Hannah O'Doyle, but he was shot first by Bernard. I was angry that night and followed him. I saw Bernard pull the trigger. Said I wouldn't say anything. I was glad Bernard killed him. Liam called me a dumb bitch too that day, right before he broke up with me. My father used to call me that when he beat me. I can't kill my dad, but I thought if I made Liam pay for it, I'd stop being angry. I just want to not be angry anymore."

"I didn't mean to call you that," Timothy stuttered. "I don't know what came over me. I'm a good person really. You know that, Miss Mason. I've helped you. Kept your secrets."

Chloe rested her arm against his neck and pressed down all her weight. She was tired of hearing him speak. He'd utter no more words. Not ever. He wheezed desperately for breath. With her other hand, she kept the shard of glass pointed closely at this face.

"You killed Clementine because you wanted power," she said into his ear. "You were going to rape me because you wanted me to think you were powerful. I'll show you what power you have over me."

Chloe slammed the shard into his chest. Timothy squirmed under her arm to get free. Sweat poured down his face and veins protruded from his forehead. She pulled the glass out of his chest and blood erupted, then she slammed it back down, again and again.

"You can't hurt me!" she roared. She wasn't a victim anymore.

Chloe stood to her feet and watched as a puddle of red spread around Timothy's dying body. He wheezed for breath, choking on his own blood, and his body spasmed like a helpless fish flopping on dry land. Her eyes were fixed for the entire time it took him to bleed to death, and for those brief moments, she imagined him to be her father.

65

GREGG RACED DOWN THE ROAD AS FAST AS HIS LEGS WOULD CARRY him. Eventually, the van came into sight, and he cocked the gun Bernard had given him. There was one man standing outside. His daughter had to be inside the van.

Just before the man's head spun round and caught sight of him, Gregg leaped behind a tree and thought about his next moves. If this man was a trained killer like Bernard claimed, then shooting first wouldn't be simple. Clearly, Gregg had gotten lucky at the construction site when he killed Rachel's driver during his failed rescue attempt. He couldn't afford to fail this time too. This was his only chance to save his daughter.

There wasn't going to be a better time than right now. Gregg took a deep breath and counted to ten. It was the longest ten seconds of his life. He pictured him and his daughter finally living a quiet life together, maybe in a small town, surrounded by nature. All that mattered was that they'd be together again.

The ten seconds were over. This was it. Time to get his daughter back. He whipped around the tree and aimed his gun. The man spotted him. They locked eyes. In the blink of an eye, the barrel of the man's gun was staring back. Who was going to shoot first? If Gregg missed, the man wouldn't. Suddenly, the man was lit by a beam of light that got brighter and brighter. Gregg glanced over his shoulder. Bernard's car was heading right for the man.

The man leapt off the road as Bernard's car skidded to a stop. Gregg dashed over and shot the man in the back before he was even up on his feet again. He wasn't dead yet. The man spun and fired half a dozen rounds towards him. Gregg ducked to the ground, but one bullet still grazed his shoulder. He clung to it in pain, but there was no time to fixate on it. He shot the man in the chest. At last, he was dead.

Bernard jumped out of the car, brandishing a gun of his own. Faintly, Gregg could make out the sound of kicks and yells coming from Rachel in the trunk of the car.

Before either of them could make a move, the blast from a shotgun came firing from inside the van, putting a hole in the back door. Gregg and Bernard ran for cover behind the car. As the van door opened, Fury emerged with his shotgun aimed straight at Gregg's head.

Gregg ducked just as a flash from Fury's shotgun took a chunk of metal from where Gregg's head had been. As Gregg crawled on the ground, he shot at Fury's feet from underneath the car.

Bernard dashed over and wrestled the gun from the large man, causing it to go off several times into the air. Gregg went and helped pin Fury down.

Finally, standing over the man he had searched for, Bernard took the locket off from around his neck and showed him the picture. "Tell me how you knew my wife."

Fury spat at the picture.

Bernard's face went pale, and he shot Fury in the kneecap, but he still barely reacted. He stood on Fury's injured leg and roared, "Tell me why you killed her!"

"Cause and effect," Fury simply said. "She got what she had coming. It's a shame really. She was one of the few I actually liked."

Fury rolled over and wrestled free the shotgun, placing it under his chin. However, before he could pull the trigger, Gregg knocked the gun away, preventing Fury from splattering his own brains across the tarmac. Gregg struck Fury across the face with his own gun, knocking him out cold.

Gregg ran to the van and opened the back. Even with her peeled skin—a lasting reminder of the horror they had endured —he recognized his daughter instantly.

At first, she looked terrified, but her eyes and smile brightened at the sight of him, and she leapt into his arms. He held her close, as though he would never let her go, and they cried together. The sweet sound of her voice was enough to melt his heart: "You saved me, Dad."

Emilie's past was a dark shade of gray,
Filled with violence day after day,
But a new role she found,
As a hitwoman, renowned.

Rachel, they called her on the street,
A killer with a heart hard as concrete,
Kidnapped a girl to get what she sought,
A dark past that she never forgot.

EPILOGUE

THERE WAS A LOT TO CLEAN UP DURING THE FOLLOWING MONTHS, especially because Gregg became Blackberry Cove's new sheriff. Marc was happy to serve as his deputy for the time being and to gain more experience.

Rachel had been placed under witness protection by the FBI in exchange for her testimony against Fury, as well as her assistance in closing dozens of cases. It wasn't yet clear how large Fury's circle of professional killers was. Gregg didn't know where Rachel was these days, but he had been assured she was somewhere far away from Blackberry Cove. Rachel claimed Bernard's wife had once been a partner of Fury, and he had killed her when she chose to quit in favor of living a quieter life with Bernard. This was currently being investigated. Bernard had fled before the police arrived. His current whereabouts were unknown.

Furthermore, Rachel was close to getting everything she ever wanted—Gregg reopened the case of Anna Jones and was hoping to find remains so Nathan could be brought to justice. Gregg had been granted a search warrant to look for remains beneath the mayor's mansion. About twenty years ago, Nathan had replaced the mansion's wine cellar with an indoor swimming pool. Hopefully, something would turn up.

Given the circumstances, Richard would not be facing any charges. He and Hannah were in the process of adopting, and they seemed to be happier than ever.

The only thing that still bothered Gregg was what happened to Chloe. According to Marc, Chloe had been taken captive by Timothy and brought to the house where Clementine had been murdered. Marc had tried to save her but had been hit unconscious. When he woke up, Timothy was lying dead in the basement, stabbed over a dozen times. There was no sign of Chloe, except for the boot prints she had left behind in the therapist's puddle of blood.

Perhaps Chloe managed to save herself and kill Timothy in self-defense, but then why had she run away? And why had she stabbed the therapist so many times? Clearly, there was an anger in Chloe that Gregg hadn't been able to see. He had examined the case files from the fire that happened when she was a girl. Apparently, there had been signs of arson, but the sheriff had produced no suspects at the time. One day, he hoped he would see Chloe again so he could ask her a few questions. In many ways, this only seemed like the beginning, with a lot more still to come. But for now, Gregg was just glad to be at home with his daughter.

ACKNOWLEDGMENTS

I had to go through many drafts of the story and owe a lot of thanks to those who read earlier versions and offered me advice and criticism, including Amanda, Brian, Eduardo, Jo, Josh, Lainey, Ray, Senthil, Stephen, and Susan. Special thanks go to Joe, who helped me craft an earlier outline of the story, and to Rena, who read and provided feedback on more than one draft.

Lastly, thanks to my friends and family, who I can always count on for encouragement and support.

ABOUT THE AUTHOR

Ben Cotterill was born and raised in Stirling, Scotland. Fascinated in understanding extreme human behaviors, he studied forensic psychology. After completing his PhD on the psychology of children's eyewitness memory, he moved to the United States to teach forensic psychology to university students. When not working or writing fiction, he spends his weekends hiking the Appalachians and his vacations exploring as much of the world as possible.

To learn more about Ben Cotterill and discover more Next Chapter authors, visit our website at www.nextchapter.pub.

Printed in Great Britain
by Amazon